CLEARING IN THE SKY

D0870484

Purchased in Berea Ky
July 9, 1994

JESSE STUART

Clearing in the Sky
& Other Stories

With a Foreword by Ruel E. Foster

Woodcuts by Stanley Rice

THE UNIVERSITY PRESS OF KENTUCKY

Copyright © 1941, 1943, 1945, 1946, 1947, 1948, 1950, by Jesse Stuart.
Foreword by Ruel E. Foster copyright © 1984
by the University Press of Kentucky.
All rights in this book are reserved.

Scholarly publisher for the Commonwealth,
serving Bellarmine College, Berea College, Centre
College of Kentucky, Eastern Kentucky University,
The Filson Club, Georgetown College, Kentucky
Historical Society, Kentucky State University,
Morehead State University, Murray State University
Northern Kentucky University, Transylvania University,
University of Kentucky, University of Louisville,
and Western Kentucky University.

Library of Congress Cataloging in Publication Data

Stuart, Jesse, 1907-
    Clearing in the sky & other stories.

    1. Kentucky—Fiction.   I. Title.
PS3537.T92516C54   1984   813'.52   83-27404
ISBN 0-8131-1510-8
ISBN 0-8131-0157-3 (pbk.)

For Mitchell Stuart, my father

Contents

FOREWORD

When literary historians a hundred years hence write a history of the American short story, Jesse Stuart's name may well be near the top. Stuart has written well in the genres of the novel, essay, and poetry, but for many of us his greatest talent has been shown in the short story which has always been his special delight. Doubtless he has written too many short stories (some five hundred at the last count), but we should not hold this against him since he has lodged so many of that five hundred everlastingly in the imagination of America. Stuart, like many American writers, has created a magic sense of place. He has brought to lasting fictional life the world of W-Hollow, the locale of most of his short stories. W-Hollow now joins Faulkner's Yoknapatawpha County, Elizabeth M. Roberts's Pigeon River country, and Thomas Wolfe's Altamont as one of the places we visit imaginatively and lose ourselves in.

The present volume, *Clearing in the Sky*, clearly has about it that talismanic sense of place which fascinates American readers. This book gives us in generous portions a mountain way of life which is now long past but which was once prickly hard with the thorny individualism of Kentucky mountaineers. W-Hollow is a world of hills and mountains, dark hills in the wintertime but marvellous flowering hills in the spring. It is a hard land where people make their living by hardscrabble farming, cattletrading, mining, timbering, or moonshining. The people are primarily of Scotch-Irish or English stock with old-fashioned names—Sam Whiteapple, Cief Salyers, Battle

Keaton, and the Powderjays, Pa and Ma and children Finn and Shan; Shan frequently functions as the first person narrator in the stories.

What has made this world of Stuart's short fiction so lively, so compelling that readers for the past fifty years have followed it with timeless fascination? Though genius can never be analyzed to its ultimate source, it can at least be annotated and described. Among the obvious virtues of Stuart's short stories are their convincing primitivism, humor, natural talk style, and epiphanic insight.

Take, for example, his hard primitivism. If the term seems needlessly abstruse, let us say his short fiction is of the earth, earthy. In Stuart's phrase he is "just a dirt-colored man." He is a "one horse farmer singing at the plow." His fictional creatures are children of the earth, a voice from the clods. His stories call us ever to the outdoors. They give a poet's voice to the far and lost land of the Appalachians. We open *Clearing in the Sky* and get the odors of new plowed ground and feel the fine mist of nature blow into our face. A father hoists a handful of rich loam from the virginal soil of the story "A Clearing in the Sky" and smells its fecund odors with a kind of ecstasy. Stuart stops under the oaktrees and prays an earth-prayer—"Give me life close to the earth." "Get close to the soil and know Him" (*Beyond Dark Hills*).

The story "Clearing in the Sky" is an excellent example of Stuart's belief that earth and nature provide a healing, annealing power to men. In that story a father conducts his son to the top of a mountain where the father has a vegetable garden in virgin soil. The father explains that the doctors had given him up, had told him he had no chance to live. He has been saved by his work in the virginal garden soil. "The best days are the first to flee" wrote Willa

Cather in *My Antonia,* translating a line from Virgil's
Georgics. This is the classic theme of the primitivist and
it is stated succinctly here by Mitch Stuart who yearns back
to the garden world of his youth. "Clearing in the Sky"
is his therapy which does for him what physicians could
not do. Later Stuart mulling over the earth tie that both
his mother and father had, wrote: "They were the least
book-educated but the best earth-educated people I have
ever known" (*God's Oddling,* p. 225).

Stuart as a short story writer learned to follow his own
life and his instincts. Like Robert Frost, Stuart can say that
almost all of his stories are based on events that either happened to him or were told to him. He has written from
within a great globe of actual event and of myth and oral
tales of which he is the center. More than that the greater
part of his work falls for the most part into readily discer-
nible categories. Stuart and his editors have already
recognized these categories by bringing out a volume of
short stories, *Save Every Lamb,* in which all the stories
have to do with farm animals. Later Stuart published
Dawn of Remembered Spring in which every story features
a snake. One familiar with Stuart's work could easily pick
stories for a volume simply on dog stories, or one on
political stories, or one on politics, moonshine, etc. Please
note that the present volume mingles several categories.
Stuart's strong primitivistic, agrarian bent is featured in
the title story, "Clearing in the Sky," as well as in
"Testimony of Trees," where Uncle Mel foils a land thief
by demonstrating that an old blaze mark never completely disappears from a tree; i.e., nature, which provides so
many norms to man, can also be a silent witness in a court
battle. Other categories found in the stories that follow are
animals, politics, feuds, and moonshine. An important

mode in the above categories is Stuart's brand of
southwestern humor. Although there is a streak of sur-
realistic or "black bile" humor in Stuart, a mixture of the
comic and horrible, this does not appear in *Clearing in
the Sky*. In the present work, Stuart's humor is a good
natured reveling in comic incongruities, as in Sam
Whiteapple's corn eating duel with Lester Pratt's game
rooster ("The Champion").

Stuart is a true devotee of animals. He finds them splen-
did, courageous, and admirable. In the present volume,
at least six stories revolve about animals and one about bees.
In "The Champion," champion eater Sam Whiteapple
matches himself against a cock-of-the-walk rooster at eating
raw corn with farcical results. "To Market, to Market" trots
out Pa and his prize bull trained to walk on his hind legs
at Pa's command. Pa takes him to market and has a run-
in with the local pin-hookers where, in classic comic
fashion, the con man gets conned. "Fight Number Twenty-
five" enlists our sympathies for a mongrel dog who has to
take on a wildcat that has slaughtered a vast number of
dogs. "Horse-trading Trembles" is a traditional tale of the
old South (A. B. Longstreet's "The Horse Swap") and of
Faulkner's *The Hamlet* translated into an Appalachian
milieu. Once again the cheater gets cheated. "No Hero"
pits a six-foot five-inch bean pole who weighs 135 pounds
against a 385-pound bear in a wrestling match which comes
to a miraculously gentle conclusion. "Battle with the Bees"
shows the organized mayhem which results when a hundred beehives are turned over by marauding hogs and the
bees invade the family farm house in a mad orgy of stinging. "Hot-collared Mule" shows how Pa learns a lot more
about mules from a retired mule skinner who cuts down
Pa's braggadocio. Essentially a third of the stories in this

book treat animals, their habits, devotion, and idiosyn-
cracies. These stories record Stuart's deep kinship with the
animals of the earth and his almost mystical feeling for
the wild life of the earth, a feeling very similar to Thoreau's
thoroughly primitive "Brute Neighbors" chapter in
Walden. This sentiment is italicized for us by Stuart's final
line in *Save Every Lamb*—"And the saddest and loneliest
countries in the world are those without wildlife" (p. 277).

Lesser categories in this volume are the stories of
politics—"Thirty-two Votes before Breakfast," "Road
Number One," and "Governor Warburton's Right-hand
Man." These confirm the Kentucky cliché that "politics
are the damnedest in Kentucky." Then there are the moonshine stories, "Coming Down the Mountain" and "Evidence
Is High Proof." The remaining stories treat feuding, social
consciousness, and young love.

Please note that all the stories in this book were published
between 1941 and 1950. The years from 1930 to the mid
1950s were Stuart's freshest and more spontaneous period.
The stories written in this period are closer to the elements
of nature that he enjoyed so much as a young man; the
dialect is stronger, the language more evocative. This early
fiction becomes in the aggregate a great sustained elegy
to a lost world of Appalachian experience, a nostalgic
greeting and farewell to an important part of America's
past.

I would argue that this short fiction is essentially op-
timistic. Stuart believes in and practices Allen Tate's con-
cept of "Knowledge Carried to the Heart." He has continued to live so close to his material that he can, as he
says, "hear it snore." As a good primitivist he is *not out
of time with nature* and his best short stories are not out
of time with nature. Even city people—in some cases

especially city people—will find the timeless archetypes of Stuart's fiction attractive. Animal fables are as old as civilization, their appeal timeless.

The reader who comes to the present work will find that the author is indeed a genuine, original, marvelously fecund writing man. These stories are well representative of his genuineness and his great vitality. They are the incarnation of a matchless individuality. Stuart says "yes" to life all along the way. He obviously belongs to what R.W.B. Lewis in *The American Adam* calls "the party of hope." These stories are a welcome part of his affirmation.

RUEL E. FOSTER

ACKNOWLEDGMENTS

The author wishes to thank the following magazines for granting permission to republish the stories listed below:

Story for "The Champion";

Household for "Clearing in the Sky";

Minnesota Quarterly for "When Mountain Men Make Peace";

Collier's for "Fight Number Twenty-five";

Esquire for "No Petty Thief," "Thirty-two Votes before Breakfast," and "Evidence Is High Proof";

Woman's Home Companion for "The Slipover Sweater";

The Commonweal for "Testimony of Trees" (previously entitled "Land Grabbing and Uncle Mel");

Pic for "Horse trading Trembles" and "Road Number One";

Tomorrow for "Land of Our Enemies" and "Battle with the Bees" (previously entitled "Drone and Little Drone");

Blue Book for "No Hero";

Salute for "Competition at Slush Creek";

The Virginia Quarterly Review for "Governor Warburton's Right-hand Man";

Profile for "The Anglo-Saxons of Auxierville";

Columbia for "Hot-collared Mule" (previously entitled "Rock and Rye");

Senior Scholastic for "Old Gore."

CLEARING IN THE SKY

The Champion

Now, Lester, you know that I can outeat you," Sam White-apple said as he followed me down the path from our house to the barn. "I ain't seen anybody yet that I can't out-eat."

Sam stood in the path and looked me over. He slapped his big stummick with his big pitchfork hands. He had walked six miles to get me to try to outeat him.

"Right here's where I put the grub," he said. "This old nail keg will hold it."

Sam laughed a horselaugh and showed two rows of yaller teeth. His beady black eyes squinted when he looked into my eyes. Sam looked tough as a shelled-bark hickory, too. His face was covered with black beard—so black that it made his yaller teeth look like two rows of corn between his beardy lips. Sam was a hard-workin' man, too, fer his overall knees were threadbare and the seat of his overalls was good as new. His overall suspenders had faded on his blue work shirt.

"I've heard you was a great eater," Sam said. "I've just come over to put you under the table. I want to show you who is the champion eater in these parts."

"It's in crop time, Sam," I said. "Any other time but now."

I

"Why not now?" Sam ast.

"It knocks me out," I said. "I don't want to be knocked out. I've got too much work to do."

"You know which side of your bread is buttered," Sam laughed. He bent over until he nearly touched the ground; he slapped his ragged overall knees and laughed. "Old Beanpole Lester Pratt can't take it. You got a mouth big enough to shovel in grub, but you can't take it. The eatin' championship goes to Raccoon Creek. There's where I winned it from Gnat Hornbuckle when I et a hog's head."

"That ain't no eatin'," I said. "I could eat that much and still be hungry."

"What about five stewed hens and all the trimmin's?" Sam said. "I winned the chicken-eatin' contest over on Uling Branch. I was full to the neck. Didn't think I could get the last bite down my gullet but I did."

"You didn't eat that many hens."

"Ast Porky Sturgill," Sam said. "He et the least—just a couple of hens. He had to pay for all the hens six men et. I'll tell you it's fun to get a real square meal and let the other feller pay fer it. I've never paid for a meal yet. I've winned every eatin' contest. I've got the nail keg to put it in and you've just got a hollow beanpole there."

Sam hit me on the stummick and laughed as I started to open the barnlot gate.

"Wonder if Sam could outeat a cow," I thought. "No, he couldn't eat corn nubbins, fodder, or hay. Wonder if he could outeat a mule. No, a mule et more roughness than anything else. Sam couldn't eat hay or fodder." Then it flashed through my mind if Sam could outeat a hog. But Sam couldn't eat the things a hog et. Sam wouldn't get down and drink slop from a trough and gnaw corn from the cob on the ground. What could he eat with?

Just then my black game rooster run across the barnlot. He could always put away more corn than any chicken I'd ever seen. He'd eat so much corn I often wondered where he put it. He was tall with a long neck and a big craw. His face was red as a sliced beet. He didn't have any comb for it was cut off so other roosters couldn't peck it when I took him to fight.

"Sam, you're braggin' about your big nail-keg stummick," I said. "You can't eat as much shelled corn as that rooster."

"You wouldn't try to be funny, would you?" Sam ast.

"No, I mean it."

"Huh, never et with a rooster but I'd just like to show you," Sam said. "If I could eat the same grub, I'd eat with a mule, horse, cow, or hog. It wouldn't make no difference to me. I've fed livestock around the barn and I know how much they eat. I know how much I can eat. I'll tell you I've got a big capacity. When I drink water in the cornfield it takes a gallon bucket full of cold water to make me a swig. You talk about that little chicken! You make me laugh."

The rooster stopped in the barnlot. He held his head up to one side and cackled. He looked at us with the glassy-lookin' eye that was turned toward us. His red face beamed. It wasn't as large as the side of a big watch. I looked at the rooster and then I looked at Sam. He stood head and shoulders above me. I didn't know he was so tall. He looked short, for his shoulders were so broad and his stummick bulged out so in front. His sleeveless arms looked like fence posts folded across the bibs of his overalls. Sam was bigger than a lot of fattenin' hogs I'd seen. Maybe he could outeat my tall slim game rooster; I didn't know. But if he did, he would have to put a lot of corn in his craw!

"Can old Sam outeat you, boy?" I ast my rooster.

My black game rooster cackled. He cocked his head to one side and looked at Sam. He cackled louder.

"He says that you can't outeat him, Sam," I told Sam. "Said he was ready to take you on!"

"That rooster can't understand what you say," Sam laughed. He looked at me as if he believed though that the rooster could understand what I said.

"Can he outeat you, boy?" I ast my rooster.

He cackled louder than ever. He cackled like he was skeered.

"W'y, that silly chicken!" Sam chuckled. "You shell the corn and I'll show you who's the champion of this barnlot in just a few minutes. I won't haf to swaller enough corn to spile my dinner to beat him."

We walked from the gate down to the corncrib. The chickens followed me to the crib, for I allus shelled 'em corn in front of the crib. The rooster walked toward us cacklin' like he was tryin' to say somethin'.

"What's your rooster sayin' now?" Sam ast.

"He's cussin' you," I said. "He says that you can't eat corn with a chicken."

"Tell him in chicken talk that I got a good gullet," Sam said. "Tell him I got a place to put shelled corn that's bigger than his craw."

I opened the crib door and got an ear of corn. I shooed the rest of the chickens back from the crib. My rooster stood there. He wouldn't shoo. He wasn't a chicken that you could shoo easily. If you shooed him too much he was liable to fly at your face and try to spur you. He never had as much as he could eat for I left 'im in fightin' trim. Now I would give him all that he could eat. He stood with his neck feathers ruffled up like he was goin' to fight. His feathers were black and shiny as a crow's wing. His spurs were straight as sourwood sprouts and sharp as locust thorns. He acted like he owned the barnlot and that he would as soon spur Sam as to outeat him.

"Now, Sam, I'll give him a grain of corn every time I give you one," I said.

"Any old way suits me," Sam said. "This eatin' contest ain't goin' to last long nohow. I'm just doin' this fer fun to say that I outet Lester Pratt's black game rooster since old Beanpole Lester was afraid to eat with me."

Sam ketched the grain of corn in his big mouth when I pitched it to him. It was fun fer Sam. He laughed and swallered the corn. Then I pitched my rooster a grain. He picked it up in his hooked bill and swallered it. He quirked and wanted more.

"He laughed at you, Sam," I said.

"Throw us the corn," Sam said. "We'll see who laughs last." Sam stood there a big giant in our barnlot. I'd throw a grain of corn first to Sam and then one to my rooster. The hens stood back. They were wantin' the corn that I was

throwin' to Sam and to my rooster, but Sam thought they were lookin' on and hopin' that their hero would win.

That ear of corn didn't last as long as frost on a hot plate. I kept shellin' corn and pitchin' to Sam and my rooster until my arm got tired. Every time a hen quirked or made a funny noise in her throat Sam thought she was makin' fun of him. He would screw up his big beardy face and look sour at something little as a hen. Sam stood by the corncrib. He never moved out of his tracks. He would stand there and crane his big bull neck and swallow.

"Ain't your throat gettin' awful dry?" I ast.

"Nope, it ain't," Sam said. "A little grain of corn just draps down my gullet. You'd better ast your rooster and see if his throat is gettin' dry."

Just then I pitched my rooster a grain of corn and he sneezed.

"My rooster says his throat is okay," I said.

Sam looked a little funny when the rooster sneezed. I could tell he didn't have the confidence that he did have when we started the contest. Sam was lookin' a little worried. Maybe it was because of all the noises the chickens made.

"Am I 'lowed to chew my corn?" Sam ast.

"Nope, you're not," I said. "The rooster ain't got no teeth and you're supposed to swaller your corn like he does. What's a little grain of corn nohow?"

"Nothin' to look at it," Sam groaned, "but a lot of swallered corn gets heavy. I can feel a heavy lump right down at the end of my gullet."

"I guess my rooster feels it too," I said. "Watch him stretch his neck when he swallers a grain."

I looked down at my feet and there was a pile of corncobs big enough to start a fire in the fireplace. There was a pile of cobs big enough to cook a big dinner in our cook-stove. I'll tell you it was horse and cat between Sam and my rooster. At first I thought Sam would swallow more corn than my game rooster. Now I doubted that he would. I wondered where my rooster was puttin' so much corn. His craw had begun to swell. When he reached down to get a grain he nearly toppled over from the weight of his craw. But he reached down and picked up a grain, stood up as straight as Sam, and swallowed it.

"I'd like to have a sip of water," Sam said. "I'd like to dampen my gullet. It's gettin' a little dry."

"My rooster ain't ast fer water yet," I said. "You've got to abide by the same rule he does. See, he's never made a sound. He just stands up straight and swallers his corn."

"It's gettin' hard to get down," Sam said as he craned his neck and twisted his head from first one side to the other.

I could see now that Sam was worried. His eyes showed it. He didn't have any confidence at all. My rooster looked cheerful. He acted that way when he picked up a grain of corn in his fightin' beak. His eyes looked bright. He was confident and in fine spirits.

"Where's that chicken puttin' all that corn?" Sam ast.

"I don't know," I said. "You will haf to ast the chicken."

But Sam Whiteapple didn't ast the chicken. Old Sam kept strugglin' with a grain of corn. He was tryin' to get it down. His eyes begin to look watery. And Sam didn't have his natural color. There was a place on Sam's cheek where the beard didn't reach and that was allus rosy-red. Now it was turning pale. Sam moved out of his tracks when he tried to get another grain down. He run a little circle like a dog followin' his tail when he lays down. I kept my eye on Sam to see that he didn't spit the grain of corn out. Finally Sam got it down. My rooster swallowed his but he acted like he was gettin' plum full up to his ears. His craw was swellin' all the time. But 'peared like he knowed what was up. And he was goin' to beat Sam.

I pitched Sam another grain of corn. He ketched it in his big mouth. I never saw a big man wrestle with a little grain of corn like Sam did. He worked, and worked and finally he got it down by screwin' up his face, gruntin' and groanin' and runnin' a little circle. Tears come to his eyes and flowed down his beardy cheeks.

" 'Pears like I got a bushel of shelled corn in my gullet," Sam said. "It's lodgin' now in my windpipe. I'm gettin' short of breath."

I had just pitched my rooster another grain of corn and he had had time to grab it when Sam fell like a tree. If my rooster hadn't been a quick one, he wouldn't've got out of Sam's way. Sam sprawled like a sawed-down oak on the barnlot. His arms fell limp as two rags. It skeered me nearly to death. I shook Sam. He wouldn't talk. He didn't move or anything. His mouth was open and I saw three grains of corn on his tongue. I felt to see if his ticker was still goin'. I thanked my God that it was. My rooster walked away with his flock of hens. He was craw-heavy, for he almost toppled over on his face. But he flew up on a fence post and crowed. He'd et more corn than Sam. I wanted to break the news to the boys on Raccoon Creek that my rooster had out-et their champion eater. But I had to get on a mule and get a doctor.

"A man's a fool that will do a thing like this," Doc Hornbuckle said. "A big, fine-lookin' man like Sam Whiteapple ought to have more sense than to eat corn with the chickens. Swallowin' corn grains that have never been chewed. Get him home!"

I harnessed the mules and hitched them to the spring

wagon. Doc helped me load Sam on the wagon. Doc strained his back liftin' on Sam. Finally we got him on the spring wagon, and I hauled him to Raccoon Creek. I left him with his people. His pa was awful mad at me about it. But I didn't have nothin' to do with my rooster eatin' more corn than Sam. I told his pa that too. He said his crop was in the weeds, and he needed Sam's help.

It was a funny thing the way people talked when Sam was so bad off the next two weeks. We'd go there and sit up all night. We'd talk about the corn Sam swallered. Some thought that Sam would have to swallow pieces of broken dishes, eggshells, and white gravels from the creek just like a chicken did, to work on the corn in Sam's craw. I told them Sam didn't have a craw and that Doc Hornbuckle would bring him out of it if anybody could, if they'd just listen to Doc's orders.

The last night I was over to the settin'-up, Doc Hornbuckle said, "Don't you ever try to outeat another chicken, Sam. You have ruint your stummick. You'll haf to go easy fer a year. You can't do much work. You'll just have to piddle about the place. I'm goin' to haf to put you on a corn-flake diet. You'll haf to eat corn flakes and warm sweet milk mornin', noon, and night."

Sam's eyes got awful big when Doc Hornbuckle said "corn flakes."

To Market, to Market

COME, BOSS," Pa said affectionately to the bull he had raised from a little calf. "We got to be goin', fellow. The truck's waitin' for us!"

Pa never had to use a ring in old Boss's nose. He never had to put a halter on his head and use a rope to lead him. All Pa had to do was speak to Boss. It seemed that old Boss could understand what Pa said. He followed him away from the barn like a dog following a man after he'd asked the dog to come along. That's the way old Boss understood Pa. That's the way Pa understood old Boss. Pa was taking old Boss to the Cannongate Livestock Market where he would be sold to the highest bidder. It looked strange to see Pa taking away an animal that he loved.

"I hate to take you, old boy," Pa said as he walked slowly down the path beneath the pines. "But the time has come when we got to do something."

The time had come when Pa did have to do something, too. Boss was no longer the pretty little white-faced bull calf he once was. That was three years ago and Pa had trained Boss to walk on his hind feet like a dog. He would walk that way around the stall and fold up his short front legs. Then Pa would open the gate and let Boss leave the stall and go to the pasture. Often Boss would stick his tongue out and look at Pa with dark bullish eyes. That was the only calf out of the hundreds and hundreds we had owned Pa could train to walk on his hind feet. Maybe this was the reason big Boss would follow little Pa, who weighed only one hundred twenty-four pounds, down the path under the pines toward the truck that was waiting for him. Because Pa had finally decided this was the best thing for him to do. Five farms joined the big range where we kept our cattle. Each of our neighbors kept a bull too. And when one of these bulls bellowed, Boss didn't bother to jump the fence. He pushed it down and went to him. When Boss put his head and shoulders against a wire fence, the wires snapped like shoestrings. That was unless the wire was new. Then Boss pushed up the posts and flattened several panels of fence. Not any fence could hold him when he heard another bull bellow.

Boss had killed one big bull for Jim Pennix. Pa had to pay for him and he had to repair three panels of new barbed wire fence. Boss had almost killed Lonnie Madden's bull when we got to him. Because Lonnie's bull had a big pair of horns and old Boss was a pole-Hereford, he made the mistake of trying to mangle Boss with his horns. Boss had him down trying to crush him between his mighty head and the ground when Pa took Boss off. Jake Thompson's, Albert Thomb's, and Alec Reed's bulls were smarter. When they bellowed and Boss went through the fences to get them, each of them took one look at Boss and he took off. That was one thing other bulls could do. They could outrun Boss. He was too big to do much running up and down the cowpaths on the wooded hills and up the grassy pasture slopes.

Not so much what Boss would do to our neighbors' bulls worried Pa as the stories we had been hearing about the fox hunters who had brought their hounds to the highest range of hills on our farm to chase the foxes that denned in the Stuartland rocks. The hunters had stood on one side of the seven-wire fence, one built to hold sheep, and had pawed the dry leaves with their brogan shoes and had imitated the sounds of other bulls. They had done this to old Boss, who was on the other side of the seven-wires, to scare Red Arrington, an old fox hunter who was afraid of bulls. He took one look at old Boss high on the mountain standing in the moonlight and this was enough. When Red Arrington ran away, as he did every time the hunters teased Boss, all the hunters would clap their hands and shout with laughter. One night Boss walked through the seven-wires to get them and each hunter took to a tree while Red Arrington ran as fast as a fox over the mountain despite his seventy years of age. Pa heard about this and he was afraid Boss was getting disgusted with men as well as rival bulls. Once when Charlie Sprouse, a neighbor, came through our barnlot, Boss tossed his head in many strange ways enough to let Pa know he didn't like it. Pa was afraid Boss would hurt some innocent man that was walking across our pasture. This was another reason he was taking him to the market.

I walked behind and watched the big bull follow my little seventy-year-old father. There was not any more difference in this big bull's following him than a shepherd dog. Except the bull was so large and Pa was so small that it made one laugh to watch them. Not if one knew how Pa had raised old Boss. It gave me a sad feeling to see Pa taking him away. I felt sad to see this big friendly animal leaving our farm. He was friendly to us even if he didn't like other bulls and fox hunters. I knew as I walked behind them that I was not half as sad as Pa was. For in the distance I could see the truck backed up against the steep bank where we had made a fence to make a loading chute. Cousin Penny Henson was sitting in the truck waiting to haul old Boss to market.

"You don't mean to tell me, Uncle Mick, that you can load that big bull without a ring in his nose?" Cousin Penny said to Pa.

"Watch me, Penny," Pa said. "I'll take old Boss onto the truck."

Pa walked into the little enclosure we had fenced to make the loading chute. Old Boss followed him inside the fenced enclosure. Then Pa walked down the little bank, the way we had to drive the cattle onto the truck after we got them inside the enclosure. Boss followed Pa onto the truck bed. Cousin Penny stood behind the truck and soon as Pa and Boss were safely inside he fastened the gate on the truck bed and roped it securely. Pa didn't get down to ride in the truck cab with Cousin Penny and me, but he rode standing on the sawdust in the truck bed with old Boss. We were on our way to the market.

I looked back as the truck jolted along to see how Pa and Boss were riding. Boss wasn't used to the truck, since it was the first automobile ride he'd ever had. Pa was saying something to him and rubbing his shoulder. Boss seemed to understand all Pa was saying. He braced his feet when the truck slowed and gained speed. Soon, we had reached Route 1. The ride was smooth from now on. Boss didn't have to brace his feet and Pa didn't have to explain. We passed truckloads of cattle going to market. We passed truckloads of hogs, cattle, and sheep.

"Have you ever been to Cannongate Livestock Market?" Penny asked me.

"Never have," I said.

"Wait until you're there today and you'll see why I'm rushin'," Penny said. "I thought we were early. But look at the people on the road. I want to get there and get unloaded soon as I can."

In a few minutes we reached Route 23, the broad national highway that took us directly to Cannongate. Cousin Penny stepped on the gas. I looked back to see how Pa was getting along. He was holding his hat with one hand. His other arm was across old Boss's shoulder. Pa was standing close beside Boss. One truckload of hogs passed us up, and the beardy-faced man sitting on the side next to our truck laughed as he pointed to Pa riding beside his bull. He yelled something that Pa couldn't understand.

In Roston we stopped to get gas. Pa climbed down from the truck bed.

"When we get to Cannongate the pinhookers will swarm around this truck," Pa said. "They'll be wantin' to know the price of my bull. What's he worth?"

"Put him on the market, Pa," I said. "Let the cattle buyers bid for 'im."

"That's what I say," Cousin Penny said. "You'll get more for 'im that way."

"But the pinhookers will be wild about this bull," Pa said. "They'll swarm around this truck soon as we get to Cannongate. They'll be askin' me my price."

"But you don't want to sell 'im that way do you, Uncle Mick?" Cousin Penny said.

"Sure don't," Pa said. "I want to put 'im on the market."

"Then put a price on 'im you know they won't take," Cousin Penny suggested.

"But I don't know how cattle are sellin'," Pa said. "I can't read the livestock report in the paper. My radio won't play. I don't know what to ask for 'im."

"Good bulls are sellin' at twenty dollars a hundred," I said. "I heard that yesterday over the radio."

"How much do you think Boss will weigh?" I asked Pa.

"Nineteen hundred pounds," Pa said.

I looked at Cousin Penny and he looked at me. We didn't agree with Pa's calculation.

"What do you think he'll weigh, Penny?" I asked.

"About seventeen hundred," Penny said. "How much do you say?"

"Seventeen-forty," I said.

"He'll weigh more than that," Pa said, shaking his head sadly.

"Say twenty dollars a hundred, Uncle Mick," Penny said, "your bull ought to be worth three hundred sixty dollars!"

"That's an awful price for a bull," Pa said. "The way I've sold cattle all my life! I never sold an animal for that much! Looks impossible to get that much for a bull!"

"But you don't want to sell him, Pa, to the pinhookers?" I said.

"That's right," Pa answered.

"Then I'd ask this much for 'im and the pinhookers won't even bite," Cousin Penny said. "You'll be able to put 'im on the market."

"All right," Pa agreed. "That's business. They'll look at the price before they buy!"

Then Pa started climbing back into the truck with Boss.

"Boss, we're goin' to ask a big price for you," Pa said softly as he rubbed the big bull's kinky head.

"Nice bull you got in that truck," said the filling-station attendant while Cousin Penny was trying to make the right change so we could be on our way. "How much do you expect to get for 'im?"

"Three hundred sixty dollars," Cousin Penny said.

"Not enough for that animal," said the small, pale-faced filling-station attendant. "A lot of fellows stop here with loads of cattle. I've never seen a prettier bull than that one. That big, fine-looking bull for three hundred sixty dollars when a little veal calf sells for sixty-five?"

"We'd better raise the price of the bull, Uncle Mick," Penny said as the filling-station attendant went inside. "What do you say we ask three hundred eighty-seven dollars for 'im? You know the pinhookers won't take you up on that price."

"Suits me fine," Pa agreed. "How does it suit you, Boss?" Pa asked, turning to the bull. "Reckon pinhookers won't laugh when we ask that much for you, Boss?"

Cousin Penny climbed in the cab and I beside him. Pa stood in the truck bed with one arm up over old Boss's neck while with his other hand he rubbed his nose. Cousin Penny stepped on the gas.

"It's a funny thing," Cousin Penny laughed, "how fillin'-station attendants think they know all about the price of cattle. That bull won't bring three hundred dollars. Wait and see! I've hauled a lot of cattle up here. Uncle Mick thinks he's got a better bull than he actually has. He won't bring the top market price. He's fooled in his weight, too. He's overguessing, but I wouldn't tell 'im so. Don't want to hurt his feelings."

When we pulled under the Cannongate overhead, there was already a half-mile line of trucks of all makes and descriptions ahead of us. They were loaded with cattle, sheep, calves, cows, steers, heifers, and hogs. The half-ton truck with one little bull in it, that we pulled in behind, was almost surrounded with pinhookers. When Cousin Penny pulled his two-ton truck in behind it with old Boss standing as erect and pretty as you ever saw a bull stand, all the pinhookers left the half-ton truck and the little bull and they swarmed around Cousin Penny's truck.

"What will you take fer 'im?" shouted a tall red-beardy-faced man, wearing a big black umbrella hat and with a crook in his hand. He started to punch Boss through an opening in the truck bed to make him stand around.

"Here, don't do that," Pa warned. "You don't have to punch this bull. He won't stand for it."

"How much does he weigh?" asked a short, broad-shoul-dered man, wearing a fur cap with attached ear muffs and carrying a mule whip across his shoulder.

"Is he your bull?" asked a small man wearing briar-scratched boots on his bowed legs.

"Best lookin' bull I've ever seen at this stock market," said a mousy little man that wore boots and spurs and carried a quirt in his hand. "He's a handsome thing! Look at 'im, won't you!"

Boss never looked better to Cousin Penny and me. We were standing behind the pinhookers who were crowding each other to get closer to the truck.

"I guess this bull to weigh nineteen hundred," Pa said.

"He won't weigh eighteen hundred," said the red-beardy-faced man. "But how much will you take fer 'im?"

"Three hundred eighty-seven dollars," Pa said.

"Odd dollars," the red-beardy-faced man mumbled to himself as if he were puzzled.

Then I saw the short, broad-shouldered man, who was wearing the fur cap with the ear muffs attached, reach into his pocket. The red-beardy-faced man saw him goin' down in his pocket after his pocketbook. At least he must have thought so for he screamed up to Pa, "Your bull is sold. I want 'im."

Cousin Penny had not stopped his truck over a minute. Pa looked down from the truck at the red-beardy-faced man as he looked up at Pa. There was a strange look on Pa's

face. But Pa had stated his price. There wasn't anything
he could do, since more than twenty men had gathered
around the truck and had heard Pa set the price on old Boss.
The man pulled a big billfold from his pocket. Pa came
down from the truck. He paid Pa nineteen twenty-dollar
bills, a five, and two ones. Cousin Penny left his truck and
he and I started walking toward the market with Pa.

"That's funny," Pa said. "The truck wheels had hardly
stopped rollin' before old Boss sold. I believe I'm stung.
Damn the pinhookers!"

Then we met Flood Hall, a short, broad-shouldered
timber cutter from Greenwood County who had quit cutting timber and had gone into the cattle business.

"Who brought that big, fine-lookin' bull in here, Mick?"
Flood asked us as he started to run past us.

"I brought 'im, Flood," Pa said.

"What'll you take fer 'im, Mick?" Flood asked as he
hurried on toward the truck where the men were still
standing around talking about old Boss. Flood's eyes were
fastened on the bull, and he went like a man walking in his
sleep.

"I've sold 'im, Flood," Pa said.

"Oh, Mick, why didn't you let me know," Flood said.
"We're old friends."

Flood stopped dead in his tracks. I thought he would sink
to the street. He acted like a man that had missed the buy
of a lifetime.

"But I set a price, Flood," Pa explained, "that I didn't
think anybody would accept. I planned to put old Boss on
the market. Raised that bull from a calf. Got the papers
right here with 'im!"

"What did you get fer 'im, Mick, if that's a fair question?" Flood asked.

"Three hundred eighty-seven dollars," Pa said.

"Now, I feel better," Flood said. The sad expression left Flood's face and he twirled the quirt he was holding in his big right hand. He was happy. "You got eighty-seven dollars more than that bull is worth. Old Sherm Potter bought that bull. Am I glad to see 'im get a stingin'! He's poured it on me a time or two!"

Now Pa's face changed from an expression of gloom to one of happiness.

"I'm hard to fool on cattle," Pa said to Cousin Penny and me. "I've lived a long time. I've sold a lot of cattle to pin-hookers. They've never made much off old Mick!"

Pa had confidence in himself now.

"Well, boys," Pa said to Penny and me as Flood Hall walked on toward the truck where the men were standing around admiring old Boss, "I'll do a little pin-hookin' now. I'll buy myself a young bull to replace old Boss."

"I'll have to get back to my truck, Uncle Mick," Penny said. "I want to stay in line so I can unload old Boss. I guess Sherm Potter plans to put 'im on the market."

Trucks were pulling around Cousin Penny's truck and getting ahead of him now. So Cousin Penny hurried back to his truck. I walked beside Pa. We started along the line of parked trucks toward the stockyard.

"Here's a nice bull," Pa said as we stopped beside a half-ton truck to look at a young Hereford bull.

"How old is that bull?" Pa asked the driver.

"Six months," he said.

"What will you take for 'im?" Pa asked.

"Two hundred dollars," he said.

"Not for me," Pa said, shaking his head sadly. "That's too high."

"Cattle are high as a cat's back, Mister," the man said very irritably as if Pa should know.

We followed the line of trucks up to the cattle chutes where they were unloading. We asked the price of all the bulls in all the trucks. The lowest price for a scrub Jersey bull was one hundred fifty dollars. Pa didn't want him. He just wanted to know the price. One Hereford bull, about half the size of Boss, that interested Pa sold before our eyes to a pinhooker for two hundred fifty dollars. The owner had papers with him. Pa had papers with old Boss too.

"I'm ruint," Pa said. "I sold too cheap. I don't care what my old friend Flood Hall said. He tried to make me feel good by sayin' those kind words. That's all."

We looked over fourteen bulls. Pa wouldn't buy any of them at the prices the men asked. Only one had papers. That was the one that sold for two hundred fifty. The others were scrub bulls of all breeds, description, colors, and kinds. They ranged in price from one hundred fifty to three hundred fifty. Pa didn't buy. When we reached the cattle chutes where they were unloading from the trucks we ran into old Professor Wentworth. He had been a rural school-teacher in Greenwood County. But he had quit teaching and had gone into the cattle business, since he had found it more profitable. Our meeting him was what caused something to happen.

"Mick, I've just seen that fine bull you brought up here," he said, running toward Pa. "He's the finest thing that's ever come to this market. Somebody told me you only got four hundred dollars for 'im."

Pa looked strangely at Professor Wentworth. He didn't tell him how much he got.

"If I could've only seen you first, Mick," Professor Went-worth said as he took a little book and pencil from his inside coat pocket, "I would have bought your bull. See, I don't do any guesswork on this cattle business. I go by facts and figures. How much did the bull weigh, Mick?"

"I guess 'im to weigh nineteen hundred," Pa said.

"Nineteen hundred at twenty-six cents a pound," Professor Wentworth said as he put the figures down and started calculating.

"Twenty-six cents a pound," Pa said.

"That's right, Mick," Professor Wentworth said as he continued to figure. "That bull will bring top price. Wait and see if I'm not right. Say he weighs nineteen hundred. He'll bring four hundred ninety-four dollars on the market."

"Well, Sherm Potter will make some money on that deal," Pa said.

"Flood Hall owns 'im now," Professor Wentworth said. "I was right there when he changed hands. I saw him pay four hundred twenty-five dollars to Sherm for the bull."

Pa didn't say another word. He turned and walked away. Professor Wentworth and I stood there watching Pa disappear into the crowd of livestock sellers, buyers, and traders.

"I wish I'd never shown your father the figures," Professor Wentworth said, looking at me with sad brown eyes. "He's a sick man over that trade."

Cousin Penny and I are partly to blame too, I thought. Even a filling-station attendant knew more about the price of cattle than we did.

I didn't say a word to Professor Wentworth. I took off through the great crowd of men wearing broad-rimmed hats, boots, and carrying crooks over their arms and quirts in their hands. There were more men at this market than I saw at the Fourth of July and Labor Day celebrations in Blakesburg. I never saw such a crowd of unshaven, beardy-faced men. They were talking cattle, sheep, and hogs every-where I hurried to find Pa. These were cattlemen, cattle buyers, traders, sellers, and pinhookers. I never saw any-thing like it. I never heard as much trading talk in my life. But I couldn't find my father. I even went to all the cattle pens looking for Pa. I first looked at the pen for yearling bulls. I couldn't find 'im. Then I went to the pens for heavy bulls. Old Boss was in a pen by himself. I asked if he had been weighed.

"Two thousand twenty-five pounds," said one of the group of men still following and admiring the bull.

Then I wondered if Pa had seen Boss in his pen. I won-dered if he knew that he'd come the closest of more than fifty men guessing his weight. I knew if Pa had seen Boss in the bull pen with a number pasted on his fat hip he would be sick now. If Pa could have heard the comments I'd heard then he would be sicker. I'd heard no less than forty men say that old Boss was the finest bull that had ever been brought to the Cannongate Livestock Market. After listening to the swarm of men gathered around old Boss's pen brag what a fine bull he was, I took off again to hunt for my father. I looked around the heifer pens for him. I looked around the cow pens. I looked around the calf pens and the yearling steer pens. I thought Pa would try to in-vest some or all of the money he got for old Boss in cattle of some sort to take home. But nowhere could I find Pa. Then I found Cousin Penny hunting through the milling, trading, buying crowd of cattlemen.

"Penny, have you seen Pa?" I asked.

"Nope, I haven't, Shan," he said. "Too bad Uncle Mick lost the way he did on that bull! I feel so guilty I'm not goin' to charge 'im anything for haulin' 'im up here."

"I feel guilty, too," I said. "I feel sick. Pa loved that bull.

Never knew him to love an animal more. I feel that I'm partly responsible too, Penny."

"Let's go find Uncle Mick," Penny said. "Let's cheer 'im up!"

Then Cousin Penny and I agreed to search for Pa until two o'clock in the afternoon. That was the time they started putting cattle, sheep, and hogs over the Cannongate Livestock Market. We agreed to meet each other every few minutes at the stock-market door and report.

Six times Cousin Penny and I met each other at the door and reported to one another. The reports were always the same. We hadn't seen anything of Pa.

When the bidding started, Cousin Penny and I went inside. This was the first time I'd ever been inside of a livestock market where cattle were driven in front of the prospective buyers and the man that bid the highest took the cattle, hogs, or sheep. There was a floor about thirty by thirty feet square and it was covered with sawdust and shavings. On each side of the floor the seats went up like baseball bleachers, only steeper. There was a gate on the south where the cattle were let in and a gate on the north where they were let out after the bidding was over and they had been sold. Cousin Penny went up in the west tier of steep seats and I went up on the east tier of seats. Cousin Penny scanned the tiers of seats on my side with his big brown eyes for Pa. I scanned the tiers of seats on his side. Pa was not inside the livestock market.

We watched them bring the yearling heifers in first. They brought them one at a time and sometimes by groups. They sold them by the head and by the hundredweight. There was not any certain way they sold them. But I saw something I had never seen before. Cattle buyers lined the wall of the arena below. And when the cattle were turned through the south gate, they started punching them with their crooks and tapping them with the leash on their quirts. They made them keep running so everybody could see them., They even used the stalks of their mule whips to gouge them between the legs and made them kick. If the cattle showed plenty of life, the buyers were more interested and the price went higher. I noticed the well-marked cattle fetched big prices too. Cattle marked like old Boss fetched the money. They brought top prices.

Cousin Penny and I watched them take the yearling heifers and steers over the market floor. We watched them take the little suckling calves, the short and long yearlings, the dry cows, the cows giving milk, the hogs, and the few sheep. At first it was hard to understand what the little auctioneer, who wore a big black hat and flowing bow tie, was saying because he sat behind a loud-speaker and he shot his words and fragments of words like bullets and fragments of bullets into this speaker. Men held up their hands, held up one finger, nodded in the direction of the little auctioneer until the bids got too high. Then the bidder called to the man that bid the highest.

Penny and I watched and waited for Pa. We thought he would surely come to watch the bidding. Then I wondered if he'd gone home alone. Cousin Penny and I waited until they started putting the bulls over the market. It was about five o'clock in the afternoon when the first young bulls came through the south gate. Well-dressed men bid on the fat ones. They bid them in for slaughter. I wanted to wait until old Boss came through. I wanted to know the price he fetched. I wanted to tell Penny too if Boss fetched a big price for Flood Hall not to tell Pa. Bulls coming through the south gate got larger. Soon they were selling the heavy bulls. Many bulls sold for twenty cents a pound. Fewer sold for twenty-two cents. And a very, very few, sold for twenty-four cents. I saw two bulls sell for twenty-five cents and one bull, the bull the owner asked Pa two hundred fifty dollars for, sold for twenty-six cents.

Then something happened that brought excitement to the Cannongate Livestock Market. Something that will never be forgotten long as any man or woman lives who was there that Friday afternoon on January fourteenth, nineteen forty-nine. The gate opened and old Boss came through. He took his time and looked over the people sitting on the steep seats above him. He looked at the line of strange specimens of cattle buyers and traders that admired him more than he admired them. They were looking at Boss and they looked at each other. Every well-dressed man in the crowd stood up. I watched Professor Wentworth. He was watching eagerly. Flood Hall stood near the auctioneer. Sherm Potter was sitting on the bottom rail.

The auctioneer started old Boss at twenty-three cents a pound. And the bidding of the well-dressed men began as they moved in closer along the bottom rails that enclosed the arena. They wanted old Boss for beef. That they were willing to pay for him was an evident fact. Just as the bidding was getting hot and the auctioneer's words and half words went into the loud-speaker like bullets and fragments of bullets, something happened. Red Arrington, who traded in cattle and fox-hunted, recognized old Boss. Old Boss recognized him too. Boss started toward him. Red was sitting on the bottom rail.

"It's the Mick Powderjay bull," Red screamed. "I know 'im. He's dangerous!"

Red fell backwards with his feet sticking up in the air. His two feet were about the level of the eyes of the spectators, traders, buyers, and sellers sitting on the first row of the steep seats on the opposite side. Just when this happened Boss put his head under the rail. Then something else happened. The keeper had opened the north door to let old Boss through, since men were gouging him with crooks and hitting him with quirts while Red Arrington was down on his head screaming. Pa walked up to the door. He was weaving like an oriole's nest hanging to a topmost wind-swayed bough.

"Get out of here before you get killed," said the north doorkeeper to Pa. "You can't come through this door anyhow. Go around!"

"Who said I'd get killed?" Pa said. "Who said I was at the wrong door? I'm comin' through."

> "To market, to market
> To sell a fine bull,
> Sherm Potter's skinned Mick
> And now he's full."

It was Professor Wentworth who recited this little ditty and chuckled in childish glee.

The keeper grabbed Pa. I knew that something had happened to Pa. He had imbibed of the spirits. This was something my father never did, due to his bad heart and high blood pressure. Now he was going around and around with the doorkeeper.

"What do you say, Boss?" Pa shouted.

"That's the old man that fellar cheated outen his bull," said a man near me. "Look at 'im now! He's in some shape!"

"I'm comin', Boss," Pa shouted.

"Do something with 'at bull, men," shouted the auctioneer into the loud-speaker.

"He's a mad bull," men shouted.

The small group of women sitting near me raced to the highest section of seats. They were screaming until I

couldn't hear what Pa was saying. Pa tore himself loose
from the doorkeeper and came inside. The doorkeeper was
left holding Pa's coat. The well-dressed buyers were getting out of the way. Old, experienced cattlemen were running out of the market. They were going through doors and
windows. For old Boss with one motion of his big head and
giant neck tore the bottom rail away to get to Red Arrington. Pa finally got over to Boss.

He rubbed Boss's neck and his forehead. Boss stopped
when Pa touched him but the cattle buyers and traders
didn't stop. They kept on trying to get out. The little
auctioneer chinned himself up and was sitting on a higher
seat.

"Walk like a man, Boss," Pa shouted. "Show 'im, Boss,
who your master is!"

When Boss rose to his hind feet and folded back his stout
forelegs, licked out his long red tongue and rolled his big,
black, shining eyes until they looked like living embers in
the dark, the auctioneer went to a higher seat. Men poured
out the doors and windows fast as they could go. Professor Wentworth ran to the last seat in the bleachers, up
among the women, to pacify them. Their screams were
frantic. Even Cousin Penny was scared. He was trying to
run this way and that, and he couldn't because there was
always somebody in any direction he started. Flood Hall
was trying to get out the door. Old Boss walked a few steps
on his hind feet while the people screamed. They thought
he was trying to charge. Little Pa, his face flushed ripe-plum
red, walked around the circle with Boss.

"Do something with that bull," Flood Hall screamed.
"Why didn't you tell me!"

"I'll give you three hundred for 'im, Flood," Pa shouted.
"That's what you told me he's worth! I won't buy 'im by

the pound. I'll buy old Boss back and take 'im home where he belongs. Won't I, Boss?"

"I've auctioned cattle thirty years and I've never seen anything like that," screamed the auctioneer. "Take three hundred for 'im, Mister, unless one of the bidders want him at twenty-three cents a pound!"

"The bidders are all gone now," Cousin Penny shouted.

"Get that dangerous bull outen here," shouted Red Arrington, still standing on his head, with his hobnailed shoes sticking straight up in the air. "Get him out before he turns this house over. Get me off my head!"

"What do you say, Flood?" Pa said. "I'm goin' to buy 'im back at three hundred dollars!"

Boss was walking on all four feet now. He drew back his tongue.

"Get back up there, Boss," Pa shouted. "Show 'em you can walk like a man! But, Boss, I'm not tellin' you to go after any of these men. They hit you with quirts and goosed you with whip stalks but let 'em go, Boss!"

"You can take 'im for that," Flood Hall screamed. "Get 'im out of here!"

Flood was backed into a corner. He couldn't get out. He was scared of Boss. He was afraid, since Pa was feeling the spirits, that he would tell Boss to charge him and Boss would do it. For Boss was walking for the second time on his hind feet. Pa was walking beside him.

"Then you're mine again, Boss," Pa screamed. "Everybody heard me buy you back, Boss, and I got the money here to pay for you. It's the same money I got for you this morning, Boss. I'll have a little money left too, Boss!"

"Get 'im out," shouted the auctioneer. "Get 'im out, so we can finish selling these cattle!"

"Come on, Boss," Pa said.

Boss dropped down on all four feet and followed Pa through the north gate. Cousin Penny and I walked down from the bleachers as the people started coming back looking strangely at the little red-faced man leading the big two-thousand-pound bull with his hand. Old Boss followed him as gently as a shepherd dog.

Clearing in the Sky

THIS is the way, Jess," said my father, pointing with his cane across the deep valley below us. "I want to show you something you've not seen for many years!"

"Isn't it too hot for you to do much walking?" I wiped the streams of sweat from my face to keep them from stinging my eyes.

I didn't want to go with him. I had just finished walking a half mile uphill from my home to his. I had carried a basket of dishes to Mom. There were two slips in the road and I couldn't drive my car. And I knew how hot it was. It was 97 in the shade. I knew from that January until April my father had gone to eight different doctors. One of the doctors had told him not to walk the length of a city block. He told my father to get a taxi to take him home. But my father walked home five miles across the mountain and told Mom what the doctor had said. Forty years ago a doctor had told him the same thing. And he had lived to raise a family of five children. He had done as much hard work in those years as any man.

I could not protest to him now. He had made up his mind. When he made up his mind to do a thing, he would do it if he had to crawl. He didn't care if it was 97 in the shade or 16 below zero. I wiped more sweat from my face as I followed him down the little path between the pasture and the meadow.

Suddenly he stopped at the edge of the meadow, took his pocketknife from his pocket, and cut a wisp of alfalfa. He held it up between him and the sun.

"Look at this, Jess!" he bragged. "Did you ever see better alfalfa grow out of the earth?"

"It's the best looking hay I've seen any place," I said. "I've not seen better looking alfalfa even in the Little Sandy River bottoms!"

"When I bought this little farm everybody around here said I'd end up with my family at the county poor farm if I tried to make a living here," he bragged again. "It took me thirty years to improve these old worn-out acres to make them do this!"

As I stood looking at his meadow of alfalfa, down in the saddle between two hills, I remembered how, down through the years, he had hauled leaves from the woods and spread them over this field in the autumn and then plowed them under and let them rot. All that would grow on this ground when he bought it were scrubby pines and saw briers. The pines didn't grow waist-high. There wasn't enough strength in the ground to push them any higher. And the saw briers didn't grow knee-high. In addition to this, the land was filled with gullies. But he cut the scrubby pines and turned their tops uphill to stop the erosion. And he mowed the saw briers with a scythe and forked them into the gullies on top the pines. Then he plowed the land. He sowed a cover crop and turned it under. Then he sowed a second, a third, and a fourth cover crop. In a few years he had the land producing good crops of corn, wheat, potatoes, and tobacco.

"But this is not what I want to show you, Jess," he said

as he threw the wisp of alfalfa to the ground. "Come on. Follow me!"

I followed him through the pasture gate. Then down a little narrow cattle path into the deep hollow.

"Where are we going?" I asked when he started to walk a log across the creek toward a steep, timbered bluff.

"Not up or down the hollow," he laughed. "But there." He pointed toward a wooded mountaintop. "That's the way we are goin'!"

"But there's not even a path leading up there," I said.

"There's a path up there now," he said. "I've made one."

I followed him across the foot log he had made by chopping down a white oak, felling it over the deep-channeled stream. It was a foot log a flash flood couldn't carry away because its top branches rested on the far side of the channel behind a big tree. He hadn't chopped the white oak all the way off at the trunk. He had left a little of the tree to hold it at the stump. His doctor had told him not to use an ax. But he had cut this white oak to make a foot log across the stream so he could reach the rugged mountain slope.

Now I followed my father up the winding footpath under the tall hickory trees, a place where I used to come with him when I was a little boy to hunt for squirrels. We would shoot squirrels from the tall scaly-bark hickories and black walnuts with our long rifles. But that had been nearly thirty years ago. And through the years, from time to time, I had walked over this rugged mountain slope and there was never a path on it until my father had made this one. It was a pretty little footpath under the high canopy of hickory, walnut, and oak leaves. We couldn't see the sky above our heads. Our eyes could not find an opening among the leaves.

In front of me walked the little man who once walked

so fast I had to run to follow him. But it wasn't that way now. Time had slowed him. The passing of the years and much hard labor had bent his shoulders. His right shoulder, the one he used to carry his loads, sagged three inches below the left one. His breath didn't come as easy as it used to come. For he stopped twice, and leaned on his cane to rest, before we reached the top of the first bluff. Then we came to a flat where the ground wasn't so steep.

"I like these woods, Jess," my father said. "Remember when we used to come here to hunt for squirrels? Remember when we sat beneath these hickories and the squirrels threw green hickory shells down at us? The morning wind just at the break of day in August was so good to breathe. I can't forget those days. And in October when the rabbits were ripe and the frosts had come and the hickory leaves had turned yellow and when the October winds blew they rustled the big leaves from the trees and they fell like yellow rain drops to the ground! Remember," he said, looking at me with his pale blue eyes, "how our hounds, Rags and Scout, would make the rabbits circle! Those were good days, Jess! That's why I remember this mountain."

"Is that what you wanted to show me?" I asked.

"Oh, no, no," he said as he began to climb the second bluff that lifted abruptly from the flat toward the sky. The pines on top of the mountain above us looked as if the fingers of their long boughs were fondling the substance of a white cloud. Whatever my father wanted me to see was on top of the highest point on my farm. And with the exception of the last three years, I had been over this point many times. I had never seen anything extraordinary upon this high point of rugged land. I had seen the beauty of many wild flowers, a few rock cliffs, and many species of hard and soft-wood trees.

"Why do you take the path straight up the point?" I asked. "Look at these other paths! What are they doing here?"

Within the distance of a few yards, several paths left the main path and circled around the slope, gradually climbing the mountain.

"All paths go to the same place," he answered.

"Then why take the steep one?" I asked.

"I'll explain later," he spoke with half-breaths.

He rested a minute to catch his second wind while I managed to stand on the path by holding to a little sapling, because it was too steep for my feet to hold unless I braced myself.

Then my father started to move slowly up the path again, supporting himself with his cane. I followed at his heels. Just a few steps in front of him a fox squirrel crossed the path and ran up a hickory tree.

"See that, Jess!" he shouted.

"Yes, I did," I answered.

"That brings back something to me," he said. "Brings back the old days to see a fox squirrel. But this won't bring back as much as something I'm goin' to show you."

My curiosity was aroused. I thought he had found a new kind of wild grass, or an unfamiliar herb, or a new kind of tree. For I remembered the time he found a coffee tree in our woods. It is, as far as I know, the only one of its kind growing in our county.

Only twice did my father stop to wipe the sweat from his eyes as he climbed the second steep bluff toward the fingers of the pines. We reached the limbless trunks of these tall straight pines whose branches reached toward the blue depth of sky, for the white cloud was now gone. I saw a clearing, a small clearing of not more than three-fourths of an acre in the heart of this wilderness right on the mountain-top.

"Now, you're comin' to something, son," he said as he pushed down the top wire so he could cross the fence. "This is something I want you to see!"

"Who did this?" I asked. "Who cleared this land and fenced it? Fenced it against what?"

"Stray cattle if they ever get out of the pasture," he answered me curtly. "I cleared this land. And I fenced it!"

"But why did you ever climb to this mountaintop and do this?" I asked him. "Look at the fertile land we have in the valley!"

"Fertile," he laughed as he reached down and picked up a double handful of leaf-rot loam. "This is the land, son! This is it. I've tried all kinds of land!"

Then he smelled of the dirt. He whiffed and whiffed the smell of this wild dirt into his nostrils.

"Just like fresh air," he said as he let the dirt run between his fingers. "It's pleasant to touch, too," he added.

"But, Dad——" I said.

"I know what you think," he interrupted. "Your mother thinks the same thing. She wonders why I ever climbed to this mountaintop to raise my potatoes, yams, and tomatoes! But, Jess," he almost whispered, "anything grown in new ground like this has a better flavor. Wait until my tomatoes are ripe! You'll never taste sweeter tomatoes in your life!"

"They'll soon be ripe, too," I said as I looked at the dozen or more rows of tomatoes on the lower side of the patch.

Then above the tomatoes were a half-dozen rows of yams. Above the yams were, perhaps, three dozen rows of potatoes.

"I don't see a weed in this patch," I laughed. "Won't they grow here?"

"I won't let 'em," he said. "Now this is what I've been wanting you to see!"

"This is the cleanest patch I've ever seen," I bragged. "But I still don't see why you climbed to the top of this mountain to clear this patch. And you did all this against your doctor's orders!"

"Which one?" he asked, laughing.

Then he sat down on a big oak stump and I sat down on a small black-gum stump near him. This was the only place on the mountain where the sun could shine to the ground. And on the lower side of the clearing there was a rim of shadow over the rows of dark stalwart plants loaded with green tomatoes.

"What is the reason for your planting this patch up here?" I asked.

"Twenty times in my life," he said, "a doctor has told me to go home and be with my family as long as I could. Told me not to work. Not to do anything but to live and enjoy the few days I had left me. If the doctors have been right," he said, winking at me, "I have cheated death many times! Now, I've reached the years the Good Book allows to man in his lifetime upon this earth! Threescore years and ten!"

He got up from the stump and wiped the raindrops of sweat from his red-wrinkled face with his big blue bandanna.

"And something else, Jess," he said, motioning for me to follow him to the upper edge of the clearing, "you won't understand until you reach threescore and ten! After these years your time is borrowed. And when you live on that kind of time, then something goes back. Something I cannot explain. You go back to the places you knew and loved. See this steep hill slope." He pointed down from the upper

rim of the clearing toward the deep valley below. "Your
mother and I, when she was nineteen and I was twenty-two,
cleared this mountain slope together. We raised corn, beans,
and pumpkins here," he continued, his voice rising with
excitement—he talked with his hands, too. "Those were the
days. This wasn't land one had to build up. It was already
here as God had made it and all we had to do was clear the
trees and burn the brush. I plowed this mountain with
cattle the first time it was ever plowed. And we raised more
than a barrel of corn to the shock. That's why I came back
up here. I went back to our youth. And this was the only
land left like that was.

"And, Jess," he bragged, "regardless of my threescore
years and ten, I plowed it. Plowed it with a mule! I have,
with just a little help, done all the work. It's like the land
your mother and I used to farm here when I brought my
gun to the field and took home a mess of fox squirrels every
evening!"

I looked at the vast mountain slope below where my
mother and father had farmed. And I could remember,
years later, when they farmed this land. It was on this steep
slope that my father once made me a little wooden plow.
That was when I was six years old and they brought me
to the field to thin corn. I lost my little plow in a furrow
and I cried and cried until he made me another plow. But
I never loved the second plow as I did the first one.

Now, to look at the mountain slope, grown up with tall
trees, many of them big enough to have sawed into lumber
at the mill, it was hard to believe that my father and mother
had cleared this mountain slope and had farmed it for many
years. For many of the trees were sixty feet tall and the wild
vines had matted their tops together.

"And, Jess," he almost whispered, "the doctors told me

to sit still and to take life easy. I couldn't do it. I had to work. I had to go back. I had to smell this rich loam again. This land is not like the land I had to build to grow alfalfa. This is real land. It's the land that God left. I had to come back and dig in it. I had to smell it, sift it through my fingers again. And I wanted to taste yams, tomatoes, and potatoes grown in this land."

From this mountaintop I looked far in every direction over the rugged hills my father and mother had cleared and farmed in corn, tobacco, and cane. The one slope they hadn't cleared was the one from which my father had cleared his last, small patch.

I followed him from his clearing in the sky, down a new path, toward the deep valley below.

"But why do you have so many paths coming from the flat up the steep second bluff?" I asked, since he had promised that he would explain this to me later.

"Oh, yes," he said. "Early last spring, I couldn't climb straight up the steep path. That was when the doctor didn't give me a week to live. I made a longer, easier path so I wouldn't have to do so much climbing. Then, as I got better," he explained, "I made another path that was a little steeper. And as I continued to get better, I made steeper paths. That was one way of knowing I was getting better all the time!"

I followed him down the path, that wound this way and that, three times the length of the path we had climbed.

When Mountain Men
Make Peace

Cief Salyers walked down the Boneyard Hollow turnpike.
At every alternate step his sassafras cane hit the ground.
His eyes did not engulf the distance ahead of him. He
looked toward the ground. His head was bowed as if he
were in a deep study. His shoulders were stooped. When
he reached Mel Renfroe's shack, he left the turnpike and
walked slowly across the yard. He knocked reluctantly on
the door.

Doshia Renfroe opened the door.

"It's not trouble Mel wants?" Cief asked Doshia.

"I don't think it is," she said.

"Better not be," Cief warned. "I'm prepared."

"It's not trouble, Cief," Mel said with a softer voice than
Cief had ever heard him speak. "That's why I've sent for
you to come to me. I'm not able to go to you."

Cief walked inside the big room, where Mel was lying on
a wooden bed in the corner of the room.

"Are you still ailin', Mel?" Cief asked.

"I'm a-dyin'," Mel said.

"Surely you're not, Mel."

"But Death has been here, Cief," Mel said.

41

"How do you know, Mel?"

"I saw him."

"What did he look like?"

"Day before yesterday, when it thundered and lightened, Death was a turkey buzzard a-ridin' high on the wind before the storm," Mel said. "I laid here in my bed and watched the turkey buzzard through the winder as he circled above this shack, a-gittin' closer and closer; but the storm didn't reach here and he sailed back over the mountain.

"Yesterday when it thundered and lightened and a powerful wind bent the treetops," Mel said as he moistened his dry lips with his parched tongue, "Death was a beardy-faced man dressed in ragged clothes, holding to that barbed-wire fence up there on the bank with his bare hands. When the storm didn't get here, he went away. Death can't fool me. He's comin' to me in a storm.

"Today is the third day and he might reach me," Mel talked on. "He's liable to come in the form of a bull black-snake crawlin' across the yard to get the wren that builds on the kitchen porch. He's liable to be a water-soaked stranger that runs into this house from a storm. But I think Death will be back today in the form of a turkey buzzard."

Mel Renfroe's children were gathered in the living room. Cief noticed as he looked at Mel that his long black beard was sprinkled with gray. Cief noticed, where the beard didn't cover his cheeks, they were the pale whitish color of fire-scorched dirt. Even the beardy cheeks were sunken and the yellow fangs from his mouth had been pulled. Cief Salyers couldn't believe now that this was the man who for many years had been his best friend. He couldn't believe this was the man who had helped him make thousands of gallons of moonshine in the gorge under the tough-butted white oaks. He couldn't believe this big, soft-talking man had knocked him completely over the still one night and chased him home trying to kill him.

"I want you to forgive me for everything, Cief," Mel said. "I've not been a bad man. I've allus known right from wrong. I've been a good apple with a few rotten specks in it. Will you forgive me for hittin' you at the still?"

"I'll forgive you, Mel," Cief said, "but I'll never forget how you treated me. I'll not forget as long as there is breath in my body."

Cief walked from beside his bed. He sat down in a rocking chair a few feet away facing Mel's bed.

"I've called Bony Keaton down to my house," Mel said. "He forgave me for all our trouble. I told 'im he could have a road any place through my farm. He confessed to me that he pizened the hog that I bought to catch his chickens. He offered to pay me for the hog and I told 'im we'd cancel the debt I owed him for his chickens. I didn't want these things to come before me when I stand before God Almighty to be jedged."

Cief sat nervously in the rocking chair while thunder grumbled beyond the mountains. Lightning spears bayoneted the sunless air near the window. A buzzard circled on the darkening air. His broad wings flapped against the turgent wind.

"There, he's back," Mel said, pointing toward the window with his big skinny finger. "I told you he'd be here. That's Death come after me."

"Oh, Mel," Doshia said, weeping. "Don't talk like that. Death's not a turkey buzzard."

"Death is a turkey buzzard," Mel said, sticking his moist tongue-tip to his parched lips. "Death can be anything when he wants a man."

Cief squirmed restlessly in his chair while the thunder grew louder and the lightning dashed like heat glimmers above a July cornfield. Cief clawed the rocking-chair arms nervously with his big fingers as he watched the buzzard through the window.

"I've come clean, Cief," Mel said. "I've confessed every wrong I've done but one. When I leave this world, I want to leave it with all my confessions made. When I meet my Maker I want to be able to look Him square in the eye and tell Him the whole story. I want to cut the last rotten speck out'n this good apple."

"You children leave the room," Doshia said. "Your Pappie has something he wants to tell Mr. Salyers."

After they had left, Mel toyed at his dry lips with his long, shriveled, big-knuckled fingers.

"Cief, I've not kilt anybody," Mel said. "I won't have that to answer for. But remember that the three dead revenooers will be resurrected from the secret graves where you laid them."

Cief squirmed in his chair; he fingered at his pistol handle.

"Go on and shoot me, Cief," Mel said. "I've not got much longer to live for Death is a-comin' closer all the time. I know you've got your pistol but you don't need to do more killin'. You've got enough to answer for. You'll have to come clean, Cief."

There was a tremendous crash that shook the window-panes near where Cief was sitting. The lightning splintered a tough-butted white oak. Clouds of strange-colored smoke moved about the riddled tree whose top of dark-green leaves had been singed to a crisp light green.

"You are right, Mel," Cief spoke thoughtfully as he put his hand over his bony face where his beard was growing again.

"One thing more, Cief," Mel said slowly, "I've got to tell you. It was harder to tell Doshia than it will be to tell you. I've made love to Nerva, your wife."

"I feel like a-blowin' your goddammed brains out there in the bed, Mel," Cief said as life surged in him and his face colored crimson among his beard stubble. "You might live a month or two yet. You might even get well."

"No, I won't, Cief," Mel said.

"If I thought you would I'd shoot you right here in your own shack," Cief said.

"Go on and shoot me," Mel said. "You'll have another dead man to answer for when you are jedged."

The great thunder rolled over Mel Renfroe's house; lightning flashes sliced the darkening air to razor-blade thinness. Cief sat sullenly, his face bloodroot red, fondling his pistol butt that was sticking above the leather holster belted on his hip.

"If life had allus been for us just like it is now," Doshia said, crying as if her heart would break. "We've had more peace together since Mel has been sick than we have had in all our married life."

"Have the young'ins come back, Mother," Mel said to Doshia. "I've made my last confession; there's not a rotten speck in this apple."

"All right, Mel," she answered him between sobs.

Doshia tiptoed softly to the kitchen door and told the children to come. They silently followed her to the living room.

"Boys, carry me out in the back yard," Mel whispered. "I want to feel the wind on my face again before the storm gets here."

"We can't carry your bed through the door," Creech said.

"Carry me by the arms and legs," he told them.

"Horace, you get 'im by one arm," Creech directed. "Othie, you get 'im by the other arm. I'll carry his legs."

Creech, Horace, and Othie carried their father through the kitchen to the back yard while Doshia walked beside Mel and held a quilt over him. Cief Salyers walked behind. They carried him beneath the big black oak where the great avalanche of wind that preceded the coming storm rustled the soap-slick bellies of the leaves.

"It's wonderful to see this," Mel said feebly, looking up at the tree with deep-sunken eyes now turned ash-colored in their pale-red sockets. "I've allus loved a comin' storm."

Cief Salyers stood looking at the man with whom he had worked making pure corn and "sugar" moonshine. Cief thought it was strange the way Mel was talking. Then Cief looked above at the threatening sky. The buzzard circled just a few feet above the oak-top, and Cief wondered if a buzzard could smell a dying man, since he remembered how they had sailed over Boliver Tussie's shack at the time people thought Boliver was dying.

"The wind has never felt better to my face," Mel mumbled. "And it's so good to breathe. I love to watch the leaves tremble in the wind. But there goes that buzzard!"

"Lord Almighty, that buzzard swooped low," Creech said.

Mel coughed and strangled. His eyes suddenly became watery.

"What can we do for you, Mel?" Doshia said, rubbing his pale forehead with her trembling hand.

Mel jerked his legs like he was trying to get to the ground. His great chest heaved. His breath went out with a muffled sound like autumn wind whining through the fine-comb-teeth stems of frostbitten crabgrass. Mel fell limp. His powerful body was relaxed forever. Waves of wind-blown rain dashed on his pale face.

"He's dead," Doshia screamed.

"Take it easy, Ma," Lucretia said. She and Melvina helped their mother back to the house while their brothers carried their father in. Cief stood there in the rain, watching until they had closed the door, then he turned and started homeward.

Suddenly the door opened again and Doshia called to him and came running out.

"You forgive him, don't you?" Doshia asked. "You forgive him now?"

"Yes, I forgive him now," Cief replied, "but you know he shouldn't have died so easy."

Doshia wiped her tears and said quietly, "It's good to see men make peace." She started back again and added, "But I don't know who's ever going to forgive you, Cief. Those three dead revenooers can't."

"Don't you ever let me hear you mention them again," Cief said fiercely and turned and hurried off. But just then he saw three streaks of lightning in the sky, and when the lightning flashed again he thought he saw three large birds flying high above the treetops. But it wasn't the three dead men, he told himself, that were going to bother him. They were spying, and they deserved what they got. But he was glad he hadn't shot Mel, even though Doshia did hear Mel accusing him of murder. All he wished now was that Mel were still alive so that he could ask Mel to forgive *him*.

Fight Number Twenty-five

I'D just taken my first shipment of hides to the Greenwood express office when Hade Stableton saw me.

"Eddie—hey, you Eddie Battlestrife—just a minute," Hade hollered at me. "I want to see you!"

"Make it snappy," I yelled. "I want to get this batch of hides on Number Three."

I didn't want to fool with Hade. For every time he'd ever stopped me in his life, he wanted to borrow something from me or he wanted me to do something for him.

"Eddie, I had bad luck last night," Hade grunted soon as he reached me.

"What happened?" I asked.

"Lost my good tree dog, old Rags, and a hundred dollars to boot," he sighed. "You caused it, Eddie!"

"How did I cause it?" I asked him.

"Remember that big wildcat you catched out on Seaton Ridge?" he asked me.

"But what does that have to do with your losin' your best tree dog and a hundred dollars?" I asked. "That wildcat went to West Virginia."

"West Virginia, hell," Hade said. "That wildcat's right up here at Auckland in a cage. I wish that wildcat's hide was among this batch of fur you're expressin'. I'd be a lot better off."

"How'd that wildcat get to Auckland?" I said. "I sold 'im to Elmer Pratt."

"You know who's got the wildcat now?"

"No, I don't."

"Jason Radnor's got 'im," Hade told me.

"Jason Radnor?" I said.

"Yep, Jason Radnor's got 'im," Hade said, shaking his head sadly. "He's got 'im in a big cage. And you pay a dollar to get in to see the cat fight a dog. If you fight a dog against the cat, you pay five dollars! And there's plenty of betting a-goin' on. Old Jason will cover any bet that the cat will whip a dog. Now he's even giving odds. Last night bets went up to five hundred dollars. Jason covered everything that the men bet against his cat!"

"I sold that wildcat to Elmer Pratt for fifty dollars," I said. "I don't need a cat. I didn't want to keep 'im. I could get more for 'im that way than I could for his pelt."

"I know it's bad, Eddie," Hade said. "But I thought I'd tell you! I thought you ought to know about it."

"Yes, I'm glad you told me," I said, as I began thinking about what the wildcat had done to Hade's dog. "I need to know about it. Where do they have that cage?"

"Over the hill from the slaughterhouse where we used to fight our game roosters. But listen, Eddie," Hade went on to warn me, "if you're thinkin' about a-takin' old Buck up there and fightin' that cat you'd better be keerful! I'm a-tellin' you, Eddie! It looked like easy money to me. And I went atter it. Old Scout kilt many a wildcat too. But he never fit one like this cat! He'll never fight another cat! Scout was the nineteenth dog the wildcat's kilt. Boys told me up there last night that old Jason was a-feedin' the wildcat beef blood to make 'im mean. Never saw a meaner cat in my life! Didn't hardly get old Scout in the cage until the cat sprang on him and laid open his side until you could see a whole panel of his ribs!"

"But that didn't kill 'im?" I said.

"Nope, but the old cat spat 'im with the other paw," Eddie said. "That finished the best dog I ever had! Had to give a man five dollars to take Scout out behind the house and shoot 'im to put 'im outen his misery. Guns barked all the time I was there. Had to take the dogs that fit the cat out behind the house and polish 'em off."

"I'd fight that wildcat myself," I said, as I thought about the poor dogs the cat had mangled. "I'll go in the cage with it!"

"Somebody'd haf to polish you off, too," Eddie said. "Now don't get riled. Don't get worked up and lose your head. If I'd a-knowed it would've upset you like this I wouldn't have told you!"

I stood a minute looking down at the toe of my shoe. I thought about the October night when old Buck put the cat up a tree and the way he ran it, full speed like he's after a fox. That was the way Buck had put many a coon up a tree. And just as soon as he treed, I hurried to the tree, thinking he'd got me a coon. But when I reached the place where he was barkin' up a great saw-timber-sized oak with branches big enough for crossties sprangled out from its bushy top, I knew it wasn't any coon. I hardly had to use my lamp, for the big wagon wheel of an October moon was as bright as day and flooded the fields and woods with light. And the wind had whipped enough of the rich wine-colored leaves from the tree so that I could about see over every limb. I walked around the tree looking up and spied the old cat, stretched out, his belly against a big flat limb. He didn't look worried to me. He looked like a cat that was full of confidence. He was a pretty thing a-layin' up there on the limb with his head a-stickin' over and his eyes shining like wind-whipped embers on a pitch-black night.

"Buck, you won't fight 'im," I said to myself. "I'll take care of him, myself." So I went up the tree with my lasso rope. The old cat didn't mind my climbing up there. He laid perfectly still. He was a-takin' himself a good rest. Buck had crowded him pretty hard in the chase. He didn't let him get to the Artner rock cliffs. That was where the wildcats denned. I climbed up at about the right distance and hung my lamp on a twig. I looked for the right opening to throw my rope so I wouldn't hit a limb and scare the cat and make him jump from the tree. I didn't want Buck to fight this cat; I wanted to take 'im alive. I found the right opening. I steadied myself and I threw my lasso.

Guess I was lucky. It went around his neck and I jerked the slack as the cat jumped. But I had him. The more he jumped the tighter the rope drew around his neck. And when his long red tongue popped out of his mouth, I drew him up to me, some weight at the end of the rope. I took him from the tree and released the lasso enough to give him enough breath to keep him alive. I tied his feet with the cords, good and tight. I kept the lasso tight enough not to give him too much wind. I put the wildcat under my arm and carried him to Blakesburg.

Old Buck wasn't satisfied because he didn't get to fight the cat, and he trailed along at my heels a little disappointed. But I knew this was a good catch for one night. It was more than a coffee sack full of dead possums, coons, polecats, minks, weasels, and foxes. If you hunt in these woods, fifty dollars for one night is not to be sneezed at. And it made me the most respected hunter in Blake County, for I was the only man that had ever gone up a tree and took a wildcat with my hands and carried him home in my arms. People knew that I did it, for I'd done it many times before. Older hunters than I was had seen me do it. I took the wildcat home, put him in a cage, and when people passed along the street, they'd come to look at him. And it pleased me when they walked over to see what kind of a looking man I was, just a little, slender, beanpole-sized man with a scraggly beard, that could go up a tree and catch a wildcat.

"Eddie, I'm a-tellin' you not to fight old Buck against that cat," Hade said. "If you'd see that thing cut a dog all to pieces once, you'd never go up in the tree and take him down any more. You'd lose your nerve. The way my poor old Scout run to the side of the cage, looked at me, and cried like a baby," Hade's voice changed until I thought he was crying, "I'll never be able to forget."

I couldn't stand to see that, I thought. I love dogs too well. But I didn't say another word to Hade. Thoughts were running through my mind. I walked into the express office and left Hade standing.

"Remember, Eddie, that my dog was the nineteenth dog that cat had kilt," Hade warned me. "Remember, Radnor'll take your money and——"

I didn't hear the rest of his words. I knew what I was going to do. I knew Buck or I, one, would fight the cat. I didn't want it a-killin' any more dogs. And I knew that I'd like to fight Jason Radnor to even up an old score. I didn't care if he did weigh two hundred and ninety. I hardly knew what I was doin' when I expressed my batch of hides. I went to the First and Peoples Bank and drew out every dollar I'd ever saved. When I got home, I went over to the corner of the house where I had old Buck tied.

"Buck, one of us has to kill a wildcat tonight," I said. "Do you think you can do it?"

Old Buck looked up at me with his big, soft, brown eyes.

Then I unsnapped his chain and started across the yard. I was on my way.

"You're not a-goin' a-huntin' this early," Mollie said when she saw me leading Buck across the yard.

"Yep, I am," I said. "There's a wildcat that's a-killin' a lot of dogs and we want to get 'im."

"Do be careful, Eddie," Mollie warned me. "If it's that dangerous and old Buck trees it, don't you go up and take it from the tree."

"I'll promise you I won't take it from a tree," I said.

I wonder if old Jason will remember me, I thought, as I walked toward Auckland, a distance of twelve miles.

When I reached the shack down the hill from the slaughterhouse there was a man ahead of me with a big English bull.

"There's the dog that'll kill that damned wildcat," a beardy-faced man said, pointing to the big broad bulldog.

The beardy-faced man looked at old Buck, then he looked at me. Buck wasn't a big dog. And he looked pinched in two, for I hadn't fed him anything. I didn't want to feed 'im anything before a fight. Buck smelled blood and trouble. He held his tail down as if he were about to spring at something. Then I heard a pistol go off behind the house and I knew another dog was finished. Buck was on his mettle, for he didn't know exactly what was taking place. I pulled my hat down low and got my six-hundred-odd dollars ready.

Soon as the big red-faced man ahead of me had paid the five dollars to fight his bulldog, I stepped up to the entrance.

"Say, feller," said the tall, hatchet-faced man at the door, "you don't aim to fight that old dog against this wildcat, do you? He's not as big as the wildcat!"

"I want to fight the dog or fight the wildcat myself," I said, and then I gave a wild laugh.

The man looked at me with his black, beady eyes like he thought I was crazy. But he let me inside the shack.

It was a big room filled with men and a few dogs. Over at the far end of the room was a big wire cage. And inside the cage lay the same old wildcat that I had taken from the oak tree on Seaton Ridge. He was a-layin' there as peaceful-like, just like any cat, with his head across his paws, as if he wanted to sleep and the men and dogs wouldn't let him. He looked just as mean as he did the night I carried him back to Blakesburg. His big tushes hung out over his lips. And his whiskers looked like old Davey Burton's handle-bar mustache. Beardy-faced men, with mean-looking eyes, stood back and looked at the cat. I led Buck up to the cage where he could get a whiff of the cat. I looked down to see what Buck thought. All he did was jerk his tail. He never even growled.

When the big, clean-shaven, well-dressed man led his bull-dog up to the cage, the bull tried to break through to the cat. He trembled all over, growled, and scratched the floor. When he barked, the slobbers flew from his big mouth.

"I'm a-puttin' up a hundred dollars on that dog," a man said. "What odds you givin'?"

And then the bets started. I looked over against the wall and there sat big Jason Radnor behind a table, counting out money to cover the bet. Since the cat belonged to Jason, no one but him was allowed to bet on the cat. Jason covered all the money that was bet on the dog, giving three-to-two odds. It was a funny way to bet, and we'd never bet that way at rooster fighting. And I guess that's why everybody wanted to see the cat killed. Jason was raking in the money. But I wanted to see the cat killed because it was killin' the dogs.

"Jason's got a gold mine with that cat," said a tall lantern-jawed man who was standing beside me.

And while the greenbacks were shelled out on top of the table, for the bulldog was a good bet, Jason pulled money from a drawer and covered each bet. I watched Jason to see if he was looking at me and if he recognized me. But he was too busy betting and making money to recognize anybody. He was sitting there with all that money around him, and I knew this kind of betting was better than playing poker on Sundays or spitting at cracks. Jason was in the money.

"Say, mister, what have you been a-feedin' that bulldog?" asked a short, dark-complexioned man.

"Beef blood and beef bones," the owner said. "I've been a-feedin' 'im that and getting 'im ready for this fight ever since Radnor first brought the cat here!"

"I'll bet a hundred then," the man said.

Jason covered his hundred while the bulldog charged at the chain.

"All bets in?" Jason asked.

There wasn't any answer.

"Let 'im in the gate, Little Man," Jason said.

A little man with a scattered, heavy beard on his weather-beaten face unlocked the cage door. And the big man patted his dog on the back.

He's a good-lookin' bull to be slaughtered by that cat, I thought.

"Take 'im, Buck, and good luck!" the man spoke with a trembling voice as he unsnapped the collar and the bulldog charged full force toward the cat. As the bulldog charged at its throat, the cat leaped high in the air, and when it came down on the dog's back, it raked a paw around his slats, his big claws, longer than a tack hammer, sinking deeper and deeper as the bulldog groaned.

"There goes my money," a man shouted.

"There goes all our money," the tall man said. "Damn, I wish we'd get a dog that could kill that hellcat. I've lost over a thousand dollars in this dang hole."

I didn't listen to all the men said. I looked down at my Buck. He was moving his tail like a cat does when it sees a mouse and gets ready for the crouch. When the poor bull-dog got the cat's claws from his ribs, he came over to the wire and cried like a baby. I never heard more pitiful crying. It hurt me through and through to hear it.

"He's through," a man said. "When they do that, they've had enough. Take him from the cage."

He didn't look like he was clawed up too badly until he came from the cage.

"Mister, you'll have to have Sherman to polish 'im off," Little Man said. "He's through. If you don't have 'im finished, he'll die by degrees."

When the well-dressed man led his bulldog out behind the house to have Sherman polish him off, another tall lanky man from Culp Creek came up with a big mountain cur. He was a long dog with a mean black eye.

You might not get to fight the cat, Buck, I thought. If I were betting, I'd bet on this dog.

"What have you been a-feedin' this dog, mister?" a little stooped-shouldered man asked.

"Corndodger," the cur's owner said. "Just what you feed a good dog."

"I was raised on it, mister," another man said. "I'm bettin' fifty on your dog!"

"Looks like a good bet to me," a tall lanky man with fuzzy chin whiskers said. "I like his build. Listen to his growlin' at that cat! Sounds like low thunder!"

But the bets didn't go as high as they did on the English bull. I looked over at Jason's table and I didn't see the stacks

of greenbacks like I'd seen there a few minutes before. And just as the last money was in and Jason was covering it, we heard a pistol fire twice. The English bull had been polished off. And the big mountain cur, with his bristles raised on his back like jutted rocks along the top of a winter-bleak mountain, charged against the chain to get to the cat.

"Ready to go, Little Man," Jason said. "Turn 'im in."

The beard-scant, weathered-looking little man who tended to the cage unlocked the door, and the tall man let the big cur inside and unsnapped the collar. When the cat saw this big black mountain cur, he never rose to his feet but laid flat on his back as the dog charged, and just as the dog started over for the cat's throat, he ripped into him from beneath with both hind feet. The cur whined, fell over, got up again, and whined as pitifully as a small baby crying. He walked slowly to a corner of the cage—I couldn't bear to look at him. I wanted to get into that cage so bad I could hardly stand it.

"It's a shame," one of the men said, "to fight good dogs against that murdering wildcat. You can feed 'em beef, beef's blood, corndodger, and anything you want to feed 'em, but that doesn't make any difference when it comes to a fight. Not one dog has stayed with that cat three minutes!"

"Lost again," another man said, not paying any attention to the poor cur that had lost his life. "Lost another fifty bucks."

Sighs went up from among the mean-eyed men when Little Man pulled the cur through the door. He was awful to look at, and to think of him now makes me mad. Old Buck looked at the poor cut-to-pieces cur disgustedly.

"Get 'im to Sherman quick," Little Man said. "Let 'im polish 'im off soon as he can, to put 'im outen his misery."

We saw two more fights. We saw the cat lay on his back and cut a pretty shepherd to pieces. There wasn't much betting on this fight, although the shepherd came the nearest getting to the cat's throat of any of the dogs. And there was a big brindle bulldog that the cat seemed to hate more than any dog that had been turned in. That bull never even got close to the wildcat. He had him cut to pieces before he got halfway across the cage. What was left of him was dragged outside by his master, a well-dressed city man from Auckland.

"I'm glad it's over," said a big fat man with a handle-bar mustache. "I'd rather see cockfighting, a boxing bout, or a wrestling match any old time as to see these good-looking dogs go in there and get ripped up."

"Yep, I'd rather go with my wife to the movies as to slip out here to this unlawful place and see this," said the tall man who had bet heavily on every fight against the cat.

"It's a wonder this place ain't raided by the law!"

"But it's not over yet," I said loud enough so the men could hear me.

They were mixing around and intermingling in the crowded room, getting ready to leave. And I couldn't blame them for that. I'd smelled enough and I'd seen enough for one evening. The smell in the shack was awful. The crowd was awful, too.

I couldn't understand how anybody could enjoy seein' dogs cut to pieces by a wildcat.

"But that dog can't do anything," one man said. "That cat'd kill 'im before Little Man got 'im inside."

"Little Man ain't a-puttin' this dog in," I said. "I'm goin' in the cage with 'im myself."

"What's that I hear?" Jason said from over in the corner, as he stacked his money away.

"I'm going to take old Buck in myself," I said.

"Are you crazy, feller?" Jason said. "Don't you know if a man gets ripped up here, we can't have Sherman to polish 'im off, and this place will be raided shore enough."

"I wouldn't be afraid to fight that cat," I said. "Give me a piece of rope fourteen feet long and I'll fight 'im."

"Don't be foolish," Jason said. "You don't seem to know much about the power of a wildcat!"

Then I heard a lot of whispers in the crowd. I heard men saying that I was off in the head.

"How much are you willing to bet that my wildcat won't kill your dog?" Jason said. "You'll be the only one to bet on your dog. No one else will!"

"I think I got about six hundred and fifty-three dollars," I said. "It's my life savings and I don't want to bet it all."

"Well, I've got ten times that," Jason said. "I'll put my pile against yours!"

Then the men who'd been moving toward the door stopped. They were surprised at the money I had. And they were surprised when Jason said he'd put up all he had against what I had. They knew he had a pile, for he had taken their money on twenty-four fights. My dog was Number Twenty-five for the cat to fight. And I knew all the men except Sherman, Little Man, Jason, and the fellow who took our money at the door would be for me. They'd want to see my dog win.

"Mister Radnor, I hate to bet all my money," I said. "If I lose, I won't have a dollar in the world left and my dog will be gone."

"Well, that's what you come here for, to fight that old mongrel, wasn't it?" Jason said gruffly as he put the last roll of bills back in the table drawer. "And I'd as soon have your money as anybody else's."

"Yes, but I didn't know you had sich a big wildcat," I said. "And I can't stand to see it a-killin' all these fine-looking dogs."

"Come on or get out," Jason said. "After all, we bet here. This isn't a playhouse. It's a fightin' house."

"Will you let me take my dog inside? If you will, I'll put my pile up against yours!"

"I'm afraid of it," Jason said.

"Let 'im learn," one of the men shouted. "We've seen about everything now. Let's see something new!"

"I'm willin' to run the risk," Jason said thoughtfully, as he arose from the table and looked me over.

Then I went over to the table and counted out my money. Jason brought his from the drawer and I made him let me look inside to see that the drawer was clean.

"You watch the money, men," I said to the fellows gathered around me. "I want this to be square and honest."

"We'll see to that," said the fellow that had lost the big English bull.

"Sure we will," said the one that had lost the cur.

"Then open the door, Little Man," I said.

Old Buck didn't growl and he didn't charge against the chain. He just looked at the cat and jerked his tail.

"He's a funny dog," said one of the men behind me.

But I didn't look back to see who had said it. I had my eye on the cat. Buck had his eye on the cat. Then I reached down and rubbed his back. I patted his head as I reached midway of the cage. The cat laid perfectly still. He planned to work on Buck like he did the big mountain cur. Then I unsnapped Buck's chain. Buck crouched halfway. But he didn't take his eye off the cat. And he never growled, but he crept slowly toward the cat as I stepped to one side. Men rushed up and stood on their toes around the cage, like something was going to happen.

Buck went close. But he wouldn't go farther.

"Watch 'im, Buck," I said. "Let 'im make the first move."

Buck held like an Irish setter—he didn't go a step. The cat looked at him with his shiny green eyes, and Buck looked back at the cat. Then all at once the cat began to crouch. Buck held his position. Then the cat made a flying charge and Buck flattened on the cage floor. As the cat went over, Buck whirled and sprang from behind like April lightning. He caught the cat across the skull and the sound went plunk. It was a light crash but the cat sprawled senseless on the floor, its legs quivering and drawing up to its body then out again, each time a little weaker.

"What did that dog do?" a man asked me.

"What about that?" another man said.

"Leave that money or there'll be another death," I heard a voice growl.

"That dog knows how to tree wildcats," I said. "And he knows how to kill them. It's been suicide on the dogs to put them in here, dogs that never fought a wildcat. Buck knows that a wildcat's skull is as easy to crush as a rabbit's. It's a little bit easier—a wildcat's skull is thinner."

"Good boy, Buck," I patted his head.

I snapped the chain into his collar and we left the cage. The wildcat had breathed his last.

"There's your cat, Jason Radnor," I said. "He'll never kill another dog. And the money you made by clawin' dogs to pieces won't do you any good."

"Who are you, anyway?" Jason said, his voice trembling. He was shaking all over.

"Jason, I'm the man that caught that wildcat," I said. "My dog treed it and I went up in the tree and brought it down with my hands. I'm Eddie Battlestrife. You remember my dad, don't you—remember, you tried to kill him? Shot 'im not four feet away between the eyes but you didn't kill him. The bullet parted his hair. He was taking a few quarters from you in a poker game that Sunday afternoon. Now don't shake, Jason, I'm not a-goin' to hurt you. I just want all that money. It's good money and I like money and I like to see old Buck kill a wildcat that's kilt twenty-four dogs."

"Easy, Radnor," said the tall man that owned the cur. "Don't move. Keep your hands up! He took your money and he took it fair."

"Fairer than the way you got it from us," the bulldog's owner said.

"Nice bank account now," I said as I picked up the rolls of greenbacks and put them back in my hunting coat.

"It's a fraud," Jason wept. "It's a stick-up!"

"Easy, Mr. Radnor," the tall man said, as I walked from the shack with old Buck. "Keep your hands up!"

"You won't have to polish this dog off, Sherman," I said as I went through the door. "You can bury your cat."

No Petty Thief

MAYBE it was the coming of the rains that caused the thing to happen. For the rains came early that November to the mountains. They were cold rains as well as I remember, dropping from the black clouds that raced over the mountaintops like thin-bellied foxhounds. Driven by high mountain winds, they lashed at the treetops, stripping them bare long before it was time to shed their leaves. It was these early rains that stopped the work on the highway they were building through the mountains.

I guess I ought to 've been ashamed of myself, too, for it was the first road ever to be built in our country. It was a real road they were making. They were going down into the deep valleys and around the rocky-walled mountains and over the mountains. Of course we had several jolt-wagon roads, log roads, cowpaths, goat paths, fox paths, rabbit paths, and footpaths. But you couldn't drive an automobile over one of these. And if the contractors could've only finished the big road and covered it with loose gravel before November, we'd a-had a real road that people could've driven automobiles over. It would've been a real road like I've heard a few counties in the mountains already had. I've only heard about these roads. I've never seen one of 'em.

And because we didn't have automobiles in our county, nice spring wagons and hug-me-tight buggies and a lot of fancy vehicles like they had in other counties and in Edensburg, the county-seat town of our county, maybe that is what caused me to do what I did. For I'd stood in the Edensburg streets many times and watched the automobiles roll over the dirt streets and out of town a little ways as far as the turnpikes went. And I watched the buggies, hug-me-tights, and the fancy express wagons. I loved to watch their wheels roll. It was a lot better than the sleds we used, pulled by a team of skinny mules on our hilly farm. The sled slid over the ground on runners winter and summer. And it wasn't any fun watching runners slide and hearing the green dogwood runners grit on the rocks and the hard dry dirt. But it was fun to watch wheels roll. I'd stand and watch them for hours, and what I wanted most in this world was to own something with wheels. Whether I could find level ground enough around our house or not for the wheels to roll, if I had just had something with wheels I could have sat and looked at it for hours, admiring the wheels and the machinery.

Now if it wasn't the rains coming early or my love for wheels and machinery, I don't know what made me do it. I do know that I was raised in a decent home. My pa never used the word "raised" when he spoke about one of his ten young'ins. He allus said he didn't raise young'ins but he "jerked 'em up by the hair on the head." And Pa was about right in a way. He did jerk us up by the hair on the head but he didn't use any monkey business. He was a strict man in a fashion, belonging to the Old Fashion Church, and when he jerked us up by the hair on the head, he did it in decency and order. That's why I hate what I've done on account of Pa and Ma. They never learned us to lie, steal, gamble, cuss, smoke, and drink. And when I tell you what happened to me, I don't want you to blame Ma and Pa. They had nothing to do with it. And I'll regret what I done to my dying day just because of Ma and Pa.

As I have said, the rains came early to the mountains in that November. And before the Big Road got too muddy, the men got the machinery out. I mean they drove the dump trucks, the caterpillar tractors, and big graders back to Edensburg where they had started the road from in the first place. But one piece of machinery they didn't take back with 'em was the big steam shovel. Maybe it was because it couldn't go back over the muddy road under its own power, and maybe it was too big for a caterpillar tractor to pull. Maybe they were afraid it would bog down even if pulled under its own power and with a tractor helping it. Anyway, they left it a-settin' there lonesome-like in the November rain.

I didn't work on the road. I had too much work at home to do. For I raised light burley terbacker on the steep mountain slope, where it was too steep to plow with mules but I dug the ground up with a hoe. And every time I had a chance to leave the terbacker, say fer a few hours, I would hurry over the mountain to watch 'em build the Big Road. I liked to watch a piece of machinery working like a man and I liked to watch the wheels roll. One of the pieces of machinery I loved most of all was the big steam shovel. And when it was left alone sitting in the rain, an idear popped into my head. And I went back home to get my monkey wrench.

You may think it was a hard job. But it wasn't too hard. I started taking off the little pieces first. I started stripping it like the wind and rain was stripping a big tree of leaves. Only I had a warm feeling for the steam shovel, and the wind and the rain didn't have any feeling fer the tree. There was something about this steam shovel that I loved. It was a beautiful thing to me. I had the same love touching it that a lot of the mountain boys have fer their pistols. It was the touch of ownership; yet I knew it didn't belong to me. But it would belong to me. It would belong to me even fer a little while. I knew that it was mine. Fer I was going to take it. And I was taking it to a place where I didn't think it would ever be found. And if it was found, it would be a place that it couldn't move out under its own power plus a dozen caterpillar tractors pulling at it.

After I'd taken it apart I started carrying the little pieces over the mountain. Maybe I'd better tell you what kind of strength I have. I'm not a little weakling what you might think. I'm not what you'd call a real tall man. I just measure a bit over twelve hands high, which is a little over six feet. But I'm almost six hands across the shoulders. And my legs above my knees are about the size of tough-butted white oaks big enough for banks timbers and below my knees they are big as gnarled locust fence posts. My wrists are big as handspikes, tapering up to my arm muscles, which are pretty powerful and I'm not a-lying. When I swell my arm muscles they're nigh as big as half-a-gallon lard buckets.

If Brother John was alive today, he could tell you the time when I lifted the back end of a jolt wagon from a chughole when it was loaded with corn. Eif Porter could tell you the time when ten wood choppers, one at a time, tried to lift the butt end of a sawlog and I was the only one that could come up with it. I didn't even get red in the face lifting it, either. I ain't a-saying that I'm the biggest and the stoutest man in the hills, but I ain't a-lyin' when I tell you I'm powerful on a lift. And everybody around home could tell you that I couldn't get a pair of boots big enough to fit me. My legs wouldn't go down into 'em. Too much calf on my leg. I was pretty well fitted fer the task that I was a-going to do.

So I started carrying my steam shovel up over the mountain and down the other side to my terbacker barn that was built on the steep slope with a high lower side and a short upper side. And I arranged my terbacker that was a-curing on terbacker sticks on the tierpoles all around the sides and the ends of the barn. I had a big open space in the middle of my barn with big brown terbacker walls all around that no human eye could see through. Right in the middle of my barn, I shoveled off a level place to set up my steam shovel.

You'd be surprised how many parts there are to a steam shovel. The best way to find this out is to start taking one apart. It's a lot of work. And it would be awfully hard if a body had to do a lot of watching out fer somebody a-trying to catch him. But I guess the road builders thought a steam shovel would be safe to leave where they had stopped working on the road. They even guarded their trucks and tractors in Edensburg, but they didn't bother to guard the steam shovel or even send anybody back to look about it. So I didn't have anybody around to bother me. And I got in some good time.

If I's to tell you how long it took me to take it down and take the parts apart, it would surprise you. I had it down in less than three days and had taken it apart. And I didn't let any dead leaves gather under my feet when I started carrying it over the mountain. I'd take a big load and I'd never set it down to wind a minute. I'd carry it right to the barn and take it back under the bright wall of terbacker to the place I'd prepared for it.

Believe it or not, I rolled the wheels, one at a time, over the mountain. A steam shovel's wheels ain't too big a thing but they are powerfully heavy. And the beam that holds the shovel is one of the pieces I couldn't carry. So I hitched my mules to it and dragged it like I's a-snakin' a big crosstie up over the mountain. I took all the parts loose from the engine I could, but the main body of the engine I hauled on my sled across the mountain. And the shovel was as big a load as any man would want to carry, but the worst thing about it was the durned shovel was so unhandy for a body to get on his back. So I hauled that over on a sled, too. I carried all of it or rolled it but these three pieces. And I got it in the terbacker barn by myself because I didn't want to let anybody in on the secret. I carried so many loads over the mountain that I made a path from where the steam shovel used to be to my barn. My shoe heels had sunk into the earth since I carried such heavy loads on my back. But I knew the sun would come out and dry the leaves and the wind would blow the leaves over the mountain again and kiver up all the trail. I knew it was too much of a job for me to go back with a stick or a rake and kiver up the path that I had made with my heavy brogans. So I left it to the wind, sun, and the rain to kiver the trail of evidence I'd left behind me.

Then came the happiest hours I ever spent in my life. I

was putting my steam shovel back together. I'd laid out all the parts careful not to get them mixed. First I put the wheels on good foundations and got up the framework. And then I used a block and tackle that I used at hog-killing time to swing up the beam and the shovel. For I couldn't get up steam and let it work under its own power in my ter-backer barn. I would have set the barn on fire and lost my terbacker crop and my steam shovel. I had to do it myself just with the help of the block and tackle. And I had by the end of November one of the prettiest things in my barn that ever my eyes looked upon when it come to machinery.

It was hard for me to believe that I had it. Sometimes it seemed like a dream. But I would pinch myself as I went to my barn to look at it again, again, and again to see if I were asleep and dreaming or if I were wide awake. But I wasn't dreaming. I was very much awake. Even my wife knew something was wrong with me, since I spent so much time at the barn. But I told her my terbacker was in "case" and I was taking it down and handing it off. She had allus helped me at this busy season with the terbacker, but she felt good and thought I loved her more when I told her that I would be able to take care of the terbacker this season. Since she was slender as a beanpole and I was such a mountain of a man, she had allus climbed up on the tierpoles and handed the terbacker down fer me to strip. She was allus afraid that a tierpole would come unnailed when I swung onto it a-climbin' up in the barn. But she didn't have all this worry about me now.

I would go to my barn in the morning and just stand and look at my steam shovel. And I'd think of the power it had. I'd think about the way I'd seen it bite into the dirt and rocks easier than I could sink my teeth into a piece of squir-rel or possum. And how it would lift a big bite of dirt and rocks onto the trucks. How graceful the long beam would swing around just by pulling a little lever, and then there was another little lever a body pulled and it would unload its bite into the truck. And how it puffed, blew, and steamed but it never sweated no matter how much dirt and rocks it moved. All day long it worked and it never tired. I guessed it could do the work of a hundred men with picks and shovels. And after it had dug a slice of road, how it would move with huffs and puffs under its own powerful power to a new place and start work. And now I loved to put my hand onto it and I had a sense of ownership and power, a feeling that nearly lifted me to the skies.

But the November rains stopped falling. The winter sun had come out again, making the day bright and warm. Though the ground froze a little at night, it wasn't enough to have stopped my steam shovel's eating away the earth. For the bright sunlight and the crisp wind had made the weather good again for road building. And as I had expected, the road builders came back and brought their machinery. Naturally, they didn't find the steam shovel.

There was a lot of excitement. They had expected it to be right where they left it. And the day I sauntered over where I had dismantled the shovel, I found a crowd gathered around and I joined them to listen to their talk. I never saw a crowd of men so confused. Nearly every man on this road gang said the steam shovel had to be taken off under its own power and there wasn't any road for it to get out except going back through Edensburg.

They had all been living in Edensburg and not one had seen a steam shovel rolling through the streets of this little mountain town. Besides, when it had passed through on its way to build us a road, all the young'ins in the town had followed it. And the old people who had never seen a steam shovel had come out to watch it, too. It was the biggest thing that had ever gone through the town. And now the road builders argued with each other how the shovel had ever been taken back through the town, popular as it was among the people, without someone a-seeing it. One man laughed, said it had grown wings big enough to fly it over the mountain back to "civilization." The men said a lot of foolish things like that. But one of the old men with hard, cold, blue eyes said he didn't think it was impossible for a man to carry it away on his back and that was the only way he believed it could have got away. When he said these words he looked me over. He looked at my shoulders and my big hands, forearms, and my legs that were cased in my overalls, stretching them like full mealsacks. Then he pointed out that the steam shovel tracks didn't leave the spot, and the ground had been tramped down like a floor around where the steam shovel had once been. But when he said these words everybody laughed and said that was impossible, but I could tell from the way this old man acted that he believed it had been carried away.

I didn't feel comfortable any longer around these men. And when I snuck away they were talking about bringing in an "expert" to find the steam shovel. I didn't go back the way I'd carried the steam shovel fer I thought they might get suspicy and come over the path to my barn. I went down another path and circled out of my way a couple of miles like a fox. Instead of going down to my barn from the north, I came in from the west. And I went in to look at my shovel again. There it was, safe, pretty, and dry. And it was in a place that I didn't think it would ever be found. Even if they had to buy a new steam shovel or stop building the road that we needed so much, I didn't care. It was a toy I loved to fondle and something I wanted to keep forever.

I guess I did neglect my wife and my two young'ins since in these last days I spent so much time at the barn. Rhoda thought my work with the terbacker was coming along mighty slow. She even tried to hurry me to get it off to the market before Christmas. But Christmas or no Christmas, I still fondled my toy. I looked at its beauty and thought of its power and forgot about Christmas although the terbacker was in case and the season was wonderful. Rhodie even threatened coming to the barn and helping me. But I told her not to mind for I had the work well under hand and that I could easily do it myself.

And I guess I would have gotten along someway if it hadn't been for the "expert" the boss-man of the road gang went out somewhere and got to help him find the shovel. And maybe it was the wind and the sun of that early December that were against me. Maybe it was the rain had failed to do its part. I could have laid it onto several things when I heard voices upon the mountain and peeped through a crack in the barn. I saw a big man in front, dressed in good clothes, whose face I'd never seen with the road builders before. He was leading the men like a pack of hounds. He was out in front on my tracks. He was following the path I had made. The rain had never erased my deep shoe prints in the dirt and if the leaves had once kivered them, the sun had dried the leaves and the wind had blown them off again, leaving my path clean as a whistle fer 'em to follow. And that old man with the cold, hard, blue eyes must have put the "expert" wise that a man could carry off a steam shovel. For they found it clean, dry, and purty in my terbacker barn.

No use to tell you more about it. Naturally I was arrested and tried in Edensburg. And people came in great droves to hear the trial. There was a lot in the papers about it. They

even had my picture in the papers. And everybody wondered how I had carried away a steam shovel. Even the
jurymen would hardly believe it until I told them the truth.
When they swore me to God that I could tell the truth that
is just what I done. I told 'em I wasn't no petty thief. I told
'em I'd never stole anything in my life before. I told them
the whole story how I'd carried it all but three pieces and
that I thought I could've carried two of them. Even I had
a time convincing the jury against my lawyer's advice that I
had done it. But I finally convinced them after the whole
jury went to the spot. They followed me over the path to
my barn where I showed them the shovel.

If you know the people and the laws in our state, it
would've been better fer me to 've kilt a man. I would have
stood a better chance of coming clear. Anyway I wouldn't

have got but one or two years in the pen even if I hadn't done it in self-defense. But when you steal something, even if it's just a chicken, let alone a steam shovel, you're a gone gosling. Why they let me off with only seven years and a day was, I was honest enough to tell the truth after they found the shovel in my barn. If I'd a-tried to got outen it, I'd been given life. The road builders fit me hard, too, fer they had to build a road to my barn to get the shovel. Not a one of the whole gang was man enough to carry it back.

The Slipover Sweater

Now if you don't get the sweater," Grace said as she followed me up the narrow mountain path, "you mustn't feel too badly. Everybody in Gadsen High School knows that you've made your letters. Just because you don't wear them like the other boys. . . ."

Grace stopped walking before she finished the last sentence. And I knew why. But I didn't say anything—not right then. I stopped a minute to look down over the cliffs into the gorge where the mountain water swirled over the rocks, singing a melancholy song without words. Grace walked over and stood beside me. And I knew the sound of the roaring water did the same thing to her that it did to me. We stood there watching this clear blue mountain water hit and swirl over the giant water-beaten rocks, splashing into spray as it had done for hundreds of years before we were born.

The large yellow-gold leaves sifted slowly down from the tall poplars. And the leaves fell like big, soft, red raindrops from low bushy-topped sourwoods to ferny ground. Dark frostbitten oak leaves slithered down among the lacework of tree branches to the leaf-carpeted ground. Two of these oak leaves dropped onto Grace's ripe-wheat-colored hair. And a big yellow-gold poplar leaf fell and stuck to my

76

shirt. They were a little damp, for they fell from a canopy of leaves where there was no sun.

Gold poplar leaves would look good in Jo-Anne Burton's chestnut-colored hair, I thought. And how pretty the dark oak leaves would look on her blouse. I was sorry she wasn't with me instead of Grace. I could just see Jo-Anne standing there with the red and yellow leaves falling on her.

I would say, "Gee, you look wonderful with those golden leaves in your dark hair."

"Do you think so?" she would answer. And I could imagine her smile and her even white teeth. She was always gay and laughing.

I didn't say anything to Grace but Grace knew how I felt about Jo-Anne. Grace and I had gone to Plum Grove grade school together for eight years. I had carried her books from the time I could remember. And then we started walking five miles across the mountains to Gadsen High School together. When we started to Gadsen I was still carrying her books. I'd carried them down and up this mountain for three years. But I was not carrying her books this year and I wouldn't be again, for Gadsen was a bigger school than Plum Grove and there were many more girls. But there was only one for me and Grace knew who she was. She was the prettiest and the most popular girl in Gadsen High School. When she was a sophomore she was elected May Queen.

Grace knew why I wanted the slipover sweater. It wasn't just to show the letters and the three stripes on the sleeve I'd won playing football three years for the Gadsen Tigers. Grace knew that Roy Tomlinson had a slipover sweater and that he was trying to beat my time with Jo-Anne Burton. Grace had heard about Jo-Anne asking me one day why I didn't get a sweater.

"You've got a small waist and broad shoulders," Jo-Anne had said, "and you'd look wonderful in a slipover sweater!"

I didn't care about having a sweater until Jo-Anne had said this to me. Now I wanted it more than anything on earth. I wanted a good one, of the style, color, and brand the other boys had bought. Then I could have my G and the three stripes sewed on, as my teammates had done. They let their favorite girls wear their sweaters. Jo-Anne was wearing Roy Tomlinson's, and that hurt me.

Grace probably knew I was thinking of Jo-Anne now. And as she stood beside me, with the leaves falling onto her dress, I couldn't keep from thinking how they would look on Jo-Anne.

Why we had stopped at this high place every morning and evening for three years, I didn't know. But it was from here on the coldest days in winter, when the gorge below was a mass of ice, that we listened to the water singing its lonesome song beneath the ice. And here in early April we watched spring come back to the mountains.

We knew which trees leafed first. And even before the leaves came back we found trailing arbutus that had sprung up beside the cliffs and bloomed. Then came the percoon that sprang from the loamy coves where old logs had lain and rotted. It was the prettiest of all wildwood flowers and its season was short. Grace and I had taken bouquets of this to our high-school teachers before a sprig of green had come to the town below.

Grace shook the multicolored leaves from her hair and dress when we silently turned to move away. And I brushed the leaves from my shirtsleeves and trousers. We started up the mountain as we had done for the past three years—only I used to take Grace's arm. Now I walked in front and led the way. If there was a snake across the path, I took care of him. I just protected Grace as any boy would protect a girl he had once loved but had ceased to love since he had found another girl who meant more to him than anyone else in the world.

"If I had the money," Grace said after our long silence, "I'd let you have it, Shan, to buy your sweater."

"I'll get the money some way," I said.

Not another word was spoken while we climbed toward the ridge. But I did a lot of thinking. I was trying to figure out how I could buy that sweater. I was not going to hunt and trap wild animals any more and sell their skins just to get clothing for my own skin. Books had changed me since I'd gone to high school. I'd never have the teacher send me home because I had polecat scent on me. I'd always bought my schoolbooks and my clothes by hunting and trapping. But I'd not done it this year and I'd not do it again. I was determined about that. Books had made me want to do something in life—for my girl. And I knew now that I wanted to be a schoolteacher and teach math in Gadsen High School. And that's what I'd do.

When Grace started from the path across to her home, a big double-log house on Seaton Ridge, she said good-by. And I said good-by to her. These were the only words spoken. We used to linger a long time at this spot by a big oak tree. I looked over at the heart cut in the bark of the oak. Her initials and mine were cut side by side inside the heart. Now, if I'd had my knife, I would have gone over and shaved these initials and the heart from the oak bark. Now I hoped that she would find some boy she could love as much as I loved Jo-Anne.

When I first realized I had to get that sweater for Jo-

Anne, I had thought about asking Pa for ten dollars. But I knew he wouldn't have it, for he raised light burley tobacco, like Grace's father, and it hadn't been a good season. Pa had not made enough to buy winter clothes for my four brothers and six sisters. And another thing, I'd never in my life asked him for money. I'd made my own way. I'd told my father I'd do this if he'd only let me go to high school. He wasn't much on education. But he agreed to this and I'd stick to my end of the bargain.

That night I thought about the people I knew. I wondered if I could borrow from one of them. I didn't like to borrow, but I'd do anything to get Jo-Anne to take off Roy Tomlinson's sweater and to put mine on in place of it. Most of the people I knew did not have the money, though.

At noon the next day the idea came to me: what are banks for? Their job is to lend money to needy people—and that's why I walked straight to the Citizens' State Bank at lunchtime. I was a citizen, a student at Gadsen High School, and I needed money to buy a sweater. If Mr. Cole asked me why I needed the money, I'd just tell him I wanted very much to buy myself a sweater so I could put my school letter on it and my three stripes—and be like the other high-school boys. I wouldn't mention Jo-Anne.

I stood nervously at the window. Mr. Cole was a big heavy man with blue eyes and a pleasant smile. "Something I can do for you?" he asked politely.

"Yes, sir," I stammered. "I'd like to have ten dollars."

"You want to borrow it?" he asked.

"Yes, sir." Now the worst was over and my voice was calmer.

"You go to high school, don't you?"

"Yes, sir."

"Thought I'd seen you around here," he said. "You're the star player on the Gadsen Tigers—you're Mick Stringer's boy."

"Yes, sir," I said.

"What's your first name?" He started making out a note for me.

"Shan," I said, "Shan Stringer."

He shoved the note forward for me to sign. And he didn't ask for anyone to go my security. If he had, I don't know who I could have got to sign. I wasn't old enough to borrow money at the bank. But it just seemed to me as if Mr. Cole read my mind. He knew I wanted the money badly. So he gave me nine dollars and seventy-five cents and took a quarter for interest.

"This note will be due in three months," he said. "This is October twenty-eighth. Come back January twenty-eighth. And if you can't pay it then, I'll let you renew for another three months. And then we'll expect all or partial payment."

"Thank you, Mr. Cole."

I hurried to Womack Brothers' store and bought the sweater. It had a red body with white sleeves—the Gadsen High colors. I would have Mom sew the white G on the front and the red stripes on the sleeves as soon as I got home. I was the happiest boy in the world. Gadsen High School had always been a fine place but now it was wonderful. I loved everybody but I worshiped Jo-Anne Burton.

That afternoon when Grace and I walked through the town and came to the mountain path, we talked more than we had in a long time. But I didn't mention what was in the package I was carrying. We stopped at our place on the cliffs and looked down at the swirling waters in the gorge. The dashing water did not sound melancholy to me. It was swift dance music like a reel from old Scotland. Even the trees above us with their arms interlaced were in love. All the world was in love because I had got what I wanted and I was in love.

The next morning Grace was waiting for me beside the old oak where we had cut our initials. Grace was all right, I thought. She was almost sure to be valedictorian of our class and she was good-looking too. But she didn't have the kind of beauty Jo-Anne had. Jo-Anne was not only beautiful— she was always happy, laughing and showing her pretty teeth. She wasn't one of the best students in the class—her grades were not high at all. But she was friendly with everybody and as free as the wind. Her clothes were always pretty, and they fitted her much better than Grace's did. I loved the way she wore her clothes. I loved everything about Jo-Anne. She held my love as firmly as the mountain loam held the roots of the wild flowers and the big trees.

"Why are you taking that bundle back to school?" Grace asked.

"Oh, just to be carrying something," I said.

Grace laughed as though she thought I was very funny.

We got to school early. When I had a chance to speak to Jo-Anne alone, I told her what I had.

"Oh, Shan!" she exclaimed. "Oh, you're a darling!"

"Brand-new," I said. "You'll like it, Jo-Anne."

"Oh, I know I'll love it," she said. "I'll put it right on!"

I handed her the package and she hurried off. I was never happier in my life. When she came back she was smiling at me, her eyes dancing. She walked over to Roy Tomlinson and handed a package to him. Everybody standing around was looking at Jo-Anne in the new sweater with the three stripes on the sleeve—the only sweater in the school with three stripes. Was Jo-Anne proud! And I was proud!

"Do you like it on me?" she asked as she walked up to me.

"Do I like it?" I said. "I love it."

She smiled happily and I was glad that Roy could see now that I was the one Jo-Anne loved. And everybody knew now that I was in love with her. Roy would probably wonder, I was thinking, how I was able to buy that sweater. He had probably thought that he would be able to keep Jo-Anne with his sweater and his two stripes because I'd never be able to buy one for her. But Roy would never know how I got it—that would be a secret between Mr. Cole, the banker, and me.

While the girls were admiring the sweater and many of my teammates were looking on, I glanced over at Roy. He stood by not saying a word, just looking at the sweater that had replaced his. I hadn't expected him to react that way, but in a few minutes Grace came in and she was wearing Roy Tomlinson's sweater.

"Boy!" Jim Darby exclaimed. "Look at Grace! Doesn't that sweater look swell on her!"

"She isn't the same girl!" Ed Patton said.

I stared at Grace. I didn't realize a sweater could make such a difference. Her clothes had never become her. But this sweater did! There were many whispers and a lot of excitement as we flocked into the auditorium. I was watching Grace move through the crowd in her new sweater when Jo-Anne edged over close to me.

"You do like this sweater on me, don't you, Shan?" she asked.

"Sure do, Jo-Anne," I said. And I walked proudly beside her into the auditorium.

That afternoon after I had said good-by to Jo-Anne I looked around for Grace. She was just saying her good-by to Roy. When she turned toward me I could see that she was as proud of that sweater as she could be. And Roy stood there looking after us as we started toward the mountain together.

We stopped at the gorge but we didn't stay long. Grace did most of the talking and I did the listening but I didn't hear everything she said. I was wild with joy for I was thinking about Jo-Anne wearing my new red sweater.

At every football game Jo-Anne sat on the front bleacher and yelled for me. And Grace yelled for Roy Tomlinson. Once when I made an eighty-five-yard run for a touchdown Jo-Anne came up to me after the game and kissed me. I could outkick, outpass, and outrun Roy Tomlinson. And I didn't brag when I said it. He earned another stripe that season and so did I. Grace sewed Roy's third stripe on his sweater with pride. She kept the sweater clean as a pin. I'll have to admit she kept it cleaner than Jo-Anne kept mine.

When Grace was almost sure to be valedictorian, Roy Tomlinson could hardly stand the idea of our walking over the mountain together. He walked with us to the edge of Gadsen. But he never climbed the mountain and looked down at the gorge. He could just as well have come along. His going with her didn't bother me, not exactly. She did, of course, seem close to me—like a sister. As we walked along together I saw the trees along the ridge where we had had our playhouse and grapevine swings. I saw the coves where we had gathered bouquets of trailing arbutus and percoon. And those initials on the oak reminded me of the days when we were little.

It was in the basketball season, just before the regional tournament, when I received a notice from the bank that my note was due. With the other little expenses I had at school even twenty-five cents wasn't easy to get.

If the interest is hard to get, I thought, what will I do about the principal? What if I have to take the sweater from Jo-Anne and sell it to make a payment on the principal?

But when my mother let me have fifty cents and I paid the interest I felt much better and didn't think about it again during the basketball season. Jo-Anne came to every game and she was always urging everybody else to come. She was as proud of me and the way I played as I was proud of her and the way she looked in my sweater.

Grace was never so talkative and gay and popular as Jo-Anne and I was always glad to hear anyone pay Grace compliments. I heard Harley Potters say one day, "You know, Grace Hinton is a beautiful girl. Think, she comes five miles to school and five miles home and makes the highest grades in her class. There's something to a girl that would go through all kinds of weather and do that."

I thought so too. All through the winters when snow was on the ground and the winds blew harshly on the mountain, she and I had walked back and forth to school. I walked in front and broke the path through new fallen snow. I had done that even when we went to Plum Grove. We had walked through the rain and sleet together and I couldn't remember a day that she had not been good-natured. And I knew she had the durability and the toughness of a storm-battered mountain oak. I didn't believe there was another girl in Gadsen High School who could have done what Grace had done. And now to the Gadsen boys and girls she was as pretty as a cove sapling. Yet I was sure I would never go back to Grace. I'd always love Jo-Anne.

I only hoped that Roy Tomlinson appreciated Grace. I

got a little tired of looking at his sweater so often. Sometimes I wondered if I were jealous of him for making his third stripe. But I was sure I wasn't because I had four, and I had the most popular and beautiful girl in the world. I decided I was tired of looking at it just because Grace never wore anything else. I could hardly remember what Grace's clothes had looked like before.

When the heavy snows of January and February passed away in melted snow and ran down the gorge in deep foaming waters, I grew as melancholy as the song of this swollen little winter river. Jo-Anne didn't know what was worrying me. Sometimes I wished she would ask but she never did. And that hurt me too. If I didn't always smile at something she said, she acted impatient with me. I'm sure I could not have told her about the note due in April, if she had asked. But I looked for some kind of sympathy because I thought I needed it and that she loved me so much she would want to cheer me up. Instead, she kept asking me if I didn't love her and if I did, why didn't I show it the way all the other boys did?

So I tried my best to cheer up. I didn't want to lose her but I did have to figure out some way to make money. I couldn't hunt now even if I'd change my mind about killing animals. Spring was on the way and animal pelts weren't good now.

One day Grace said to me, "What is the matter with you, Shan?" That was in late March as we were watching the blue melted snow waters roll down the gorge where the white dogwood sprays bent down to touch them. "I know something is bothering you."

"No, it isn't," I said, "I'm all right."

"If I can ever help you, I'll be glad to," she said. "Just let me know."

Her words made me feel better. I didn't want to tell her that I'd never been in debt before and that a debt worried me to death. So I didn't say anything.

After the snow had melted from the mountain, I grew more despondent. Neither the sight of Jo-Anne nor of Grace could cheer me. My grades went down and some of the teachers asked me what had happened to me. Everyone around me seemed happy, for April had come again. And Jo-Anne seemed gayer than ever. Several of my teammates had their eyes on her constantly and it only made me more despondent.

Grace coaxed me again one day to tell her what was wrong. "You always like spring on the mountain," she said.

Then I decided I had to tell somebody my trouble and she was the one to tell. "Grace," I confessed, "I need money —ten dollars!"

"I don't have it," Grace said quietly. "If I did, you could have it. But that doesn't help. Maybe I'll think of a way. . . ."

I didn't think she would, but it made me feel better—just to share my worry.

On April fifteenth something happened to me that the whole school witnessed. We were gathering for assembly period when Jo-Anne handed my sweater back to me!

"I'm tired of it," she said, without the pretty smile on her lips. "And I'm tired of your ways. You go around with your lower lip drooped as if the world had turned upside down and smashed you. You never have anything to say. You've just become a bore and everybody knows it." She left me standing there with my sweater in my hand.

I was stunned. I couldn't speak. My face grew hot and I felt everybody looking at me. When I looked up I saw Grace and Roy standing at the other side of the auditorium.

They were looking in my direction and Grace suddenly started to talk to Roy and neither looked my way again. I don't know how I got through that day at school.

After school I didn't wait for Grace. I hurried out and away from them all. But just as I started up the mountain, Grace overtook me.

"I've thought of something, Shan. I know a way to get ten dollars."

I looked at her without speaking. I was still stunned.

"You know there's a big price at Dave Darby's store for roots and hides and poultry," she said, speaking quickly. "I noticed that sign yesterday. And you know the coves above the gorges are filled with ginseng, yellowroot, and May-apple root."

She waited for me to speak. I walked in silence for a while, thinking it was all too late now—thinking I'd sell my sweater for whatever I could get for it.

"When is the note due?" she asked.

"Ten more days," I said. "April twenty-eighth."

"We'll have it by then," she said.

We, I thought. I looked at her and thought of Jo-Anne. Jo-Anne was pretty and gay and popular but her face had changed in my mind. I began to wonder if all that gaiety was real—and what she had meant by "love." I was too puzzled to think anything out.

Grace and I walked along silently. We didn't stop at the gorge because Grace had suggested that we go into the cove. I just followed along and started to hunt ginseng after Grace had started.

I never saw anyone before who could find three-prong and four-prong ginseng like Grace. We found patches of yellowroot and May apple. We filled our lunch pails with these precious roots and I took them home, strung them the way Mom used to string apples and shuckbeans to dry, and hung them on nails driven on the wall above our stove.

We stopped every evening that week and gathered wild roots, and I brought them home to dry. On April twenty-seventh, one day before my note was due—and I had already received the notice—I took a small paper sack of dried May-apple roots, a small sack of yellowroot, and more than a pound of the precious ginseng roots to Dave Darby. When he was through weighing the roots he did some figuring. Then he said, "It all comes to sixteen dollars if you trade it out in the store."

"How much if I take cash?" I asked.

"Fifteen dollars," he said.

"Let me have the cash."

I went straight to the Citizens' State Bank and paid off my note. And I had five dollars for Grace. I never felt better, not even when I was so much in love with Jo-Anne.

As I walked home with Grace I told her how much the roots had brought. "This is not your half," I said as I gave her the five dollars, "but we'll dig more until we get your share. I paid my note."

"Wonderful," she said, smiling at me.

I looked at Grace. Whatever had been wrong with me, I wondered. Why didn't I see before that she had beauty such as Jo-Anne could never have? Grace was as beautiful as our mountain was in April, prettier than a blossom of wild phlox or a mountain daisy. She was as solid as the jutted cliffs, I thought, and as durable as the mountain oaks.

"Now ask me if there is anything more I want from you," I said as I took her arm to help her up the mountain toward the gorge and the wild-root coves.

"What is it?" she asked quickly.

"Take off Roy Tomlinson's sweater," I said. "I'm awfully tired of looking at it."

"But what will I do without it?" she said. "It keeps me warm."

I didn't answer. I started to pull off mine. Then I felt her hand on my arm. "No, Shan," she said. "Keep it a while. I couldn't wear it yet."

We stood silently on the mountain path and looked at each other. "I couldn't wear it yet," she had said. And that was all the promise I needed. I knew how fine she was and I was proud that she would not discard Roy Tomlinson's sweater as Jo-Anne had done, without a word to him first.

I didn't know what she was thinking as we started down the path and she didn't know what I was thinking. I didn't ask her, she didn't ask me. But I was thinking that our high-school days would soon be over and I could build a house, if she'd want it there, right on Seaton Ridge on the path that leads from her family's house to mine.

Thirty-two Votes before Breakfast

Mr. Silas Devers was the man that hired me. He was the man that made all the plans. Even before daylight that morning, when we were a-gittin' ready to start with Al Cancy, Mr. Devers got out a map. He had me to hold the flashlight while he went over the map. It was a map of Blake County. And he had little blue, red, and black pencil marks running all over the map. While he ran his big forefinger over these lines, I couldn't help but watch 'im. He went from one voting precinct to another. I happened to know all the precincts because I'd worked in many elections before. But never before had I worked in an election when we got up at three o'clock in the morning and were on the road before four o'clock. I knew something was in the wind. As Mr. Devers looked over the map, when his forefinger went to a voting precinct, he stopped and held his finger there while he checked in a notebook with his other hand and read some directions. He had a lot of stuff written down I could hardly read. But I did make out a different name for each precinct.

It took Mr. Devers several minutes to go over his map and read his notes. But that wasn't none of my business. I was working for my party, the Greenough party, and I was a-gittin' paid besides. A ten-spot for the use of your car on election day isn't to be sneezed at. But Al Caney just sit there in the back seat of the car and rolled his quid of terbacker around in his jaw and I didn't see how he could do it that early in the morning before he'd had his breakfast. But he did. He didn't do any talking when Mr. Devers was goin' over the map. He didn't even try to look on. Sometimes he rubbed his big bony hand over his beardy face to wipe a sliver of brown ambeer from his lip. Al Caney just didn't seem to mind what was goin' on. I wondered if he didn't have an understandin' with Mr. Devers same as I had. But what stumped me was, I thought I could remember when Al Caney was a Dinwiddie. I knew all the other Caneys were Dinwiddies. I didn't exactly understand what he was doin' with us. But I would soon find out.

"It's a close election this time, boys," Mr. Devers said, as he took a last look at the map, folded it carefully, stuck it in his coat pocket, and settled down in his seat. "We gotta start, Dave."

"Okay, Mr. Devers," I said, as I started the motor and turned on my lights.

Mr. Devers turned off his flashlight and stuck it in his pocket. Then he climbed in the front seat.

"Which way, Mr. Devers?"

"To the Blackoak precinct first," he said.

"But Mr. Devers," I said, "that's on the other side of Blake County!"

"Never mind where it is, Dave," he said. "You're getting paid and you must listen to reason."

"Okay," I said.

"Step on it," he said. "We want to be there by six. Want to be the first ones there when the polls open!"

I stepped on the gas. I went down the road like a bat out o' hell. There was not a light in any of the windows. Everybody must've been asleep. And I cut the curves from one side of the road to the other. I drove so fast I almost scared myself. But Mr. Devers didn't mind. He was so big that he took up most of the front seat beside me, and when I hit a chughole the watch chain across his vest gave a little tinkle like a sheep bell. And Al Caney sat in the back seat, never saying a word, chewin' his quid and spittin' out the window.

"While the Dinwiddies sleep, we work," Mr. Devers said, and then he laughed like a big-throated bullfrog.

"I'm gittin' hungry, Silas," Al Caney said, as he rolled his quid with his tongue from his mouth onto his hand and threw it from the car. "I've not had any breakfast, you know!"

"I've not had any, either," Mr. Devers said. "We've got to make Blackoak first. Then we'll talk about breakfast."

It's chewin' that green burley twist that's making him hungry, I thought. But I didn't say what I thought, since it wasn't any of my business.

Al Caney groaned and complained with his stomach and said he was about half sick.

"I'll fix all that half-sickness, Al," Mr. Devers said. "Just wait till we get to Blackoak. I know what you need. Our party'll have it on hand!"

Just before we got to Blackoak, Mr. Devers got out his notebook and looked at the name again.

"Remember, Al, your name is Casper Higgins, and you live on Sand Suck, if anybody questions you," Mr. Devers instructed Al. "Can you remember?"

"Sure can, Silas," Al Caney said.

When we drove up to the Blackoak school, there was a

light in the windows. The polls had opened. But I didn't see a crowd hangin' on the outside like we always saw in Blake County on election days.

"My name's Casper Higgins, and I live on Sand Suck," Al Caney said when he got out of the car.

"That's right, Al," Mr. Devers said, as he rolled out like a big barrel.

Just to see what happened, I got out and went in too.

"We don't vote here," Mr. Devers told one of the election judges. "We're bringin' a man here to vote."

"Name, please?" one of the women clerks asked.

"Casper Higgins," Al said.

"Casper Higgins?" the clerk repeated. "Ain't he dead?"

"Dead! Am I dead?" Al asked. "I hope to tell you I'm not! Isn't my name on the record?"

"It's been marked out," she said.

"Mark it back in," Al said. "I'm goin' to vote! How dare you mark it out!"

"Well, if he's not dead," one of the judges said, "he's entitled to vote same as any taxpayer!"

See, we had two Greenough judges at each precinct, and the Dinwiddies had one. Our county judge was a Greenough, and he appointed the election judges.

"You see I'm not dead," Al complained, as if he were mad as a wet hen.

"Let 'im vote," the second judge said.

Mr. Devers seemed pleased. I saw him wink at one of the judges as Al went into the booth, a place surrounded by bed sheets, to vote.

Just as soon as Al had voted, we hurried out the Blackoak schoolhouse, and were on our way.

"You did fine, Al," Mr. Devers said, reaching him two brand-new one-dollar bills. "Smooth talk."

"But about my breakfast, Silas?" Al complained, rubbing his stomach. "Peers like I have a hard time gettin' my breath when I get hungry!"

"We'll take care of that at Plum Forks," Mr. Devers said. "Sorry I fergot to get you somethin' back there!"

"To Plum Forks next, Mr. Devers?" I said.

"That's right," he said. "Step on the gas."

I wondered how we was goin' to get any breakfast for we were ridin' up Lambert River where there wasn't even a country store.

Before we got to Plum Forks, Mr. Devers looked at his paper and map.

"You're Columbus Mitchell, Al," Mr. Devers said. "And you live on Hoods Run!"

"Okay, Silas," Al said. "I can remember that all right. I ust to know old Columbus!"

"Name, please," the woman clerk asked Al.

"Columbus Mitchell," Al said.

"Columbus Mitchell," she spoke politely. "W'y, I thought he'd passed on."

"Nope, right here he is," Al said, grinning and showing his front discolored teeth. "I'm here to vote!"

I saw Mr. Devers wink at one of the judges.

"Oh, yes, Columbus," the judge said. "Go on and vote!"

One of the judges looked puzzled when Al went back to vote.

Mr. Devers was mighty pleased when Al walked from behind the sheet.

"Say, you couldn't spare us a little nip, could you, Bill?" Mr. Devers asked the judge that he'd winked at a minute before. "We've not had any breakfast!"

"Shore," he said, and he got up from his chair while the other judges and clerks watched us.

He walked beside us to the doorsteps, talking in low whispers to Mr. Devers. Then he slipped Mr. Devers a big bottle that he pulled from behind his coat lining, where I heard more bottles rattle.

When we got back to the car Mr. Devers took a swig first, and then he passed the bottle to me, and I nipped because I didn't like too much on an empty stomach, and then he passed the bottle to Al. I was glad he let me nip before he did Al, because Al's mouth looked like the mouth of a deserted coal mine propped up with decayed posts.

"Now, Dave," Mr. Devers spoke in a big way, "I'll let you in on the plan! We want to get all the precincts on Lambert River by eleven. Then we'll come down Sutton River, and get all the precincts by three this afternoon. In the next three hours we can finish all the precincts in Blakesburg and down Big River!"

"You mean we're goin' to take in all thirty-two precincts?" I asked.

"That's what we're a-goin' to do," he said.

"Impossible," I said.

I could tell by the way Mr. Devers puffed up, I'd said the wrong thing.

"Oh, I guess we can make it if they don't ask Al too many questions," I said. "I mean if they don't hold us too long questionin' Al. . . ."

"Never mind that, Dave," Mr. Devers said. "You leave it to me! I've got that all fixed up!"

Before we reached Farewell precinct, Mr. Devers consulted his map and notebook.

"Who am I now, Silas?" Al asked.

"Buck Stump," Mr. Devers said. "And you live on Dry Ridge."

I never knew a Buck Stump, but I knew a lot of Stumps

lived on Dry Ridge. I'd fox-hunted with 'em. That was the home of the Stumps. Mr. Devers had fixed his notebook and map all right.

"Buck Stump," the clerk said, "I thought he was run away from here for stealin' chickens!"

"I never stole a chicken in my life," Al said, looking hard at the woman. "How dare you say that!"

But one of the judges tried to smooth it out for the woman.

"It must have been another Buck Stump," he said. "You know there's more Buck Stumps on that Dry Ridge. There's Old Buck, Little Buck, Red Buck, Black Buck, White Buck, and Zeke's Buck, and Cy's Buck . . . and a lot more I can't think of now."

Everybody laughed while the judges let Al go behind the sheet.

Al seemed awfully hurt when he returned from voting. The clerk who had made the mistake tried to apologize and be nice to him, but he refused all apologies. He got out as soon as he could, and we followed him.

"Well done, Al," Mr. Devers said. "Smooth talk."

"But ye forget something, Silas," Al said.

"Breakfast, ah, breakfast," Mr. Devers said. "We shall have that, Al!"

"No, it's not that," Al said. "I'm not a bit hungry now!"

"Oh, oh, yes, I did forget, didn't I?" Mr. Devers said, as he went down in his pocket for a roll of greenbacks bigger than the calf of my leg. He shelled off four new one-dollar bills for Al.

I didn't say anything. But I thought a lot. Here I was driving my car over this rough road and was only gettin' ten bucks. And just to think if Al did make all the precincts, it would be sixty-four dollars for him! There wasn't anything fair about it. But I wouldn't say anything. I'd wait until the end of the day! Somebody'd have to make things right.

Al voted at Wolf Pen as Lonnie Ailster, who was a Dinwiddie. The clerk said Lonnie was working in St. Louis. Al told her he'd never worked in St. Louis, that he'd never seen the place. Well, the judge that Mr. Devers winked at apologized for the clerk to make her feel better after she'd made the mistake. At Grassy, Al voted as Duff Anderson, and the clerk didn't question him, but congratulated him on coming back to his wife after disappearing for five years. At Riverbend, Al voted for Alvin Miller, a Greenough who was away cutting corn in Ohio.

"See, the farther out you get among the hills, the easier it is," Mr. Devers said. "Hardly anybody around Riverbend ever sees Al Miller. Hardly anybody knows 'im. See what I mean!"

"Yes, I see," I said.

But I said that just to be nice to Mr. Devers. I knew he could make that one little mistake.

But we went to the eleven precincts up Lambert River by eleven-thirty. Just thirty minutes behind schedule. Al voted at Kenton for Tim Wurts, a Greenough, who worked away in the West Virginia coal mines. He voted in Woodland for Tom Snyder, who had been sent to the pen at Atlanta for making moonshine several years ago. The clerks didn't question his registration or his identity, for they were so glad to see him back with his family. At Three Prong he voted for Hugh Gullet. He was questioned by the clerk, who said she was sure that Hugh Gullet had moved away.

"Moved away," Al said. "I've never moved away. How did that get started?"

And a friendly judge said he hadn't moved away, and he apologized for the clerk's mistake.

At Whetstone, he voted for Brice Tremble, a "lifelong" Dinwiddie. One of the judges said Al didn't look like Brice. But Al said he was Brice, and two of the judges let him vote. We wondered what the real Brice would say when he got to the polls. But Mr. Devers said he wouldn't get to the polls until late in the afternoon. Said he was over on Sand Suck where he'd been cutting timber and wouldn't spend a whole day for the election. At the Head-of-Lambert precinct, the last one up the river in Blake County, Al voted for John And-Seven-Eighths Smith, another longtime Dinwiddie, who was down on Willow Run running a sawmill. John's father had given him the middle name to distinguish him from so many John Smiths living in the Head-of-Lambert precinct.

When we finished with this precinct, Al had twenty-two pretty one-dollar bills stuffed down in his overall pockets. I thought plenty but still didn't say anything. For we'd just driven away from Head-of-Lambert precinct, on our way over the ridge toward Sutton River, when Al took some sort of a fainting spell. Maybe it was because he'd made all this money, and maybe it was because he'd chawed green twist so early in the morning, and on top of that drank some bad hooch. It had given me something like the blind billiards. I could tell Mr. Devers didn't act the same, and we hadn't drank near as much as Al.

Maybe it was just as well it happened as we were about to reach the big hill that separated the two rivers. For we wouldn't have wanted anybody around. There'd been a lot of people hanging around the polls who heard the argument when Al went in and said he was John And-Seven-Eighths Smith. And now if Al got sick on us and the real

John And-Seven-Eighths Smith did get back from the saw-mill, we'd be in bad shape. But we opened the car door when Al passed out, and we carried him up on the bank by the side of the road and fanned 'im for a spell. When he came to, his face was whiter than any sheet we'd seen around the booths.

"Pay no attention to me, boys," Al spoke with little short gasps of breath. "I'm havin' trouble gettin' my wind!"

But I was glad when Al stumbled back to the car.

"Reckon he's all right?" I asked Mr. Devers. "Suppose we can make the fourteen precincts on Sutton River?"

"What are you talkin' about?" Mr. Devers asked me. "You know Al can make it all right. We're goin' to stop at the Porter store on North Fork as we go down," he talked on, "and get some cheese under our belts. We're a little behind, but we can make all thirty-two precincts! That'll be a record, won't it?"

"Guess it will," I said, thinking about how a few men had been able to vote in five or six precincts in one day, but that I'd never heard in my life of one making eleven precincts. We already had a record.

We stopped at the store and got cheese, brown sugar, sardines, and crackers. We did most of our eating in the car, and Mr. Devers and I did most of the eating.

"Don't be douncy, Al," Mr. Devers warned. "We've got a lot to do. You've got a lot more dollars to earn. Thirty-two votes may win this election! So, eat, my good friend!"

"Grub don't taste right," Al said.

Al only took a few bites, then he washed it down from the long-neck bottle he stuck in the cavern that was his mouth until his whiskers and mustache hid the bottleneck. He gurgled and gurgled, and his Adam's apple ran up and down his neck like a tree frog. And after he'd washed the cheese and crackers down his gullet, he bit off more green burley from his twist. Then I saw a little color come back to his face.

"We'll take these precincts as they come, boys," Mr. Devers said, when he reached sight of the Sutton River.

At Blue Licks, Al voted for Lewis MacKenzie; at Hoptown for Marcus Overton; and at Argill for Tom Kidwell. At Honeyville, he voted for Cief Hampton; at Centerview, for Tom Cromwell; at Enoch's Chapel, for Eif Fannin; and at Five Rivers, for Larry Watkin. At Twin Forks, Al voted for Milford Kilgore, a Dinwiddie, who had gone to a funeral. At Three Mile, he voted for Jim Welch; and at John's Run, for Jack Pruitt.

But at Pee Pee-Dee, Mr. Devers turned pale as a mushroom when Al gave his name as Mart Spencer, and one of the clerks asked, "When did you get back from the pen?"

"I'm not the Mart that stabbed your brother," Al said. "I'm not even akin to 'im. I just happen to live among those Spencers."

The clerk was pleased. So were the judges. Al voted.

At Willow Grove, Al voted for Gus Powers; at Lundsford, for Demp Bush; and at Putt-Off Ford, for Hawk Seymore.

"Twenty-five precincts, and fifty dollars," Mr. Devers said, giving Al another two new one-dollar bills. "Seven more to go!"

Boy, that burnt me up. Here Al had made fifty bucks. A Dinwiddie by blood and belief had taken that much from our Party, and I got a measly ten-spot! But I still kept my mouth shet. I knew Al had been through a lot, too. He'd been twenty-five different men. And he'd had several faintin' spells in the back of the car. He'd been complaining about his stomach, and once or twice he said his ticker was flutterin' like a mockingbird's wings.

"We're comin' to Blakesburg No. 1," Mr. Devers said, "where we'll get our legal and lawful votes! That'll make twenty-eight votes for the Greenoughs from us this mornin'!"

Mr. Devers had the look of victory on his face after we'd voted at Blakesburg No. 1.

"When we get to Blakesburg No. 2, you're goin' to be Reverend Spencer Hix that ust to hold the big revivals under the tent," Mr. Devers said.

"Did you hear me, Al?" Mr. Devers asked, since Al hadn't answered.

"Yep, I hear you," Al groaned. "I'm Reverend Hix in Blakesburg No. 2."

"Right," Mr. Devers said, as I brought my car to a stop.

I never saw so many people around at any of the voting places. They were swarming around Link Bratton's vacant store building like bees around a hive.

We walked inside and Al had to stand in line to vote.

"Name, please?" the woman clerk asked Al.

"Reverend Hix," Al said. "I've voted 28 times for the Greenoughs, and I aim to vote again!"

"What Reverend Hix?" she asked, looking Al in the eye.

"The Reverend Spencer Hix, that used to hold the tent meetings," Al shouted.

"Sure, this is Reverend Hix," Mr. Devers said, as he looked at a Greenough clerk and winked.

"No, you're not Reverend Hix," the clerk said. "I go to his church. I heard him preach last Sunday. Against the Greenoughs too! No, you're not Reverend Spencer Hix! I know you're not! This is fraud!"

"I know I am," Al shouted. "And I'll show you that I am! I'll show you I'll vote."

"Al Caney," Mr. Devers said, but it was too late.

Al started to dive behind the sheet when a big man grabbed him. Then the election judge caught Al around the legs. And down on the floor went all three men while more ran in to help.

"That thing's not Reverend Hix," a big woman shouted and raised her green parasol above her head to hit Al. "I'll brain 'im," she screamed.

But Mr. Devers, who'd kept out of the tussle, ran up and caught her parasol.

"That awful man!" another woman shouted. "Thinks he's Reverend Hix! He must be drunk or crazy!"

Soon the voting place was filled with men and women. They knew Reverend Hix. They belonged to his church.

I never saw such a mad scramble in my life! Al Caney was screaming that he was the Reverend Spencer Hix. Women and men were trying to get to him while he fought with the men on the floor.

"He's drunk," one man said. "Let's have 'im arrested!"

"He's off in the head," another shouted. "Reverend Hix just voted a few minutes ago!"

"Who brought 'im in here?" a big beardy-faced man asked.

"That's the feller," said a tall beanpole man with scattered beard on his face, as he pointed to Mr. Devers.

"Yes, that's the man," said a woman, who was in the voting line. "That's the man over there!"

"Something strange goin' on here," said the big beardy-faced man, "and I'll see what it is. Can't do Reverend Hix like this! Look, this man, Al, has passed out. He's drunk!"

Mr. Devers must have jumped fifteen feet out at the door.

I was a few steps behind him, but I couldn't run like he did. I didn't know any man could run as fast as Mr. Devers. It looked like he was takin' steps on the wind. For his feet were up in the air, working like pistons. If they ever hit the ground it was so fast I couldn't see 'em.

"Here's my car, Mr. Devers," I screamed, but he was so excited he didn't hear me.

He ran to some stranger's car with about two dozen women and a dozen men after him. They were yelling and screaming! And Mr. Devers opened the door of the wrong car and got in. He thought it was mine. But I couldn't go after him. I had to save my own skin. They weren't after me yet.

"He's in Reverend Hix's car," a woman shouted. "We've got 'im!"

When I turned on the switch and started the motor in a hurry, I looked toward Reverend Hix's car, and I saw Mr. Devers trying to get him to drive on like he'd been doin' me. But Reverend Hix sat under the steering wheel and laughed while the mob of voters surrounded the car.

I gunned into the highway, and I was off like a flash of lightning cutting the night. I never looked back. I knew I'd keep on goin' as long as my ten Greenough dollars lasted.

Testimony of Trees

WE had just moved onto the first farm we had ever owned
when Jake Timmins walked down the path to the barn
where Pa and I were nailing planks on a barn stall. Pa stood
with a nail in one hand and his hatchet in the other while
I stood holding the plank. We watched this small man with
a beardy face walk toward us. He took short steps and
jabbed his sharpened sourwood cane into the ground as he
hurried down the path.

"Wonder what he's after?" Pa asked as Jake Timmins
came near the barn.

"Don't know," I said.

"Howdy, Mick," Jake said as he leaned on his cane and
looked over the new barn that we had built.

"Howdy, Jake," Pa grunted. We had heard how Jake
Timmins had taken men's farms. Pa was nervous when he
spoke, for I watched the hatchet shake in his hand.

"I see ye're still a-putting improve-ments on yer barn,"
Jake said.

"A-tryin' to get it fixed for winter," Pa told him.

"I'd advise ye to stop now, Mick," he said. "Jist want to
be fair with ye so ye won't go ahead and do a lot of work
fer me fer nothing."

"How's that, Jake?" Pa asked.

"Ye've built yer barn on my land, Mick," he said with a little laugh.

"Ain't you a-joking, Jake?" Pa asked him.

"Nope, this is my land by rights," he told Pa as he looked our new barn over. "I hate to take this land with this fine barn on it, but it's mine and I'll haf to take it."

"I'm afraid not, Jake," Pa said. "I've been around here since I was a boy. I know where the lines run. I know that ledge of rocks with that row of oak trees a-growing on it is the line!"

"No it hain't, Mick," Jake said. "If it goes to court, ye'll find out. The line runs from that big dead chestnut up there on the knoll, straight across this holler to the top of the knoll up there where the twin hickories grow."

"But that takes my barn, my meadow, my garden," Pa said. "That takes ten acres of the best land I have. It almost gets my house!"

The hatchet quivered in Pa's hand and his lips trembled when he spoke.

"Tim Mennix sold ye land that belonged to me," Jake said.

"But you ought to a-said something about it before I built my house and barn on it," Pa told Jake fast as the words would leave his mouth.

"Sorry, Mick," Jake said, "but I must be a-going. I've given ye fair warning that ye air a-building on my land!"

"But I bought this land," Pa told him. "I'm a-goin' to keep it."

"I can't hep that," Jake told Pa as he turned to walk away. "Don't tear this barn down fer it's on my property!"

"Don't worry, Jake," Pa said. "I'm not a-tearing this barn down. I'll be a-feeding my cattle in it this winter!"

Jake Timmins walked slowly up the path the way he had come. Pa and I stood watching him as he stopped and looked our barn over; then he looked at our garden that we had fenced and he looked at the new house that we had built.

"I guess he'll be a-claiming the house too," Pa said.

And just as soon as Jake Timmins crossed the ledge of rocks that separated our farms Pa threw his hatchet to the ground and hurried from the barn.

"Where are you a-going, Pa?" I asked.

"To see Tim Mennix."

"Can I go too?"

"Come along," he said.

We hurried over the mountain path toward Tim Mennix's shack. He lived two miles from us. Pa's brogan shoes rustled the fallen leaves that covered the path. October wind moaned among the leafless treetops. Soon as we reached the shack we found Tim cutting wood near his woodshed.

"What's the hurry, Mick?" Tim asked Pa who stood wiping sweat from his October-leaf-colored face with his blue bandanna.

"Jake Timmins is a-tryin' to take my land," Pa told Tim.

"Ye don't mean it?"

"I do mean it," Pa said. "He's just been to see me and he said the land where my barn, garden, and meadow were belonged to him. Claims about ten acres of the best land I got. I told him I bought it from you and he said it didn't belong to you to sell."

"That ledge of rocks and the big oak trees that grow along the backbone of the ledge has been the line fer seventy years," Tim said. "But lissen, Mick, when Jake Timmins wants a piece of land, he takes it."

"People told me he's like that," Pa said. "I was warned against buying my farm because he's like that. People said he'd steal all my land if I lived beside him ten years."

"He'll have it before then, Mick," Tim Mennix told Pa in a trembling voice. "He didn't have but an acre to start from. That acre was a bluff where three farms jined and no one fenced it in because it was worthless and they didn't want it. He had a deed made fer this acre and he's had forty lawsuits when he set his fence over on other people's farms and took their land, but he goes to court and wins every time."

"I'll have the County Surveyor, Finn Madden, to survey my lines," Pa said.

"That won't hep any," Tim told Pa. "There's been more people kilt over the line fences that he's surveyed than has been kilt over any other one thing in this county. Surveyor Finn Madden's a good friend to Jake."

"But he's the County Surveyor," Pa said. "I'll haf to have him."

"Jake Timmins is a dangerous man," Tim Mennix warned Pa. "He's dangerous as a loaded double-barrel shotgun with both hammers cocked."

"I've heard that," Pa said. "I don't want any trouble. I'm a married man with a family."

When we reached home, we saw Jake upon the knoll at the big chestnut tree sighting across the hollow to the twin hickories on the knoll above our house. And as he sighted across the hollow, he walked along and drove stakes into the ground. He set one stake in our front yard, about five feet from the corner of our house. Pa started out on him once but Mom wouldn't let him go. Mom said let the law settle the dispute over the land.

And that night Pa couldn't go to sleep. I was awake

and heard him a-walking the floor when the clock struck twelve. I knew that Pa was worried, for Jake was the most feared man among our hills. He had started with one acre and now had over four hundred acres that he had taken from other people.

Next day Surveyor Finn Madden and Jake ran a line across the hollow just about on the same line that Jake had surveyed with his own eyes. And while Surveyor Finn Madden looked through the instrument, he had Jake set the stakes and drive them into the ground with a poleax. They worked at the line all day. And when they had finished surveying the line, Pa went up on the knoll at the twin hickories behind our house and asked Surveyor Finn Madden if his line was right.

"Surveyed it right with the deed," he told Pa. "Tim Mennix sold you land that didn't belong to him."

"Looks like this line would've been surveyed before I built my barn," Pa said.

"Can't see why it wasn't," he told Pa. "Looks like you're a-losing the best part of your farm, Mick."

Then Surveyor Finn Madden, a tall man with a white beard, and Jake Timmins went down the hill together.

"I'm not so sure that I'm a-losing the best part of my farm," Pa said. "I'm not a-goin' to sit down and take it! I know Jake's a land thief and it's time his stealing land is stopped."

"What are you a-goin' to do, Pa?" I asked.

"Don't know," he said.

"You're not a-goin' to hurt Jake over the land, are you?"

He didn't say anything but he looked at the two men as they turned over the ledge of rocks and out of sight.

"You know Mom said the land wasn't worth hurting anybody over," I said.

"But it's my land," Pa said.

And that night Pa walked the floor. And Mom got out of bed and talked to him and made him go to bed. And that day Sheriff Eif Whiteapple served a notice on Pa to keep his cattle out of the barn that we had built. The notice said that the barn belonged to Jake Timmins. Jake ordered us to put our chickens up, to keep them off his garden when it was our garden. He told us not to let anything trespass on his land and his land was on the other side of the stakes. We couldn't even walk in part of our yard.

"He'll have the house next if we don't do something about it," Pa said.

Pa walked around our house in a deep study. He was trying to think of something to do about it. Mom talked to him. She told him to get a lawyer and fight the case in court. But Pa said something had to be done to prove that the land belonged to us, though we had a deed for our land in our trunk. And before Sunday came, Pa dressed in his best clothes.

"Where're you a-going, Mick?" Mom asked.

"A-goin' to see Uncle Mel," he said. "He's been in a lot of line-fence fights and he could give me some good advice!"

"We hate to stay here and you gone, Mick," Mom said.

"Just don't step on property Jake laid claim to until I get back," Pa said. "I'll be back soon as I can. Some time next week you can look for me."

Pa went to West Virginia to get Uncle Mel. And while he was gone, Jake Timmins hauled wagonloads of hay and corn to the barn that we had built. He had taken over as if it were his own and as if he would always have it. We didn't step beyond the stakes where Surveyor Finn Madden had surveyed. We waited for Pa to come. And when Pa came, Uncle Mel came with him carrying a long-handled double-bitted ax and a turkey of clothes across his shoulder. Before they reached the house, Pa showed Uncle Mel the land Jake Timmins had taken.

"Land hogs air pizen as copperhead snakes," Uncle Mel said, then he fondled his long white beard in his hand. Uncle Mel was eighty-two years old, but his eyes were keen as sharp-pointed briers and his shoulders were broad and his hands were big and rough. He had been a timber cutter all his days and he was still a-cuttin' timber in West Virginia at the age of eighty-two. "He can't do this to ye, Mick!"

Uncle Mel was madder than Pa when he looked over the new line that they had surveyed from the dead chestnut on one knoll to the twin hickories on the other knoll.

"Anybody would know the line wouldn't go like that," Uncle Mel said. "The line would follow the ridge."

"Looks that way to me too," Pa said.

"He's a-stealin' yer land, Mick," Uncle Mel said. "I'll hep ye get yer land back. He'll never beat me. I've had to fight too many squatters a-tryin' to take my land. I know how to fight 'em with the law."

That night Pa and Uncle Mel sat before the fire and Uncle Mel looked over Pa's deed. Uncle Mel couldn't read very well and when he came to a word he couldn't read, I told him what it was.

"We'll haf to have a court order first, Mick," Uncle Mel said. "When we get the court order, I'll find the line."

I didn't know what Uncle Mel wanted with a court order, but I found out after he got it. He couldn't chop on a line tree until he got an order from the court. And soon as Pa got the court order and gathered a group of men for witnesses, Uncle Mel started work on the line fence.

"Sixteen rods from the dead chestnut due north," Uncle Mel said, and we started measuring sixteen rods due north.

"That's the oak tree, there," Uncle Mel said. It measured exactly sixteen rods from the dead chestnut to the black oak tree.

"Deed said the oak was blazed," Uncle Mel said, for he'd gone over the deed until he'd memorized it.

"See the scar, men," Uncle Mel said.

"But that was done seventy years ago," Pa said.

"Funny about the testimony of trees," Uncle Mel told Pa, Tim Mennix, Orbie Dorton, and Dave Sperry. "The scar will allus stay on the outside of a tree well as on the inside. The silent trees will keep their secrets."

Uncle Mel started chopping into the tree. He swung his ax over his shoulder and bit out a slice of wood every time he struck. He cut a neat block into the tree until he found a dark place deep inside the tree.

"Come, men, and look," Uncle Mel said. "Look at that scar. It's as pretty a scar as I ever seen in the heart of a tree!"

And while Uncle Mel wiped sweat with his blue bandanna from his white beard, we looked at the scar.

"It's a scar, all right," Tim Mennix said, since he had been a timber cutter most of his life and knew a scar on a tree.

"Think that was cut seventy years ago," Orbie Dorton said. "That's when the deed was made and the old survey was run."

"We'll see if it's been seventy years ago," Uncle Mel said as he started counting the rings in the tree. "Each ring is a year's growth."

We watched Uncle Mel pull his knife from his pocket, open the blade, and touch each ring with his knife-blade point as he counted the rings across the square he had chopped into the tree. Uncle Mel counted exactly seventy rings from the bark to the scar.

"Ain't it the line tree, boys?" Uncle Mel asked.

"Can't be anything else," Dave Sperry said.

And then Uncle Mel read the deed, which called for a mulberry thirteen rods due north from the black oak. We measured to the mulberry and Uncle Mel cut his notch to the scar and counted the rings. It was seventy rings from the bark to the scar. Ten more rods we came to the poplar the deed called for, and he found the scar on the outer bark and inside the tree. We found every tree the deed called for but one, and we found its stump. We surveyed the land from the dead chestnut to the twin hickories. We followed it around the ledge.

"We have the evidence to take to court," Uncle Mel said. "I'd like to bring the jurymen right here to this line fence to show 'em."

"I'll go right to town and put this thing in court," Pa said.

"I'll go around and see the men that have lost land to Jake Timmins," Uncle Mel said. "I want 'em to be at the trial."

Before our case got to court, Uncle Mel had shown seven of our neighbors how to trace their lines and get their land back from Jake Timmins. And when our trial was called, the courthouse was filled with people who had lost land and who had disputes with their neighbors over line fences, attending the trial to see if we won. Jake Timmins, Surveyor Finn Madden, and their lawyer, Henson Stapleton, had produced their side of the question before the jurors and we had lawyer Sherman Stone and our witnesses to present our side, while all the landowners Jake Timmins had stolen land from listened to the trial. The foreman of the jury asked that the members of the jury be taken to the line fence.

"Now here's the way to tell where a line was blazed on saplings seventy years ago," Uncle Mel said, as he showed them the inner mark on the line oak; then he showed them the outward scar. Uncle Mel took them along the line fence and showed them each tree that the deed called for all but the one that had fallen.

"It's plain as the nose on your face," Uncle Mel would say every time he explained each line tree. "Too many land thieves in this county and a county surveyor the devil won't have in hell."

After Uncle Mel had explained the line fence to the jurors, they followed Sheriff Whiteapple and his deputies back to the courtroom. Pa went with them to get the decision. Uncle Mel waited at our house for Pa to return.

"That land will belong to Mick," Uncle Mel told us. "And the hay and corn in that barn will belong to him."

When Pa came home, there was a smile on his face.

"It's yer land, ain't it, Mick?" Uncle Mel asked.

"It's still my land," Pa said, "and sixteen men are now filing suits to recover their land. Jake Timmins won't have but an acre left."

"Remember the hay and corn he put in yer barn is yourn," Uncle Mel said.

Uncle Mel got up from his chair, stretched his arms. Then he said, "I must be back on my way to West Virginia."

"Can't you stay longer with us, Uncle Mel?" Pa said.

"I must be a-gettin' back to cut timber," he said. "If ye have any more land troubles, write me."

We tried to get Uncle Mel to stay longer. But he wouldn't stay. He left with his turkey of clothes and his long-handled, double-bitted ax across his shoulder. We waved good-by to him as he walked slowly down the path and out of sight on his way to West Virginia.

Horse-trading Trembles

I SEE Bart comin' up the road," Mom said as she pressed her face against the windowpane. "He's not had any luck today!"

"What's he ridin' home, Mom?" I asked as I ran to the window to see Pa riding back from the Greenwood Stock Sale Day.

"He's ridin' a big black horse," Mom said.

Mom and I always waited for Pa at the window on the late afternoons of the first Monday in every month. This was his tradin' day. And we could always tell whether he had done well tradin' by the way he rode home. If he was limber in his saddle and his body swayed with the movements of his horse, we knew he'd had a good day. If he sat stiff as a poker in the saddle and looked at the ground, we knew that he had been cheated. Pa was sitting in the saddle stiff as a board. And he never looked up.

"Pa's been cheated, Mom," I said.

"He'll be mad for a month," Mom said. "He won't be in a good humor until the first Monday in next month!"

Now he was close enough until we could tell what was wrong. We could see little white clouds of fog coming from the horse's nostrils in quick spurts just like wind from a bee smoker on a cool October morning.

"No wonder he's sittin' stiff in the saddle, Mom," I said. "Somebody's traded him a 'heavie' horse!"

When Pa reached the front yard, he stopped by the gatepost. And it was something to hear the horse breathing. He made more noise getting his breath than a bee smoker when one was pumping smoke fast into a mean swarm of wild honeybees.

"I'll bet Old Erf Sizemore swindled Pa," I said. "He swindles Pa everytime!"

"I've warned Bart about tradin' with that man," Mom said. "Yet, he goes right back and tries to get even with Old Erf!"

"And everybody knows Old Erf Sizemore is given up to be the greatest trader in these parts," I said. "But Pa won't agree!"

Then I thought about the seven farms Erf owned in Greenwood County. And he owned two storehouses and a big garage in Greenwood. Beside, he had money in the bank and he had loaned his neighbors money for good interest and had taken mortgages on their property, even their livestock, for security. I knew Pa'd helped him pay for all these things. He'd made enough over the thirty years he'd been trading with Pa to buy one of these farms.

"Who cheated you this time, Bart?" Mom asked soon as she opened the door. "Did Old Erf cheat you again!"

"That polecat," Pa said, as he slowly climbed from the saddle, "lied to me like a dog! He told me this horse wasn't a 'heavie' horse!"

Pa fastened the bridle reins over the gatepost. Then he stood back and looked over the horse he'd just ridden home. Mom and I looked him over too. We stood on the porch and looked at the pitiful old plug Erf Sizemore had traded Pa.

"You didn't trade your mule colts for that horse, did you?" Mom asked.

"Yes, I did," Pa said. "That's what makes me sick!"

"But you got some boot, didn't you, Pa?" I said.

"No, I didn't," Pa said as he still looked at the horse and wouldn't face Mom and me. "That's what makes me still sicker. I gave twenty dollars to boot!"

"Oh, Bart," Mom said. "Oh . . ."

Mom knew that Pa tried to make our extra cash by trading. And Pa had made some good trades! He had made some money. But he'd never made money like some of the other traders. Old Erf Sizemore was the best of the traders! He was one that had made the money! And Mom knew that we wouldn't have any spending money for a month now.

"Sall," Pa said, "I don't blame you for feelin' the way you do! Look at that horse! Old Erf Sizemore robbed me! I'm goin' to quit tradin'. I'm goin' to give that horse away and quit!"

"Give 'im to me, Pa," I said. "Let me go to the Greenwood next month! Let me try my luck! Let me trade with Old Erf Sizemore!"

"No you won't, Finn," Mom said. "I never want you to be a horse trader! Look at your Pa! See how we have lived from hand to mouth!"

"But, Mom," I said. "Pa's been cheated too many times by Old Erf Sizemore! Let me try tradin' with 'im once!"

"I'd just like for you to try it, Son," Pa said. "I'd like for you to take this old plug horse to the jockey ground once! I'd like to see what you came home with!"

And Pa laughed for the first time. He turned and faced Mom and me. He thought what I said was funny.

"Let him learn early, Sall," Pa said to Mom. "That's the best way to keep 'im from bein' a horse trader!"

Then Mom looked at me and she looked at Pa.

"If I thought it'd keep 'im from bein' a horse trader, I'd be for givin' him the horse and lettin' him try his luck next Sale Day," Mom said with a twinkle in her gray eyes.

"Then I'll give you this horse," Pa said. "I'm through tradin' after the shellackin' I got today from Old Erf. I wish I knew how many times that man has cheated me," Pa talked on thoughtfully as a frown came over his face. "His father, Old Bass, used to cheat my father the same way Old Erf cheats me. It just ain't in the signs for a Tremble to trade with a Sizemore! And, Finn, I don't believe the signs have changed any in the third generation!"

I didn't listen to any more talk. I took the bridle rein from over the gatepost. My horse was breathin' easier. I took him to the barn. I rubbed his face. "You're a young horse," I lied to him as I rubbed his nose gently. "If you're not young now, you will be young in a month from now!" For I had some ideas of my own. I wouldn't tell them to my father. I didn't want him to know my secrets. For I wanted to trade with Old Erf Sizemore. I wanted to trade with him more than I wanted anything in the world. I thought about tradin' with him as I fed my horse corn and hay. I thought about tradin' with him as I used the curry-comb and brush and sleeked Fred's hair down over his bony body. "Fred, you won't be this bony at the end of this month," I told my horse. "I'll be good to you. I'll make you feel better and look better. I've got faith in you, fellow!"

When I went to the house, Pa was in bed.

"What's the matter, Pa?" I asked.

"Just sick," Pa said. "Sick over that trade! It's done something to me, Son," Pa moaned. "I don't believe I'll ever get out of this bed unless something good happens to lift my spirit! I'm through as a trader! I've lost all hope!"

"Pa, I've been tellin' my horse that he's a nice horse and that he will look better and feel better at the end of the month," I said. "And he will too."

"But that won't help matters one bit, Finn," Pa said. "I'm an old trader. And I know when you get a 'heavie' horse on the jockey ground you've got a white elephant on your hands. No matter how well you feed old Fred and what you do for 'im, you've still got a 'heavie' horse! And you've got something on your hands."

"Pa, one of the reasons you've never done too well tradin' with Old Erf Sizemore," I said, "is you lie to him and he lies to you! Why don't you tell him the truth once!"

Though Pa was in bed sick over his trade, he laughed louder than I had heard him laugh for a month. He laughed so loudly that Mom came runnin' into the room to see what was wrong. She'd not heard Pa laugh that way for so long that when she heard him laugh, she laughed too. Then Pa stopped long enough to tell her what he was laughin' about. Then they both laughed at what I said about tellin' the truth about my horse when I traded.

"Of course," Pa chided me after he stopped laughin', "horse traders never tell the truth. They brag on their horses. They might not exactly lie. But they never speak of their horses' faults. They just tell the good things! When you tell a horse trader that your horse has got the heaves, your trade will be finished!"

"Maybe so," I said. "But I'm not goin' to tell him a lie if he asks me! I might tell 'im the truth before he asks me!"

"Sall, you'll never have to be bothered with another horse trader in this family," Pa said to Mom. "Finn won't be on

the tradin' ground two hours before he'll be walkin' around
without a horse and not a penny in his pocket!"

Then Pa laughed again. He sat up in bed. But he didn't
get up. For when I left the room he started to thinkin' about
Old Erf Sizemore and that made Pa sick. He just couldn't
get over what Erf had done to him. And that night in his
sleep I heard him drivin' the young mule colts he'd traded
to Old Erf for Fred. Pa had them harnessed, pulling a small
pole of wood around with them. He talked all night about
his young colts and what a great span of mules they'd make.
He said this was one team Old Erf would never get. He'd
never let Erf Sizemore cheat him out of them!

As I lay awake in the next room and listened to Pa carry
on over the young mule colts Old Erf had cheated him out
of, I shed tears. I couldn't help it. I cried as hard as I'd ever
cried in my life. And this put more ideas in my head. I'd
never be able to get the span of fine mule colts back for Pa
but I'd try to get him an animal he'd like. I got to thinkin'
so much about the first Monday in October that I dreamed
about tradin' with Old Erf Sizemore and that he did to me
what Pa had told me he would do. I dreamed I walked
across the jockey ground without my horse or a penny in
my pocket and that the old horse traders laughed and whispered to one another, loud enough for me to hear, what the
Sizemores had done to the Trembles.

Next mornin' when I awoke, I was glad it was just a
dream. I fed Fred, curried, and brushed 'im. I filled his stall
with dry September leaves that had just fallen from the
trees. I knew when he lay in his stall at night on these bright
fresh leaves they would make his hair look good. Then I
polished his bridle and I put a red tassel on each side the
bridle. I made a pretty bridle out of the old one.

The next day, I used shoe polish on my saddle. I shined

it until it looked like a new one. I did these little things from day to day while the month passed and while I was getting better acquainted with Fred. And, anyway, I didn't like to stay around the house. Pa was still in bed and he was still a-takin' on something awful about his last trade. He talked about Old Erf Sizemore in his sleep and called him bad names and threatened him. Next day when Mom would tell him about it, Pa wouldn't remember his dream. But the trade had done something to Pa. I knew I had to do something. And I felt that when I did do something, Pa would get out of bed. I didn't think he was sick except in his head. He just couldn't take the worst robbing he'd ever got in a trade in his lifetime.

First work I did on Fred was his teeth. I used a brush to scrub the yellow stains from his front teeth. And, believe me, the soft gray wood ash I used first and then the charcoal that I used after to whiten his teeth really made Fred's teeth look like a new set of ivories. When he opened his mouth, he didn't look like the same horse. Fred seemed to know I was improving his mouth for he didn't mind how much I polished his teeth. Next thing I did, I used jet oil on Fred's fetlocks and mane. I put the jet oil on with a little brush, and this did away with the gray hairs mixed with the black and salt-and-pepper-colored hairs in his mane and fetlocks. This made Fred look ten years younger. Then I went over his tail with jet oil. I didn't fail to give the inner hairs on his long tail a good blacking. When I finished with Fred, he was a nice-looking horse. I had fed him well and put pounds on him too. His ribs didn't show like they did the day Pa brought him home.

"Well, I can't cure you of the heaves, Fred, old boy," I said. "I wish I could!"

And then I thought about what Pa had told me about a

"heavie" horse on the jockey ground. Finally, it came to me what to do. It came to me while I curried and brushed Fred and went over his fetlocks, mane, and tail to give them new coats of black. I didn't even tell Pa what I was going to do. For Pa wasn't any better. When he went to bed, Mom thought he would be out of bed in a few days. But Pa was worse off than Mom thought. He was very nervous now and wanted to smoke his pipe, one time after another. He sat up in bed with pillows propped behind him and smoked like a furnace. And when the first Monday in October came round, Pa wanted to go to the Greenwood Stock Sale Day with me. But he wasn't able. And Mom was glad. I was glad he couldn't go for I knew he'd be tryin' to tell me how to trade. As I rode past the house on my new polished saddle and my worked-over horse, Pa and Mom looked at me through the window. When I rode past the house, I looked back and saw their faces still close to the windowpanes. I left home early on that October morning, for I had something in mind.

I had five miles to ride. And I didn't want Fred to be heaving for breath when I reached the Greenwood. That's the reason I let him walk. When I reached the highway, Fred hadn't raised the sweat. And I'd ridden nearly to Greenwood before any traders passed me. Their horses were slobbering at the mouth and their hocks were dripping with sweaty foam. Their riders were putting the spur to them. They were rushing for the jockey ground. These were young traders. The old traders never tried to be first at the jockey ground. They came later, stayed longer, and made the day count. When I rode onto the jockey ground, though the trading had started, I didn't see Old Erf Sizemore. He hadn't come yet. Proctor Williams, another old trader, hadn't arrived. Booten Call wasn't there. Willie Kilgore hadn't come. I rode slowly up and down the jockey ground and looked the men and their horses and mules over. I just let Fred walk. He hadn't raised the sweat. I watched that.

Then I heard the crack of a whip at the jockey-ground gate. And I looked and here came Old Erf, riding a pacing sorrel mare with a flaxen mane and tail. He had a rope tied to the link in his saddle, and hitched to this rope were four mule colts. Two of them were Rock and Rye, the mule colts Pa had wept a month over losin'. I knew them soon as I saw their heads lifted high, the proud way they lifted their feet when they trotted, and the way they looked at you. They were pretty mules and Old Erf had brought them to the jockey ground to sell or trade. He reined his pretty saddle horse with one hand and with the other he cracked his long black snakeskin whip to get the attention of all the traders. For this was the way Old Erf always came onto the jockey ground. I'd seen him come many times before when I'd been with Pa. And when he came onto the jockey ground everybody stopped, looked, and listened.

"I've got four of the finest mule colts in the land," he shouted, then he cracked his whip.

Everybody watched Old Erf ride around the jockey ground. They watched him crack his long whip and they listened to him shout about the fine young mules he had. I let Fred go into a slow trot as I rode across the jockey ground to meet Old Erf. But I didn't stop when I got near him. I passed him as if he were not on the jockey ground. And many traders turned their eyes toward me. They looked at me more than they did Old Erf. For I held Fred's bridle rein tightly and he held his head high.

"Look at that pretty horse," I heard a young man say.

And when I rode past Old Erf, he turned in his saddle

and looked at me. Then he cracked his whip and rode on.
He rode in one direction around the jockey ground and I
rode in the opposite direction. Some young trader stopped
Old Erf and asked him his price on the pair of mule colts
that held their heads high and walked with pride.

"Three hundred dollars," Old Erf said. "Are you interested, my friend? Best young mule colts in the state!"

"Too high," the young trader said as he rode on.

When I passed Old Erf again I didn't look toward him.
I rode straight on.

"There's a nice-lookin' horse," I heard a man say. "Wonder what he'd take for 'im."

I rode on as if I didn't hear the man. And as I came back
around this man stopped me.

"What'll you take for this horse?" he said.

"Three hundred," I said.

"That's pretty high, isn't it?" he shook his head.

"No, that's not too high for a horse that's thirty years old,
a horse that's got the heaves and about everything else
wrong with 'im," I said as I sat in the saddle and laughed.

"Thirty years old, huh," the young man said as he pulled
Fred's lips apart and looked at his teeth. "This horse has a
seven-year-old mouth! Look at these teeth. White as hound
dog's teeth!"

"He's thirty," I said.

"Quit your kiddin', fellow," the young man said. "Have
you come out here to tantalize traders with a fine-lookin'
horse 'r have you come out here to trade?"

"I've come to trade," I laughed.

"Say, Mr. Sizemore," the young man said as Old Erf rode
around again, "stop here a minute and look at this horse's
teeth! You've traded a long time! You can tell horses' ages
by their mouths. Look at this one!"

Old Erf, flattered because the younger trader had asked him his opinion, jumped down from his saddle. He raised Fred's lips and looked at his teeth.

"He's a six-year-old," Old Erf said. "He's comin' seven in the spring! Who's tradin' for this horse, sonnie?" he asked me.

"No one," I said. "Not exactly. This fellow asked me my price and I said three hundred dollars!"

"Say, you've got a nice-lookin' horse," he said.

"Thirty years old," I laughed. "And he's got the heaves!"

"Oh, don't get funny," Old Erf said. "He's no more got the heaves than I have."

Then Old Erf laughed and laughed.

"You don't want to trade 'im?" Old Erf said. "That's it?"

"Nope, I've come to trade and sell," I said.

"Whose boy are you?" he asked me. "I've seen you some place before?"

"Bart Tremble's boy," I said.

"Bart Tremble's boy," he said, looking at me. "Where did you get this horse?"

"Pa got 'im last sale's day from you," I said.

Then Old Erf laughed and laughed.

"I never saw this horse before," he said, laughing. "But I do like to trade with the Trembles!"

Then he reared back and took a cigar from his vest pocket. He lit the cigar and started puffing clouds of smoke from one end and chewing the other. He put his big thumbs behind his suspenders and pulled them out and then let them fly back and hit him as he looked at my horse.

"How'll you trade this horse to that small span of mule colts?" he asked me.

"I'm not interested," I said as I started to climb back into the saddle.

"Just a minute," he said. "Let's do some tradin' here. I'd like to trade for this thirty-year-old horse with the heaves!"

When Old Erf started to look at Fred's white teeth again, several traders gathered around to watch Old Erf trade with me.

"He'll fix that boy," I heard somebody whisper. "Old Erf just ruint his pappie, Bart Tremble, last sale's day."

"Where's Bart, sonnie?" Old Erf asked me.

"He's sick over the way you robbed him last sale's day," I said. "He's at home in bed sick!"

"Ah, tell us some more jokes," Old Erf laughed as he looked carefully at Fred's teeth.

"Say, I cleaned his teeth with wood ashes," I said. "Then I polished 'em with charcoal!"

Everybody laughed like they thought it was funny. They thought I was a great joker.

"This horse has a five-year-old mouth, I do believe," Old Erf said.

"Look at his mouth again," I said. "He might be three. But I know he's over thirty."

Everybody laughed and laughed and Old Erf laughed and puffed clouds of smoke from his cigar and chewed the end in his mouth.

"Say, which span of my mule colts do you like?" he asked me.

"I like that one better," I said, pointing to Rock and Rye, the mule colts Pa talked about in his sleep.

"Tell you what I'll do," Old Erf said. "I'll trade you this span of mule colts for this horse!"

"No you won't," I said. "Not even tradin'."

"Then, how much boot?" Old Erf asked.

"Not a cent less than a hundred dollars," I said. "Do you

think I'd trade my thirty-year-old horse with the heaves, whose teeth I've been polishing for a month, for a pair of young mule colts without a hundred dollars to boot?"

Then everybody laughed. They slapped their thighs with their big hands and laughed. They slapped Old Erf on the shoulder and laughed. And Old Erf slapped them on the back and laughed with them.

"That boy's some trader, ain't he?" Booten Call said to Old Erf.

"Now get on my horse and take a ride," I said to Old Erf. "And if the sponges don't fly out of his nostrils, you'll never know he's got the heaves!"

Proctor Williams lay down on the ground and howled. Old Erf chuckled with glee and hit Booten Call with his blacksnake whip until Booten flinched. They all laughed like I'd said the funniest thing they'd ever heard.

"I'll just try that horse, Tremble," Old Erf said as he climbed into the saddle. He rode Fred to the far end of the jockey ground and back.

"I never owned that horse," Old Erf said.

"He's some horse," the traders agreed when Old Erf dismounted and walked among them.

"I'm ready to give you three hundred for that horse," the young man said that had first stopped me.

"Just a minute, fellow," Old Erf said. "I'm tradin' here yet. I'm not through. Remember we have a proposition here! And I'm taking this young Tremble up!"

Everybody watched Old Erf put his hand in his hip pocket and get his billfold.

"My mule colts and a hundred dollars to boot," Old Erf said as he peeled me ten tens from his big stack.

"Here," he said. "And here's your young mules!"

Rock and Rye, I thought. I'll take you home to Pa. He

won't believe this. He'll think it's a dream. But wait until I show him! Pa'll come out of the bed now. He won't be sick any longer! And what will Mom think of me?

"Don't run old Fred too hard, Mr. Sizemore," I said. "If you do, he'll blow the sponges from his nostrils and start heaving again!"

Then everybody started laughing again.

"You ought'n to cheat a boy like that, Erf," Booten Call said as I walked away with my mules.

"He asked for it," Old Erf said. "A-tryin' to be funny. I'll put one over on that Tremble family every time I get the chance! My pap used to put it on this boy's grandpa. They're easy marks for the Sizemores!"

I walked across the jockey ground leading Rock and Rye when I saw Old Erf climb into the saddle. I stood and watched him crack his whip and he took off riding Fred and leading his sorrel mare with the flaxen mane and tail and the young mule colts. I watched him race around the jockey ground three or four times. Then I went toward home with my colts and money. Just as I reached the street that went past the old Greenwood Flour Mill, I saw Fred fall and Old Erf pitched headlong over his head and sprawled on the ground as Fred went down. I saw young and old traders runnin' toward Old Erf.

"There's the sponges," one man said as he kicked one with the toe of his shoe. "That young fellow told the truth. That horse is 'heavie'!"

"Are you hurt, Erf?" Booten Call asked.

"Just the wind knocked out of me," he said as he drew a good breath and limped around old Fred, who was heaving more than he did when Pa had ridden him home a month ago.

"Boy, he fixed Old Erf," I heard Willie Kilgore say.

"I ought to have that young Tremble arrested," Old Erf said.

"But he told you the truth, Erf," Bill Broomfield said. "And you, like the rest of us, wouldn't believe him. The truth was funny."

Then I heard somebody explode with laughter. And it caught on like firecrackers exploding. As I left Greenwood for home, it sounded like a hundred exploding firecrackers down on the jockey ground.

Road Number One

I DON'T want to disturb you," were Pa's first words when he opened the bunkhouse door, "but there's something I don't want you boys to forget! I want you to remember Toodle Powell for county judge this November!"

"Pa, this war's not over," Finn said. "Remember, I'll not be here to vote. Soon as my LST is repaired, I'll be headin' back to the Pacific!"

"And remember, the Navy won't give me a leave to come back here to vote in any county election," I said.

"He'll make the best county judge this county has ever had," Pa bragged. "He belongs to the Right Party and he's really big timber for a county judge!"

"He's big timber all right," Finn laughed. "How much does he weigh?"

"I didn't come out here to get insulted," Pa said. His lips quivered and his face flushed the color of a ripe persimmon. "If we get Toodle Powell for county judge we won't be sittin' out here in the mud. I've been talkin' to 'im. And I know what he's a-goin' to do. His slogan's 'a road for every hollow.' And it will be a graveled road, too. You boys remember damned well that the Wrong Party never even put the grader on our roads! We had mud roads under their rule!"

"And if we get Toodle Powell for county judge, we'll still have mud roads," Finn told Pa. "Don't tell me he's goin' to build a road up every hollow in this county and gravel it! He couldn't do that in ten years!"

"The hell he can't," Pa said, his face getting redder than a turkey's snout when he gobbles. "Old Toodle can do anything! He's good timber. He's the best timber we got in the Right Party for a county judge. And the Wrong Party ain't got a piece of timber that'll touch 'im. Old Toodle is a 'common' man. He shakes hands with everybody. He's a man of the people!"

"War or no war," Pa said indignantly, "we want good men in these county offices! You sit out here on your can in this mud all winter and you'd be working for a good piece of timber for county judge! You don't know what it is to be on a muddy road all winter!"

"Damn it, Pa," Finn said, "I've seen the time I'd give twenty-five dollars to see this muddy road in winter! I've seen the time when I'd give five dollars just to hold a ball of this muddy dirt in my hand and squeeze it for one hour! Six times I've crossed the Pacific on an LST."

Finn's face was getting red. He was getting riled. And I winked to keep him quiet.

"Well, as I said a while ago," Pa said, "I didn't come out here to disturb you boys! I know you've not seen one another in a couple of years. And I know it's the first time you've been home in two years, Finn. But whenever I can and wherever I can, even if it's with members of my family, I put in a good word for old Toodle Powell, best friend I ever had, best friend the people in this county ever had."

"Pa, just to be frank with you," Finn said, "if I's here and could vote, I'm sure I'd not vote for Toodle Powell. Yes, he can shake your hand, nearly pull it off when he shakes hands with you, and he's got the nicest smile I ever saw in a man's face. But what about his education? How well can he handle the county taxpayers' money?"

"Leave education out of this," Pa said. "Old Toodle don't have much more education than I have! But he does have horse sense. He can build roads! And this county needs roads more than anything else! For sixteen years," Pa almost shouted, pointing his skinny index finger at Finn's nose, "the Wrong Party had the power. What did they do? A man didn't have to work. He was a pensioner! Many of 'em didn't even bother to lift a shovel. Worked on their farms and drew their monthly pay! We'll break that up with old Toodle Powell. Son, he'll be our next county judge!"

"To hell with Toodle Powell," Finn said as he got up and left the bunkhouse.

"What's the matter with Finn?" Pa asked me. "Has the war changed him? He's not like he used to be. Reckon he still belongs to the Right Party?"

"I think he votes independent anymore," I said. "He checks the men on both tickets and votes for the ones he thinks are the best qualified!"

"Yeah, his a-goin' to Michigan before the war wasn't too good for 'im," Pa said. "He oughta belong to the Right Party and support it to the man! I can't understand why he doesn't like old Toodle Powell!"

"He likes Toodle as a man, Pa," I said, "but he doesn't think he can gravel the roads up all these hollows!"

"He'll do it," Pa said. "He's told the people that he will! And you will see! Old Toodle will be elected! And he's a man of his word!"

"Pa, if I have a chance, I'll vote for 'im," I said, as I thought of his opponent.

Pa was pleased when I said these words.

"I'll go do a little more explaining to Finn," Pa said. "Something's come over that boy. He's all right but he doesn't understand what's a-goin' on here!"

"I wouldn't say anything to him, Pa," I said. "He's just got two more days. Let him rest!"

Pa left me alone in the bunkhouse and went to hunt Finn. Finn was in the house and when he saw Pa come through the back door, he went out the front door. Then he came around the house and back into the bunkhouse.

"What's the matter with Pa anyway?" Finn asked me. "Out here electioneering with us!"

"Toodle Powell's an old friend to Pa," I said. "Don't pay any attention to Pa. He's ridden a mule up every little creek in the radius of ten miles of here and stopped at every shack asking people to vote for Toodle Powell. He tells them what Toodle is going to do! But Pa's working for himself. Toodle has promised him a graded road up this hollow. And he's promised to gravel it soon as it's been graded!"

"Ah, hell," Finn said. "When I see a gravel road up this hollow, I'll think I'm dreaming. I know I won't be in a conscious state of mind!"

For the next two days while Finn and I were back from the Navy on leave, Mom had to keep Pa quiet. She told him not to mention Toodle Powell or anybody else running on the Right Party ticket or the Wrong Party ticket while Finn was home.

"But, by hell, I will mention 'em," Pa said as he went to the barn to get his mule. "There's a lot of voters that want to hear the gospel truth!"

And for the last two days of our leave we only saw Pa at night. For he worked for Toodle Powell. He rode a mule up the hollows and over the hills and along the ridges. We didn't see too much of Pa.

Finn had reached his LST and was two days on his way back to the Pacific when the war ended. And I was back on my dry-land duty in the U.S. But he couldn't get home to vote and I couldn't get home to vote. Neither of us was interested anyway. And that November Toodle Powell was elected our county judge, not by the landslide that Pa had prophesied but by a narrow margin. And the Right Party almost elected a "full house." Toodle Powell got a majority of fiscal court members elected too. He had full reins. Now there wasn't anything to hinder him from fulfilling his promises.

In January I was discharged from the Navy. That was the month the Right Party members took office. When I reached Greenwood, a midwinter thaw had hit the country and the "bottoms" had dropped from the county's dirt roads. I had to wait in Greenwood for a freeze before I could drive home. When Pa heard that I was in Greenwood, he walked over the mountain to see me.

"Shan, I'm glad to see you back," Pa said, pumping my hand as fast as an automatic pistol can shoot. "Now is the time to go before Judge Toodle Powell and the new fiscal court. They're meeting today. We want that road, you know! Son, it'll be the last time you'll ever have to wait for that road to freeze! The Wrong Party's being in power for the last sixteen years and their having so many damn pensioners on the payroll has almost ruint us!"

Pa was in high spirits. Sixty-seven years of age didn't mean anything to him. As we walked down the street toward the courthouse, every few steps he'd jump high in the air and crack his heels together twice. He talked so fast praising Toodle Powell and the members of the Right Party that I couldn't ask him how Mom's health was. I couldn't ask him about what had been done on the farm and what condition our house was in, since we'd just drawn the blinds and left all the worldly possessions we had in it, when I went into the Navy.

"Ah, boy," Pa said, "when old Finn gets back from Japan and sees the gravel road up the hollow, he'll remember how he talked to me in the bunkhouse last July! He'll see what I told him about Toodle Powell was the truth. I told 'im he'd be elected, didn't I? And I told him we'd get a road. Well, things are coming to pass just like I prophesied. Judge Toodle Powell!"

When we arrived in the courthouse, we didn't find Judge Toodle Powell in his office where Pa had expected to see him. We found Judge Toodle Powell and the members of his fiscal court around him like King Arthur and his Knights at the Round Table, in the big room where quarterly court was held. His office would not have held one-twentieth of the people there to see their judge and fiscal court members on their opening day.

"What are all these people doing here?" I whispered to Pa.

"Damned if I know," Pa said as he looked bewildered at the big crowd.

"You don't suppose they're all wanting roads?" I whispered to Pa.

"You're damn right we're a-wantin' roads," said some big beardy-faced man behind me. "And we're a-goin' to git 'em now!"

There was a lot of whispers in the crowd. And everywhere we could hear the word "road." But before us sat Judge Toodle Powell dressed in a clean pressed suit and a collar and tie. It was the first time I'd seen him wear a collar and tie. And there was the handsome smile on his face. Even his big blue-wall eyes seemed to smile as he looked over the crowd before him. He had lost one or two front teeth since I had seen him last, and he hadn't bothered to have these teeth replaced. And when he talked, I could see his tongue working in his mouth. But he still was a handsome man. And in this man was vested the power by county voters to build their roads and handle the taxpayers' money. In this hour of triumph for him, he was our man of destiny. He was the King Arthur at the Round Table with his Knights. Seated in a semicircle around him were his cohorts of Destiny. It was a pomp of heraldry, a boast of power. Pa was flabbergasted when he saw Toodle Powell, for whom he had ridden his mule up the dark hollows, sitting as the man of Destiny in this hour.

The proceedings started. Order was called. Yet men kept coming after order was called until there wasn't a seat left. Men stood in the aisles. They stood in the two doorways that lead to this big room. And many couldn't get their bodies inside the packed room. They stuck their heads inside, stretching their long red necks like rubber.

Many people wanted to sell the county something. But Judge Toodle soon disposed of them so he could get to his regular customers. Many people had come for a small pittance of county charity. Judge Toodle had them given what they wanted in a hurry. Then he came to us "wanters." The Judge had to confine each talk to a few minutes. Each man was wanting his road. Everybody wanted a road.

"Damn, this is somethin'," Pa whispered to me. "When it comes our turn, you do the talkin'."

Hours passed before our time came to state what we wanted. And when Judge Toodle called on Pa, I stood up and told the Judge and the fiscal court members what we wanted. I told them that I was waiting for the road to freeze so I could drive my wife and daughter home, that I had just been back three days from the Navy. And when I said we were waiting for a freeze so we could get home everybody laughed. I heard comments in low tones among the crowd, "Why don't they walk home like the rest of us?" And then I heard a whisper, "That Navy makes a man from these hills mighty damned soft. He can't take it when he gits back. He ain't got no wind when it comes to hill climbing. I don't blame 'im for waitin' for a freeze. I can understand it."

But Judge Toodle pounded on his desk with his gavel for order.

"Now about your road, Shan," he said, soon as talk and whispers had subsided, "we can't do anything to that road now. You know that. Our machinery will bog down. But that is one of our 'must roads' and we'll be in there in March if the weather permits! That's as early as we can come!"

"Good enough, Judge Toodle Powell," Pa spoke pleasantly. "That's all we ask. We know you are a man of your word! You'll be right there!"

Now that we knew when we would get our road, Pa and I left so some of those that had been standing for hours could get our seats. And the fellows standing with their bodies outside and their heads inside could move up and take the standing places of those that had gotten our seats. And other fellows in the hall could come up and stick their heads in at the door.

"See what I told you," Pa said as we walked down the courthouse corridor. "We'll get the road, son! I'd like to have that road before Finn gets home! I want to show that young doubter a few things! I'll never get over the way he talked about Toodle Powell!"

I didn't leave Greenwood with Pa. I waited two more

days and the freeze came and I drove home. It was rough driving, for jolt wagons had cut ruts. And these frozen ruts were hard to drive over. Only twice in January could I drive the car to Greenwood. Both times I stuck and had to get Pa's mule team to pull me out. In February I didn't take the car out at all. It was too far for my wife to walk to Greenwood, and she didn't even leave the hollow this month. But I walked over a mountain and carried the light supplies. We had to use two mule teams to the wagon to haul drums of kerosene and sacks of dairy feed. It was all one team could do to pull the empty wagon. Then I understood why Pa had worked so hard for Toodle Powell. And in February Pa and I saw Judge Powell twice and talked over our road plans.

"You'll get that road, Mick," Judge Powell assured us. "Just don't worry. Think I'll be able to get your road on the Rural Highway. If I do, the State will build it. They have the equipment to make a better road. We'll not only put gravel on it, but you'll have a black-topped road."

"Damn, what about that," Pa said as we puffed, climbing the mountain. "Just to think of a black-topped road up the hollow. Shan, when I came to this country in 1896 there was only a path up this hollow. Some change in fifty years!"

"Will be if we get that," I said.

"Get it," Pa said, "it's in the bag. You don't doubt Judge Toodle Powell, do you?"

"I'm not sure of anything until I see it," I said. "Sometimes the bird gets out of your hand!"

"Bird, hell," Pa said. "You're getting like Finn!"

Then Pa laughed a wild laugh.

"We'll have the road before Finn gets back," he said. "Now they've sent him to Chinee! We'll surprise that young doubter! He'll not be an independent voter any longer. He'll fergit what he learned in Michigan. He'll be back with the Right Party. He'll have the faith! Toodle Powell will restore that faith!"

In late March the grading crew came into the hollow. When we heard the roar of the "cat" pulling the big grader, everybody on the creek turned out to watch the big event. Big rolls of dirt were heaped here and there. When Pa followed the grader, he shook his head.

"I've never seen grading like that," Pa said, shaking his head sadly. "They're not opening the ditches. They're filling them up."

Just as they had finished grading the road, a heavy spring rain fell. Since there weren't any ditches to carry the water, our road was flooded. Little lakes were everywhere. We couldn't think of trying to get a car over it even if there came another freeze. People couldn't walk over the road. We couldn't take a wagon over it. We couldn't even ride a mule through some of the muck lakes.

"We'll have to see Toodle," Pa said. "Hell, the road's worse than it's ever been!"

"Now don't you worry about that road, Mick," Judge Toodle Powell said. "We'll put a man on that grader. We'll fix that road. Just don't be too impatient. Just give us time!"

"Patience, hell, Judge," Pa said. "You put a bunch of greenhorns on that grader. They wouldn't know a road when they saw one! Seventeen-year-old boy a-doin' the gradin'. Who is he?"

"One of the Right Party, Mick," the Judge said. "He'll soon learn."

"Let him learn on some other road," Pa said, his face getting red.

When Finn came home in late March, he tried to walk over the road. But he had to take to the hills and fight his way through the underbrush. When he got home, the cuffs of his naval officer's uniform were covered with yellow mud. His shirt and coat were torn by brush and briers and his face and hands were bleeding from brier scratches.

"What the hell has happened to the road, Pa?" he asked. "This is awful."

"Ah, they sent a greenhorn crew out here," Pa apologized. "But we'll get the road. I've got assurances!"

"That's all you've got," Finn laughed.

"In another two months you won't be a doubter, my son," Pa said. "I still have faith in old Toodle Powell. He's still good timber."

Pa walked away from Finn. He didn't want to hear any more from Finn.

They didn't touch the road in April. The heaps of dirt dried like so many miniature hills and ridges across the road. But the lakes didn't dry, though we had plenty of sun and dry weather. Twice we went to see Judge Toodle Powell. And twice he promised us we'd have our road in "no time." June came and the road was still impassable. Then Pa went once a week to remind Judge Toodle Powell something had to be done to undo what had already been done. In late June, the small grader came with a little man driving the cat and a big man doing the grading. He carried a big pistol in his holster. He worked two days on the road and leveled the hills and filled the lakes so we could get over it. Now the road was like it was in the first place and six months of the year had passed.

In July Pa and I went again to see Toodle Powell.

"That road has to be done, Judge," Pa spoke seriously. "You know you promised me. And you know how I worked fer you!"

"Right-of-way is now holding us up, Mick," Judge

Toodle said. "You know we've got to have a thirty-foot right-of-way and we don't have it between Blink Jacon and Eif Dannon. We should get a slice from Eif Dannon but he said he wouldn't give a foot."

"I'll see Eif," Pa said. "I'll take care of that."

Pa bought the land from Eif Dannon and he checked the other farms along our road. Everybody was willing to give the land for a road. And now, after a month's work, Pa had taken care of this. Then we went to see Judge Toodle Powell again.

"That's fine, Mick, that you got the land," Judge Toodle said. "But there's a lot of draining on that road and if we build the road we can't buy the pipes!"

"But you promised me. . . ."

"How much will the pipes cost?" I asked.

"From five hundred to a thousand dollars," he said.

"Where can I get 'em?" I asked.

"Union Pipe Company," he said.

"I'll get the pipes," I said.

Then we went again to see Judge Toodle Powell.

"Now Mick, I know what you're after," Toodle Powell said soon as we walked into his office where he was comfortably seated in his big swivel chair behind a neatly varnished desk. "And I guess I've got bad news for you. But I still think we can get the road!"

"What's the news?" Pa asked solemnly.

"We're out of money," he said. "And we've rented the county equipment, the grader, trucks, and cats to the State!"

"But you promised. . . ."

"Can't you borrow some money?" I broke in. "Other counties do. How much interest do you pay?"

"Borrowed some already," he said. "Borrowed it at four per cent."

"How much do you need?" I asked.

"Ten thousand," he said.

"In thirty minutes I'll see that you have your money," I said.

"No, no," he said. "Come to think about it, we pay two per cent."

"I can't get it for that," I said.

"But you promised, Judge. . . ."

"Are there any individually owned dump trucks in this county?" I broke in again.

"Yep, several," Judge Toodle said.

"How much an hour for each truck?" I asked.

"Two-fifty," he said.

"Will the county steam shovel load the gravel from Smitton Creek on the trucks," I asked.

"Oh, yes," he said.

"Then put the little grader over our road," I said. "Open the ditches, and I'll have a hundred and sixty loads of gravel put on that road before winter. I'll pay for it myself."

"Wouldn't want you to do that," Judge Toodle said as he spun first to his right and his left in the big swivel chair. "No one else in the county has offered us anything on a road! You're going out of your way!"

"You'd go out of your way, too, Judge Toodle," Pa said, "if you lived where we live. You live in this town with a hard road six feet in front of your door. You have forgotten what it is to live on a road that is impassable all winter. And we can't all live in town and be in public offices!"

Judge Toodle's face got red. But it wasn't half as red as Pa's.

"Now I'll see that you get the ten thousand dollars for less than four per cent," I said.

"Come to think about it," he said, "we can't exceed our

budget. Couldn't borrow any more money even if we didn't have to pay any interest."

Pa's face got redder and redder. Where his shirt collar was unbuttoned, his neck looked like the settin' sun and I knew it was time to go.

"Let's go, Pa," I coaxed. "I've got work at home to do!"

"Don't be in a hurry, boys," Judge Toodle said with his face lit up in a happy glow and there was a big smile on his face.

"Next year we'll build you a good road," Toodle Powell spoke sweetly. "Remember your road is not a number one road."

"It's road number one to us," Pa said.

"And before I forget it, Mick," Judge Toodle said, "the governor wants us to get behind Willie Horton for Congressman in this district. I know you're a good party worker and you have faith in the Right Party!"

Judge Toodle was getting nervous, though he kept the happy smile on his face as Pa and I left silently in a hurry.

Coming Down the Mountain

At last we found Pappie in the most unexpected place. He was sitting at the roots of a little pine. His back was leaned against it, but his head and neck didn't touch the tree. His neck was as limber as a wilted milkweed, and his head drooped like a big sunflower on a hot September day. Pappie's mouth was open and his eyes were closed. If his eyes had been open, he wouldn't have seen anything but a few yellow hickory leaves that had drifted down from the tree near him and a few pine needles that had fallen from the tree above him. But Pappie couldn't see anything. Not even the posted sign above him on the pine tree. It said KEEP OUT in big letters, and down below in smaller letters: NO HUNTING ALLOWED. Below these words was a name Pappie had never liked. Bill Payton. Beside of Pappie was something we had expected to find. It was always there when we had to go bring him from the fox-hunting woods. His gallon jug with the brown body and the white neck. It was Pappie's favorite jug. And old Sooner, his favorite hound, was sleeping on the leaves near him.

"He's dead to the world," Little Edd said. "Look at his face. He's pale as a ghost!"

"Pappie! Pappie!" I said, as I shook his shoulder.

But he didn't hear me. He was in a world of dreams,

where Sooner was winning the fox chase for the first time in his life.

"We'll have a time with him," Little Edd said. "We'll never get him sober this time!"

"But Mammie said for us to fetch him home," I said.

"What would he do if he didn't have us to take care of him?" Little Edd asked. "He'll never be able to sit around with other fathers and talk about what a time he had with his sons. Instead we could sit around with the fathers and tell them what a time we had taking care of our father."

Little Edd looked at Pappie and shook his head. Then he laughed a wild laugh.

"What's so funny?" I asked. "We won't be laughing if Bill Payton comes up and catches him and old Sooner in his sheep pasture."

"No wonder our neighbors all call Pappie 'Uncle Fox,' " Little Edd said. "I never noticed before that Pappie looks so much like a fox. Look at his long, thin, red nose! Look at his little pointed ears and the red beard and the long red hair. His arms are covered with red hair just like a fox's forelegs."

"Don't talk s'much," I said. "Let's try to sober him up and get him home."

Little Edd and I went to work. We shook Pappie again and again. But we couldn't get him to move. And he didn't say a word. I felt of his pulse to see how his ticker was beating, for I got uneasy. Not even his eyebrow twitched when the wild flies lit on his face, so I thought he could be dead. But Pappie was as warm as an oven biscuit, and his ticker was working as smoothly as a sharp crosscut saw in green tulipwood.

"He's all right, Little Edd," I said. "He's alive and normal. He's just too far along to be sobered."

Then Little Edd pulled Pappie's ears. He stretched them until they looked thin enough to see through. When he let go, they snapped back to his head like old rubber that would still stretch but not as well as it once had.

"Even that doesn't work," Little Edd said. "Now we'll have to find cold water."

"We'll have to go down to Sulphur Spring Hollow to get it," I said.

We took Pappie's empty jug and went through the briers and wild grapevines and brush to the Hollow. We filled the jug with water cool enough to ache your teeth and hurried back to Pappie. We poured the water over the top of his head and face and it ran down his neck beneath his shirt collar and down his spine and it soaked the seat of his overalls. But it didn't faze Pappie. He didn't bat an eye.

"Nothing is going to rouse him," I said. "We'll have to wait twelve hours or longer and let him wake up naturally."

"We can't wait that long," Little Edd said. "Mammie will be uneasy—and we must be home before dark."

"There's but one way to get him home," I said. "We'll have to get a mule and rope him on."

"If we walk seven miles home to get the mule, it will be after dark before we could get him from the mountain."

"We've borrowed a mule from Bill Payton before—we can do it again. He has a good mule—one that steps like a billygoat. Never slips or falls."

"Aaron, the last time we borrowed a mule from him he warned us never to come back. He said he'd never let us have one again."

"Well, he doesn't like Pappie and Pappie doesn't like him, and he tries to keep Pappie from fox hunting on him. He's got sheep and Pappie's got fox hounds. And maybe he won't let us borrow a mule again, but it's the only way to get Pappie home before dark."

"Then you go ask for the mule this time," Little Edd said.

I followed a sheep path down the spur of the mountain into the valley where Bill Payton lived.

"What do you want?" Bill Payton asked as soon as I stuck my head in at the barn door where he was oiling mule harness.

"I need a mule to get Pappie home," I said.

"So he's passed out again," he said. "I posted my sheep range and told hunters to stay outen there. Your pappie don't have any regard for posters."

"Pappie doesn't read," I said.

"He ought to know what a keep out sign looks like." His voice was trembling. "Last night his hounds stampeded my sheep and ran from the mountaintop to the barn. I had to get out of a warm bed in my night clothes and put them in the barn to quiet them. I'm not lettin' you have a mule. I'm going to get a warrant out for old Fox Bailey. Boy, I don't mean to be rude to you," he said, speaking softer, "for I feel sorry for you and your little brother havin' to hunt that old sot and take him home. You boys and your mother would fare better if he's behind the bars. All he does is fox-hunt and drink."

Tears came to my eyes, and I begged him not to get a warrant. Even if he did fox-hunt and drink, he was my father and I loved him. So did Little Edd and so did Mom. When Pappie was sober he could tell jokes and keep us all laughing. And Pappie laughed at everything when he was sober. I couldn't let him go to jail—we'd all go crazy without him—and I told Bill Payton so. I couldn't help crying.

"You just want him sobered so you can get him home?" he asked in a kindly voice.

"Yes," I said, "we'd like to have him sober enough to walk home."

"All right. I'll fix things up. You wait and see. I'll let you have the mule." And he told me laughing what he was going to do. "And after he gets home—after he gets sober—I want to see him. He's got to stop this huntin' on me. I'm tired of having my sheep butchered by his hounds."

"I'll tell him, Mr. Payton," I said.

Mr. Payton took a pretty long-legged mule from his stall. He must have been sixteen hands high. He bridled him and groomed him—threw a big gray blanket over his back that had a gold star in each corner. Then he put a nice saddle on the mule and spent a long time fixing everything.

"We could have laid Pappie across his bare back and rope him as we've done before," I said, worried.

"By fixing it up this way, son, he'll be a sober man sooner. Maybe it will help to make him a sober man in the future. You'd like that, wouldn't you?"

"I'd give anything in this world for that," I said.

Mr. Payton gave me a rope to tie Pappie across the saddle. "Let the mule walk up the mountain," he said. "He'll have enough to do to carry Fox home."

"All right, Mr. Payton. Thank you ever so much." And I started off with the mule. He was friendly, and I rubbed his nose as we climbed up the mountain together. When I reached the pine where Pappie was sitting, Little Edd was pouring another jug of water on Pappie.

"What's kept you so long, Aaron?" Little Edd asked. "I've carried ten jugs of cold water and poured on Pappie."

"Look at this saddle," I said. "Look what Mr. Payton did."

"Gee, he must've had a change of heart. Put a saddle on the mule! Red tassels on the bridle! Boy, what a pretty mule!"

When I led the mule up close to Pappie, he snorted.

"He got a whiff of Pappie's breath," Little Edd said. "He doesn't like it. I never saw a mule yet that liked the smell of moonshine."

"Whoa, whoa, Rock," I said, rubbing his nose. "You're a good mule and you'll take Pappie home all right."

Rock seemed to know what I was saying. He stood perfectly still while Little Edd got Pappie by the feet and I got him by the shoulders and we lifted him across the saddle. His legs fell limp on one side of Rock and his arms fell limp on the other. But poor Pappie didn't know he was lying across a soft springy saddle. We tied the rope around him and around the horn on the front of the saddle and through the two rings back of the saddle, and the rope was tied around the mule's belly. We tied everything tight so there wouldn't be any falling off.

I unsnapped the rein from one loop of the bridle and it was about fifteen feet long. I could walk far ahead of Rock as I led him.

"Get the jug and call Sooner, Little Edd," I said. "I'll lead Rock."

We started for home. Sooner followed behind the mule with his tail down, because Pappie couldn't talk to him. And little Edd walked beside me swinging the jug.

"The times we've taken Pappie home, like this," Little Edd said. "But never on such a pretty mule and in such a fine saddle."

Old Rock let out a little snort and jerked his head up.

"Come on, Rock," I said. "Quit your foolishness."

All of a sudden Rock raised his head high in the air and

walked on his hind feet like a man. I never heard such noise come from the mouth of a mule.

"Hold him, Aaron," Little Edd shouted, because the mule was lifting me up on the rein. "Give the rein more slack!"

I gave it enough slack so he could walk on his hind feet. Then he came down on his forefeet and lifted his hind feet straight in the air and I never saw such kicking.

"He's a buckin' mule," Little Edd said. "He doesn't like his load."

He went back up on his hind feet and came back on his forefeet. He kicked something awful to see. And he snorted something awful to hear.

"Do you reckon we can get Pappie off?" Little Edd asked.

"Reckon the rope will hold him?" I asked. "If it doesn't, Pappie's liable to be killed."

But the rope didn't give an inch no matter how much Rock bucked. Pappie was on Rock's back to stay. And when Little Edd tried to untie the rope, Rock snorted and bit at Little Edd.

"Stay away from that mule," I said. "Pappie's on there to stay!"

"Will we have to take him home like this?" Little Edd asked. "If we should get him home, how'll we ever get him off the mule?"

"I don't know," I answered. "Let's don't worry about that. Let's hope he's alive! That old Bill Payton!"

While Rock bucked, we moved along the ridge. We'd already come over a mile. We'd reached Six Hickories. Rock was still bucking, and the sweat was dripping from his flanks. I'd never heard an animal snort like this one. As we moved toward Piney Point, he reared up and came down on his forefeet and kicked with his hind feet—and we had to let him rest because his sides were going in and out like a bee smoker and when they did, they moved Pappie up and down. Even the sweat broke out on Pappie's red face—big as raindrops.

"Look, Aaron, Pappie's moving his hands and kicking his feet," Little Edd shouted. "He's stirring. Life's coming back to him."

"Oh, my," Pappie groaned just as we reached Piney Point. "Where am I? What is this?"

"Take it easy, Pappie," Little Edd said. "We're taking you home."

"H-how?" Pappie moaned as Rock went up in the air and came down.

"In a brand new saddle," I said. "You're on a mule."

Pappie wasn't quite awake. He groaned and bellowed and took on something awful when we started down the mountain toward Low Gap. And when he took on, it made old Rock madder than ever. He shook himself like a mule shakes dirt from his back after he wallows, to get Pappie off. But the rope held. Then he tried to stand on his head. He sat down. And Pappie yelled like it was killing him.

"If the Lord will only let me," Pappie said, "I'll never. . . ."

Pappie didn't get to finish his words. Rock tried to stand on his head with Pappie. And he couldn't do that. So he went on over in a flipflop. It didn't hurt Pappie for he was down in the saddle, but his feet and hands hit the ground and he let out a wild scream.

"Take me off! Take me off!" he yelled. "I'm being killed!"

Pappie's neck lost its limberness and got still. He looked

up with his keen fox eyes. "Where did you get this mule?" he screamed.

"Got him from Bill Payton," Little Edd said.

"It's a plot to kill me," Pappie shouted. "Get me offen this mule!"

We had now reached Low Gap.

"Quiet, Pappie," I said. "Your screaming makes Rock worse."

"We're almost to the Creek road," Little Edd said. "It's easy sailing then. The road's level."

"But it's in the creek all the way," Pappie said. "If he falls with me in one of these holes, he'll drown me."

Along the road Rock bucked and splashed a big spray of water that covered Pappie's head. Pappie looked like a water-soaked shepherd with his long red hair falling across his face.

"Can't you take me offen this mule?" Pappie wailed again.

"Let's try again, Little Edd," I said.

"You sober now?" Little Edd asked.

"Sober," Pappie screamed. "I've been sober since we reached Piney Point. But when he turned that flipflop, I woke up."

I held the bridle rein close to Rock's mouth. He snorted in my face, champed the bits, and kicked up big sprays of water. Little Edd started to untie the rope.

"Work easy, Little Edd," I said.

But as soon as Little Edd touched his flank, Rock thought it was Pappie and reared up, lifting me high into the air. I gave the rein slack, hit the ground just in time to get out of the way. He came down and flipped over in the road into a big waterhole. But he didn't shake Pappie off.

"Take him on, take 'im on," Pappie screamed, with water

dripping from his hair, feet, and hands. "Maybe I can stand it till we get home!"

Rock snorted till Mammie could have heard him a mile down the hollow if she'd been listening. He danced in the road, and pawed, kicked, brayed. Pappie kicked, moved his arms, cussed, then started praying. It was the first time we'd ever heard Pappie pray. Rock was trying to get down and roll in the sand with him. It scared Little Edd and me. I kept pulling at the bridle while Pappie prayed and Little Edd shoved from behind. Finally we got Rock to moving on down the hollow.

"If I get home alive," Pappie said. . . .

"I can see the shack, Pappie," Little Edd said. "I can see the chimney above the willows!"

"Thank God! Thank God!" Pappie said.

Rock walked a few steps as a mule should. Then he walked on his hind feet again and started bucking. Pappie was so tired he stopped praying. He just took it easy until we reached the shack. Rock took another bucking spell when Mammie ran to meet us. Mammie waved her hand and screamed something awful.

"Don't let 'im kill Dave," she screamed. "What's wrong with that mule? Hold 'im, Aaron—hold 'im! Hold 'im until we get Dave off."

"But we can't get Pappie off, Mammie," Little Edd said. "We've tried it twice."

"Oh—this fox-huntin' and drinkin', Dave," Mammie shouted.

"Don't worry, honey," Pappie moaned. "If I ever get free this time, I've promised God. . . ."

Old Rock put on an act for Mammie, who held her hands in the air and screamed. He brayed and kicked, then pawed and snorted. He walked as straight as a man on his hind feet.

Then he came over on his front feet and kicked high at the wind. He even tried to lie down again and roll with Pappie. And it was all Little Edd and I could do to keep him up on his feet. I pulled at the reins and Little Edd shoved from behind.

When old Rock wanted to walk toward our barn, I let him. He walked like a tired mule ought to have walked. And Pappie was about gone. Rock walked into the barn entry and just stood there calm as the air after a thunderstorm. He acted like he wanted the saddle off. And that's just what Little Edd and I did. We unbuckled the bellyband, took off the saddle with Pappie roped to it. And the blankets slid off with the saddle.

"Thank God," Pappie said as Mammie rushed up and started to untie the rope that bound Pappie. "My sweetheart is safe."

"Minnie," Pappie said, "I promised God and I'll promise you—this is my last time. I've never had a thing like this to happen to me in my life."

Mammie had untied the rope and Pappie was free.

I put the blanket and saddle on Rock's back while Mammie brushed the sand from Pappie's hair and kissed his cheek. And while she petted him and loved him now that he was safe with her again, and he had made her a promise he'd never made before, I climbed to the saddle and rode away on a mule that was as gentle as a child. I had in my pocket, so that Pappie and Mammie and Little Edd would not see them, the handful of cockleburrs that Bill Payton had slipped under the saddle. Pappie and Mammie and Little Edd looked at me and the gentle Rock too dumfounded to speak.

Land of Our Enemies

PAP will never ride another log raft down this river," Pa said, as he looked from the train window at the Big Sandy River. "I've gone down this river to Gate City with 'im many a time when I was a little shaver. I've seen a big poplar log break loose from the raft and I've seen Pap jump from the raft onto it and the spikes in his boot heels wouldn't ketch and the log would dump 'im in the icy water. Pap would come up a-spittin' water and a-cussin'. But he'd get his log back to the raft. It makes a body have a funny feelin' to remember all of these things."

Our train was lumberin' and creakin' around the curves farther up the twisting Big Sandy. The sun had gone down and twilight was settling over the deep valley. Here and there we could see a light in a shack beside the railroad tracks. Soon the thin-leafed mountain slopes faded into twilight and gradually into darkness, until we could no longer see the outlines of the mountains and the white streams of water. We were riding into darkness, a darkness so thick that it looked like from the train window one could reach out and slice it into black ribbons with a pocket-knife.

"Lindsay, Lindsay," the conductor said as he entered our coach. "All out for Lindsay!"

160

"Do you reckon anybody will be at the station to meet us?" I asked Pa.

"Somebody'll be here," he said. "Somebody'll be at this station to meet every train. Powderjays will be a-comin' back here on every train."

"When will they bury Grandpa?" I asked Pa.

"Shhh! Not so loud," he whispered, as he glanced over his shoulder.

I looked around to see two beardy-faced men with mean-lookin' eyes listening to what we said.

"You never know whether you're a-talkin' before a friend 'r an enemy here," Pa whispered to me.

The two beardy-faced men got up from their seats and followed us from the train.

"Air ye a-goin' to Cousin Mick Powderjay's funeral?" one of the men asked Pa soon as we had stepped off the train.

"That's where we're a-goin'," Pa said. "Is he akin to you?"

"We're brother's children," the man said. "I'm Zack Powderjay. And this is my brother, Dave Powderjay! We're Zack Powderjay's boys."

"I'm Mick Powderjay," Pa told them. "Pap's eleventh child by his first wife!"

"We've heard of ye," Zack Powderjay said. "See, we had to leave the Big Sandy a long time ago."

"When did you leave?" Pa asked.

"In President Hayes's administration," Dave Powderjay said.

"I left in Grover Cleveland's second administration," Pa said.

"Why did you leave?" Dave Powderjay asked Pa.

"Trouble with the Hornbuckles," he said.

"Trouble with th' Hornbuckles and Dangerfields caused us to leave," Dave said.

"Did Cousin Mick die a natural death?" Zack Powderjay asked Pa.

"I ain't heard yet but I know Pap didn't die a natural death," Pa said. "He had more enemies than he had ailments of the body."

"Ye're right, brother," a husky voice sounded in the darkness now that the train had gone. "I'm Keith Powderjay, son of Jimmie Powderjay, oldest son of Mick Powderjay. I've come to meet this train to direct any and all Powderjays and their bloodkin to the right spot."

"Then Pap was killed?" Pa asked Keith Powderjay, who had come close enough for Pa to recognize him.

Keith was a mountain of a man towering above us.

"He was beaten to death with a club," Keith told us. "Wait until ye see 'im."

"Who kilt Cousin Mick?" Dave Powderjay asked.

"We know but we ain't a-sayin' now," Keith said. "Two men done it. And we got men out atter 'em tonight. Ye may hear of two deaths before mornin'."

"It makes my blood bile," Pa said. "But I've been expectin' somethin' to happen to Pap fer many years. He's been a-fightin' a long war."

"We're all riled a-plenty," Keith said. "We'd better git goin'."

"Do you have a lantern?" Pa asked. "I can't see well in the dark."

"But ye can't have a lantern, Uncle Mick," Keith said. "Lanterns air good targets at night."

"I've been away a long time," Pa said. "I jist fergot. Hit's all a-comin' back to me now."

And as we followed Keith Powderjay through the darkness, Pa's words came back to me. I remembered when we used to sit around the fire on winter nights at home how Pa would tell about going to the railroad station or to church and how he would walk in the darkness because he was afraid to carry a lantern. He would tell us how men had waited for him because he was a son of old Mick Powderjay and how he had been shot at many times. Once a bullet came so close he felt the wind from it on the tip of his nose.

"No talkin' here," Cousin Keith told us. "Quiet until I tell ye when to talk."

Everybody got quiet and we had to walk hand in hand with Cousin Keith leadin' us. But he had been over this path so many times, he could feel the path with his feet.

I'm glad Grandpa Powderjay moved to the Little Sandy River in Cleveland's first administration, I thought. I'm glad Pa didn't go back with Grandpa when he got homesick for the Big Sandy and moved back to fight with his enemies. I'm glad Pa stayed on the Little Sandy and I was born there.

Grandpa had been a soldier; he had fought in Pennsylvania, Maryland, and Virginia. Gettysburg was a name to him that he would never forget; Antietam, Bull Run, Cold Harbor, Fredericksburg, Richmond were names that I had heard him talk about since I could remember. He had fought through the war from beginning to end and the only scars he had were around his wrists where he had been hanged by the arms to the joist of an old house. Captured twice and hanged once, he had come out of the war a living man.

But this was not the war that got Grandpa into trouble. When he came home he fought a long war. It was a war that never ended. He waged war on the guerrilla bands, who had captured, killed, and plundered while he and other mountain men were away fighting in Northern and Southern armies. These guerrilla bands didn't belong to either army. Grandpa had fought them since eighteen sixty-five, all but the three years he had lived on the Little Sandy. Now they had gotten 'im in the end as they said they would.

"We're a-past the dangerous places," Cousin Keith said. "We're a-past the Hornbuckles and Dangerfields."

"How much fudder do we haf to go?" Dave Powderjay asked.

"About three miles," Cousin Keith said.

"When will they bury Pap?" Pa asked.

"Two o'clock in the mornin'," Cousin Keith said.

"It's too bad to haf to bury Pap at night," Pa sighed.

"But this is a land of our enemies," Cousin Keith said. "Grandpa died a-fightin' his enemies. He told me two days before he's kilt that if all his bloodkin had stayed with 'im he'd a-winned this war in the end."

"But brother Zack and I were glad to get out'n it," Dave Powderjay said. "Glad to get into the mountains of West Virginia. We left soon as Pap and brother Tom were kilt, and we have lived in West Virginia and raised our famblies in peace."

I had never heard of a funeral at night but I had read in my history book in school where General Braddock was buried at night so the Indians wouldn't find his grave. I guess the reason that we buried Grandpa at night wasn't that his enemies would bother his grave but that his enemies would bother his bloodkin that had gathered to see him buried. I knew if we couldn't walk from the railroad to the shack where Grandpa lived and carry a light we couldn't have a funeral in the daytime. I knew that we were among our enemies. Though we had killed many of their people, there wasn't a family among us but Pa's where one, two, or three men had not fallen from the ambush shots of our enemies.

Why are we such hated people? I thought.

"I'll tell you where Pap made his mistake," Pa said. "He made it when he married his second wife, Mattie Henson. She's a first cousin of Anse Dangerfield and Tobbie Horn-buckle! I can't understand what made Pap marry an en'my!"

"That's right, Uncle Mick," Cousin Keith said. "Ye hit the nail on the head. If our men air lucky tonight, ye'll know tomorrow that this is the truth."

I couldn't tell when we reached Grandpa's shack. There wasn't a light from any window. Cousin Keith knocked three times on the door; it was opened by Pa's oldest brother, Uncle Cief. "Come in," he said softly.

And we followed him into the crowd of our people—beardy-faced men and women with deep-lined faces. There was silence in the room, and everybody's face was clouded.

"Where's Mattie?" Pa asked.

"She's not here anymore," Aunt Arabella said. "Pap and her's been separated fer some time."

And now I saw assembled for the first time Pa's people—my bloodkin from the East Kentucky mountains. They were my bloodkin that I had heard about but didn't know very well; many of the men had scars on their faces and hands and many of them limped. I was glad, after I looked at them, that I had not been through a long guerrilla war.

"Come this way," Cousin Keith said, beckoning to us.

We followed him into the room where Grandpa was in his homemade coffin.

"Look at this, won't ye!"

Cousin Keith pointed to the wide blue marks across Grandpa's battered face where he had been beaten to death.

And then he bent over and opened his coat and shirt and showed us the pulp-beats on his chest. I had never seen a man beaten as he had been beaten—this mountain of a man who had died in the battle he had been fighting forty-six years. His face was clean shaven and his mustache neatly trimmed and his gray hair parted on the side. His mouth was set firmly. I had seen him in life when his mouth was set as it was now. His mouth was like this in life when he spoke of his enemies.

Pa turned and walked away. He couldn't stand to look at Grandpa. He went back into the room where the old crippled soldiers sat, wearing their tattered uniforms and holding their rifles in their hands. They had fought with Grandpa. Now they had come for his funeral. Pa called them by their names and shook their hands. They were white-haired, white-bearded, and grisly old warriors who had seen their best days and had come to see an old comrade buried. They seemed to have risen from a dim and distant past.

"Your pap wuz as good a soldier as ever lived," one spoke feebly to Pa. "But one war wuz not enough fer 'im. He oughta quit then. No use fightin' all his life."

"He was the best wrestler in Grant's army," another said. "I never saw him rode in all the bouts he had."

There were low whispers among my people in the small, crowded, three-room shack. Heavy quilts were hangin' over the windows so not a ray of light could be seen from the outside. Wind came between the log-cracks, and the flames of oil lamps sputtered and smoked the lamp globes. I remembered while I stood here among my people and these old soldiers in their faded uniforms what Pa had told Mom. He had told her how Grandpa wouldn't sleep in a room unless a lamp was burning. Said he put quilts over the windows so they wouldn't be a target for his enemies shooting with rifles from the thickets on the mountain slopes.

We were quiet enough in the shack to hear the roosters crow for midnight. And as soon as they had finished crowing from their roosts outside the shack, Uncle Jason came into the room.

"It's about time fer us to start," he announced.

Six of my cousins, sons of Pa's older brothers, picked up Grandpa's coffin and stepped out into the darkness. They were tall beardy men with broad shoulders. The muscles in their forearms bulged as they carried the big coffin and the big warrior in it from his shack out into the darkness. Aunt Emerine blew out the lamps and the crowd of Powderjays, their in-laws and friends, followed the coffin into the darkness. Cousin Keith led the way up the mountain path and we followed. A moon came from behind a dark bread-loaf-shaped mountain where jutted rocks were outlined against the misty sky. There were whispers among us as we walked along slowly. Twice my cousins had to let six more cousins carry the coffin, since it was such a load in the darkness to carry up a mountain slope.

"Not one of Pap's eight young'ins by Mattie air here," Uncle Cief told Pa. "And hit's good they ain't here. Thar's too much en'my blood in 'em to suit us."

I didn't know the part-guerrilla Powderjays from the real Powderjays. But I knew that the real Powderjays didn't have any use for them even if the same blood did flow through their veins. I heard Pa and Uncle Cief talking about them as the crowd moved slowly along. I was with my people and it seemed like a dream. I didn't know there was a world like the one I was in.

Suddenly our stumbling, whispering funeral crowd

stopped on a lonely mountaintop. I could see rows of brown sandstones that had been chiseled with pickaxes and broad axes marking the rows of graves. And I saw men standing by a fresh-dug grave holding their picks, adzes, and long-handled shovels. An owl flew over us on outspread wings we could hear fanning the night wind. And on a distant mountaintop we heard a whippoorwill. But there was not a light nor a sound among us while my cousins placed Grandpa's coffin beside his grave. "Tonight, we're a-buryin' a soldier who has had many fights," an old soldier said after Grandpa's coffin had been placed beside the grave. "He has fit through a long war in the land of his enemies and he has fit well."

From among men and women of our silent funeral crowd two men walked toward the old soldier. As they walked toward him, Uncle Cief put his hand on his pistol until he recognized them. One whispered something to the old soldier in charge of Grandpa's funeral.

"And I am glad to tell you Mick Powderjay's death has been avenged," the old soldier announced. "Eif Danger-field and Battle Henson 've paid fer thar crime!"

That was all that was said for Grandpa. There wasn't a preacher to preach his funeral and there weren't any songs. The old soldiers fired a farewell volley across his grave, and the fire from their rifles was the only light we had seen except the moonlight shining dimly through the sheets of white mists rising from the valley below us. Grandpa's coffin was lowered into his grave with leather checklines on a mountaintop where only Powderjays, their bloodkin, and in-laws were buried—a mountain high enough to over-look the rugged land of our people and our enemies.

No Hero

WHEN I could look over at the bright lights of Landsburg, I stopped to catch my breath and do some thinking. For behind me lay the dark unfruitful hills where my crops had failed. And in a shack among these hills, seven miles away, I'd left Mollie with our three little ones. "Hester, we have to have bread," was the last thing she'd said to me. "We can't go another day without some kind of relief." And when I started walking to Landsburg in the late afternoon, Mollie couldn't understand. I couldn't tell her what I had in mind.

For nature had been against me. It wasn't that I wasn't willing to work. I was willing to work. The drouth had killed my crops. I couldn't make it rain. There just wasn't anything I could do about it except see my garden truck, corn, potatoes, and tobacco wilt in the hot June and July sun. All I'd worked for was lost.

Nature was against me in another way that I couldn't help. I'd grown up tall as a beanpole and slender as a poplar sapling. In August I'd tried to get work with an extra force, when the Railway Company was needing men. The foreman took one look at me and said, "Not heavy enough for your height. The lifting of crowbars, crossties, and T-rails would break you in two." Then I tried to get a job at the Auckland Iron Works, where they needed men. They gave me an examination and then put me on the scales. "Underweight," the doctor said. "We can't use you." It was that way every place I tried to get work.

Nature was against me more ways than one. And now I had to do some more thinking about Mollie and our three little ones before I tackled what I had in mind to do. Jim Harris told me about something in Landsburg. It was something they begged a man to do. It was hard to get a man to do it. But it was great fun for the people to see. Jim said the Landsburg Law had threatened to close the place up since one man, Hawk Weaver, was sent to the hospital.

In the distance below me I could see the bright lights along the streets and I could see one real bright spot in the town. This was the spot where I was going. For this was the fairground. I could hear the shouts of happy people coming from this spot and I could hear the music of the merry-go-round. "This way, this way," I could hear a man shout. "Three balls for the little dime, ten cents. Knock down three kitties and get yourself a quarter!" But this wasn't what I was going to do. It was harder than throwing balls at the kitties. It was something all the brave boys were afraid to do. And I wasn't brave either. I just needed the money. I had to have some money. And when I thought about it, my heart went up into my mouth.

But I'll be game, I thought. I'll try it. If they'll only let me try it after they see how tall I am and almost as light as the wind.

Then I started toward the brightest spot in Landsburg. My long beanpole legs soon covered the ground when I started walking. In a few minutes I'd reached the bright spot I'd looked over from the ridgetop. The Greenwood County people and the city people of Landsburg had filled the fairground. People were almost running over each other. They were standing in line to buy baseballs to throw at the kitties. They were standing in line to buy rings to throw over pegs where knives, alarm clocks, blankets, and pans were hanging. They were waiting to ride the merry-go-round and the merry-mixup. They were standing packed like sardines in front of a tent where two women danced and where a man beat a drum. And when the drummer and the dancers went into the tent and the announcer told them the "greatest show on earth would be inside the tent" they pushed each other down trying to get tickets before the tent was filled. Money was flowing like water and everybody was happy. I wished for a little of the money I saw coming from the fat pocketbooks. But my time was coming. Not now.

For Lefty Simmons, Landsburg's local boy, stepped upon the platform in boxing trunks and sparred with Slugger Stevens.

"Ladies and gentlemen, last evening Lefty Simmons and 'Slugger' Stevens fought an even match," the announcer shouted through a megaphone, "and this evening they will fight to a finish. It's your local boy, Lefty, against the great and powerful 'Slugger' Stevens! Ladies and gentlemen, right this way to see one of the greatest fights of all times!"

When Slugger and Lefty went inside the tent, the crowd rushed for tickets. I knew that my time would come next. It would come after this fight. For the people that loved to watch a fight would love to watch what I was going to try to do. Some of them might want to see a man killed. Though I wasn't sure about that. Yet, for years afterward they would talk about seeing Hester King's body mangled at the Landsburg Fair. But I didn't want to die. I'd thought this thing through and it was the only way I could see to make some quick money. I'd heard all my life, "Wherever there's a will, there's a way." I had the will. And I'd thought of the way.

There was one more night of the Landsburg Fair. And when I waited outside for the fight to be over, I heard screams and shouts of the people inside. "Kill 'im, Lefty, kill 'im!" I could hear men and women shout and scream. It must have been some fight, and a lot of people got worked up about it. For the Landsburg marshal and two deputies had to go inside the tent. But when the manager brought the fighters back onto the platform, he held up both their hands and said it was another draw and they would fight it out to a finish tomorrow night, the last night of the Landsburg Fair. They had fought to five draws, this made.

"Your local Lefty is some fighter," the announcer said. "He's stayed with the mighty Slugger for five nights!"

A great roar of applause went up from the people. For Lefty's face looked red and beaten and there was blood on his lips and nostrils.

"Don't leave now, folks, don't leave," the announcer shouted through his megaphone. "Stand by for an important announcement!"

I knew what was coming now.

"We are looking for a man to stay with old Bruin five minutes tonight," the man shouted. "Is there a man in the crowd that will wrestle the greatest wrestler in the world! Is there a man that will take a chance wrestling this three-hundred-and-eighty-six-pound bear? If there is a man that will stay in the cage with him five minutes, he will receive twenty-five dollars! If a man will stay with him ten minutes, he will receive fifty dollars. He will receive twenty-five dollars for every five minutes he stays with old Bruin! That's a lot of money, folks! And if he wrestles Bruin," he shouted, "he will get an extra one hundred dollars."

"I'll try it, sir," I said, holding up my hand high above the crowd.

I looked around me and not another hand was up.

"That damn bear'll kill you, man," a big fellow said to me. "Hawk Weaver is in the hospital over a-tryin' to ride that bear! Ain't you afraid of 'im, Slim?"

"Yes, I am," I said.

"What are you a-gettin' in the cage with 'im for, then?" the man asked.

I didn't answer him. And I heard sighs go up all over the fairgrounds.

"Another victim," said a little man standing near me.

"Then come up here, Slim," the announcer said. "Let the crowd have a look at you!"

When I walked upon the platform, everybody laughed. The announcer looked me over and he laughed. Maybe he laughed at my big feet and long hands. But the whole crowd laughed, and they pushed up closer.

"How tall are you and how much do you weigh?" the announcer asked me.

"Six feet five and weigh one thirty-five," I said.

"Ever do any wrestling, Slim?" he asked me.

"Never did," I said.

"What do you do for a living?" he asked me.

"Right now I'm unemployed," I said.

Then the announcer asked me my full name and where I lived and I told him.

"This is Hester King from Buckrun Hollow back in Greenwood County," the announcer shouted to the crowd through his megaphone. "He's six feet five, weighs one thirty-five and he's never done any wrestling! And right now he's unemployed."

"He'll be employed when old Bruin gets a-hold of 'im," some man shouted from the crowd.

"Stomp old Bruin with your big number thirteens," another man laughed.

"Slap his face with your big fire-shovel hand," another man screamed.

Then everybody laughed. More people gathered in to have a look at me. It was the first time I'd ever faced a crowd like this. Everybody on the fairground was shoving closer.

"Nobody's stayed with that bear three minutes," said a big man that stood below me, resting his hand on the platform. "That's the catch. See, you don't get anything unless you stay five minutes! Hogg Morton stayed the longest. He stayed two minutes! Had the bear down once! But it liked to 've kilt old Hogg before the referee could get 'im off! It's a mint of gold for this fair!"

"Buddie Walker didn't stay ten seconds," said a man standing beside the man that had spoken of Hogg Morton. "Bear just knocked him against the cage once and that was all there was to it!"

"How long do you think you can stay with Bruin?" the announcer asked me.

"Five minutes," I said. "Maybe longer."

"Hester King says he can stay with Bruin five minutes, maybe longer," the announcer shouted gleefully.

"That's what Hester King thinks," a man shouted from the crowd. "That bear's a man-killer and shouldn't be al-. lowed to wrestle civilized men at a street fair!"

"Then Mr. King says he'll stay with the bear five minutes or longer and you say he won't," the announcer said. "Let's see who is telling the truth! Maybe this tall man will surprise us!"

"Old Ichabod, the beanpole, will soon find out," somebody shouted from the crowd. "There won't be any draw in this wrestling match!"

"He wants to wrestle mighty bad," another man shouted. "Or he must need the money!"

"Wait until you see this man in wrestling trunks," the announcer said. "You'll see something. Worth the price of admission, folks!"

I followed the announcer from the platform down into the tent. The crowd surged up to buy tickets. When I went into a little dressing room and started taking off my clothes, I thought about Mollie, little Naomi, Sophie, and Hester, Jr. Then I thought about going into the cage with the bear. I wondered just what would happen. And what if I can stay with 'im five minutes, I thought. Ten minutes! Fifteen, twenty, twenty-five minutes! One hundred and twenty-five dollars! What a fortune!

While I put my skinny legs into the big wrestler's trunks, I heard people pouring into the tent like honeybees into a hive. Only the people made more noise. It was a louder buzzing and there was so many jumbled words that I couldn't understand what anybody was saying. I could hear the word "kill" pretty often.

When I was ready, the manager told me the referee, Johnnie Norris, who owned the bear, would see that Bruin didn't hurt me, for he could handle him. He warned me not to be too scared and to stay with Bruin two minutes if I could.

"I must stay longer than that," I said. "I must stay five minutes!"

The manager laughed as he pushed back a flap of the tent and we walked into the arena beneath the big tent where the people were crowded close to the cage. The big black bear was inside the cage, walking around, looking between the iron bars at the people. He'd hold to the iron bars with his paws as he circled the cage and looked at the crowd.

"He'd like to get among us," said a well-dressed woman. "My, if I's a man, I wouldn't want to wrestle that ugly thing!"

When I walked among the crowd, everybody screamed with laughter.

"Ichabod Crane wrestling that heavy bear!" someone screamed.

People looked at my long skinny legs and wondered how they'd hold me up. They looked at my little waist measure.

"Not any bigger around the waist than the coupling pole in a jolt wagon," a big man said as I passed him.

"But look what feet and hands," another man said.

"Bear won't care for them," said a freckled-faced man with a bow tie that went up and down with his Adam's apple as he talked.

"Hate to see that poor man get what Hawk Weaver got," I heard someone say in a low voice. For I was near the cage door.

"Timekeepers here?" the announcer asked.

"Yep, we're here," said a tall man. "Kim Kiefer of Landsburg will help me keep the time!"

"All right, Al, you and Kim start your watches," Johnnie said, as he unlocked the cage door.

I thought of Mollie and my three little ones. That was the last thought I had before I stooped nearly double to go through the cage door.

"Shake hands with Bruin," Johnnie said. "He expects it. If you do, it will be easier for you!"

Bruin knew what his duties were. For he came up to meet me and Johnnie stepped aside when he reached me his paw. I shook his paw gently. And everybody in the tent became so quiet you could have almost heard a pin drop on the dirt-packed floor outside the cage. And my shaking Bruin's paw gently didn't help matters a bit. He backed away and then he came clumsily toward me with the full force of his three-hundred-odd pounds. He pushed me against the side of the cage with a wallop. He acted like he wanted to finish me in a hurry.

"Won't be long," said the freckled-faced man with the bow tie that worked up and down on his Adam's apple. He held his face close to the cage and peeped between the bars. But he was surprised when I got back to my feet and ran in between old Bruin's outstretched forepaws. That's the spot all the wrestlers didn't want to get. Old Bruin tried squeezing on me but I was too small for him to get the full power of his powerful arms. I hugged close to Bruin and put my hands gently on his back. Then he shoved me back and slapped at me again. He knocked me against the side of the cage. But it didn't hurt me and I didn't stay long. I ran back into his arms.

"Three minutes," said Kim Kiefer. "Longest anybody has stayed yet!"

The people surged closer. They packed around the cage.

"Down in front!" I heard them yell from the far sides of the arena. "Down in front!"

"Will he stay five minutes?" I heard wrestling fans asking each other.

I have to stay five minutes, I thought. And if I can just do. . . .

But old Bruin slapped me awfully hard and I hit the bars of the cage and saw stars.

"Four minutes," Kim Kiefer said.

"Three minutes and fifty seconds," said Al, the Street Fair's timekeeper.

"You're a little off," Kim Kiefer said. "My watch is right."

I was clinched with old Bruin again and I let my hands fall gently up and down his back like you'd rub a piece of silk on a washboard. Bruin wasn't as rambunctious with me as he had been. Johnnie Norris looked at us clinched there, and my chin down on old Bruin's head. We stood in the middle of the cage and the long lanky muscles of my beanpole legs hooved higher than they ever had before. It looked like we were each trying to throw the other on the cage floor.

"Five minutes," Kiefer shouted.

"Seconds yet," Al said.

We stood there paw-locked and arm-locked and time was fleeting. Once Johnnie Norris passed around us and he had a worried look on his face. But I watched the referee to see that he didn't prod the bear to make him try to finish me. Spectators were watching through the bars. Women were sitting upon men's shoulders so they could see into the cage. They were watching Johnnie Norris too. Hundreds of eyes were trained on him as he moved around through the cage with a mysterious air and a worried look on his face.

"Nine minutes," Kim Kiefer shouted.

Al didn't say anything.

One minute more, I thought. Just one minute more.

Then Bruin started pushing me. And I braced my feet away out from him for I was tall and I leaned like a prop. Yet, I had my chin on his head.

"Ten minutes," Kiefer said.

"Lacks ten seconds of being ten minutes," Al grunted.

Then Bruin put his red tongue out like a tired dog. I felt his hot breath sizzle past my ear. The sweat was pouring from my face and running in little streams down my body. Holding a bear up as big as Bruin wasn't an easy task.

"Has he hypnotized that bear?" someone shouted.

And just about that time, Bruin pushed me to the floor. But he didn't come down on me. I stayed down to rest a minute. He panted harder and everybody could see his long red tongue and his full set of pretty white teeth. He stood in the middle of the cage like a very tired wrestler.

"Fourteen minutes," Kim Kiefer said.

Then there were shouts that went up from the people.

"He might even wrestle old Bruin yet," the fellow said who was wearing the bow tie. He said the words so fast the bow tie jumped up and down his neck with his Adam's apple like a tree frog.

I came back to my feet and Bruin came to meet me, slapping gently with his paws. I did a little footwork around the cage until his front paws were spread apart and then I rushed in and clinched Bruin.

"Fifteen minutes," Kiefer said.

Seventy-five dollars, I thought. Give me five minutes more.

And when I put my chin back on Bruin's head and braced my feet with my big hands planted on Bruin's back, this time Bruin went down and I went down beside him. Johnnie Norris ran up to look at our shoulders. Al ran up and looked between the bars. And the crowd screamed loud enough to raise the tent.

Bruin's weight on my left arm hurt a little. But my right arm was around his neck. My chin was still on top of his head. And we lay there, stomach to stomach, side by side, in wrestling embrace.

"What's wrong here?" Johnnie Norris said to the Fair's timekeeper. "Al, you go get the boss!"

"But who will keep time with Kiefer?" Al asked.

"I will," Johnnie said, as Al started pushing his way through the crowd.

"Referee can't serve in two capacities at one time," a big man with a handlebar mustache said as he put his face against the cage bars.

Shouts went up again from the people.

"Nineteen minutes," Kiefer said.

"Ten seconds till," Johnnie Norris said.

"Who said old Ichabod Crane couldn't wrestle," said the man with the Adam's apple. "He'll ride that bear yet!"

They didn't know it, but I knew Bruin was ready for a rest on the floor even if we were in a wrestlers' clinch.

When the boss, Solway Meadows, came running into the tent, his face looked as sour as if he'd bitten a green persimmon when he looked inside the cage and saw us lying side by side.

"Twenty minutes," Kiefer shouted.

"What's wrong, Johnnie?" Solway Meadows asked.

"Old Bruin just can't ride 'im," Johnnie said.

"Now you're a-talkin'," somebody shouted. "Old Ichabod Crane will ride that bear yet! He's some wrestler!"

"Old Bruin didn't find Hawk Weaver when he got hold of old Ichabod," said the big sports fan with the handlebar mustache. He tried to stick his face between the cage bars, and he worked his mustache like a rabbit works its whiskers.

"Twenty-four minutes," Kim Kiefer shouted.

"Old Ichabod said he'd stay with old Bruin five minutes and maybe longer," the big sports fan shouted and wiggled his handlebar mustache. "He's a-doin' more than he said he would!"

"Twenty-five minutes," Kiefer shouted.

Then the bear rolled over on his back.

The loudest scream of all went up from the crowd. There were screams, shouts, and whistles.

"Look at the shoulders there, referee," the old sports fan shouted. "Let's have the count. Bruin's down! He's down!"

Bruin didn't offer to get up. His big mouth was open and you could count the white teeth in his mouth and take a look at his pretty red tongue.

"You must have played my bear foul," Johnnie Norris said.

"I did not," I panted. "You'll see Bruin's not hurt. He's tired but happy!"

"First time that bear was ever ridden," Solway Meadows said.

"First time anybody ever stayed with 'im over two minutes," Al said.

But from the screams of the people it was hard to hear another word. When Johnnie Norris got Bruin up from my arm, he found out whether he was hurt or not. Bruin gave him a lick on top the head that sent Johnnie reeling toward the other side of the cage where he staggered a few times, shook his head, and seemed to do a little dance on wobbly legs as he slumped down to the floor.

"What do you know about that?" Al said.

"You see I didn't hurt old Bruin," I said to Solway Meadows. "He's a hard bear to handle!"

"Two hundred and twenty-five dollars!" said the freckled-faced man wearing the bow tie. "Think of it! Ichabod Crane rode old Bruin!"

Solway Meadows let me through the cage door, while Al dragged Johnnie outside where he'd have a more comfortable sleep.

"Same thing old Bruin done to Hawk Weaver," a tall beardy-faced man said as the old sports fan with the big mustache and the young man with the bow tie and as many others as could gather around me lifted me upon their shoulders. They carried me out of the tent and over the Landsburg fairgrounds, shouting "Here's Ichabod Crane! He rode the bear!"

And everybody laughed and screamed and shouted. They waved their hands at me and the women and girls threw handkerchiefs toward me. I was a hero for that night. But they didn't know how I did it. They paid me the money but told me the bear wouldn't wrestle on Saturday night. I didn't tell them or anybody what a friend I'd made of Bruin. I didn't tell them I had once owned a pet bear in the upper Peninsula of Michigan when I was trying to cut cord wood, and that I knew a bear liked to be rubbed between the ears and on the tummy. I suppose it wasn't exactly fair, but Mollie and the kids had to eat. Gentling old Bruin was an easy dollar.

Competition at Slush Creek

WE'LL be going back to Blakesburg in another ambulance
if you don't slow down," I said to Franklin Foster as he
steered the big ambulance around the sharp turn from
Blakesburg's main street to the Little River Road. "And
we won't be going back in your ambulance. It'll be a heap
of junk! And you don't know whether we're goin' to get
the body or not."

"Ah, boy, I know we are," Franklin said, chewing and
smoking his cigar at the same time. "It's competition! If
I don't get the body, Marvin Clayton will. He's probably
been tipped off by this time, and we got to get a head start!
You know how he drives when he tries to beat me!"

He couldn't drive any faster than this, I thought, as I
watched our speedometer swing over to seventy miles an
hour. And when we took the second curve I thought I
could feel the big ambulance leave the road. I held to the
dashboard with a death grip. For Franklin was taking the
curve on the wrong side and I didn't know what we'd meet
head-on when we rounded the curve.

Ah, I breathed a sigh of relief when I saw the road beyond the curve was clear. And over this straightaway I
watched the speedometer swing over to ninety miles.

"Look ahead," Franklin said. "Look at the road. If you

185

sit and watch the speedometer, you'll think I'm driving too fast! You'll even get dizzy!"

"How far do we go?" I said. "Where is the body?"

"Slush Creek," Franklin grunted, as he turned the siren to make the little creepy car ahead of us lay over. When the siren screamed, he gave us nearly all of the road! And as we passed him like a bullet from a rifle he looked to see if we had anybody in the ambulance.

Franklin puffed clouds of smoke from his cigar and he chewed the end like a rabbit nibbles clover. With the siren screaming, we went around the curves on two wheels and the trees and houses beside the road passed in such rapid succession that I could hardly tell a tree from a house or a telephone pole from a tree. All the traffic laid over to the far side, and many drivers who saw us in time drove their cars off the road to let us pass. I don't believe any ambulance ever went over any street in Blakesburg or any road in Blake County as fast as we were going. I was afraid to look at the speedometer now. I did just as Franklin Foster told me to do. I looked at the road ahead, for I didn't want to get any dizzier than I was.

"Boy, when you've been in this business long as I have," Franklin spoke calmly, holding the accelerator on the floor, "you'll learn that you have to move to beat a competitor like I have. That Marvin Clayton is a hustler. He's at the house by the time the last breath leaves a man. He's got the instinct of death same as a bird dog has for birds or a hound dog has for foxes. He's got the instinct, but I get the tips and I got the speed! I've got the fastest ambulance that ever rolled a wheel. Got 'er geared for speed, boy!"

The cigar smoke rolled in tiny clouds past the end of my nose out of the lowered glass on my side, where it disappeared on the wind that tried to follow us. But the wind didn't have the speed. We must have hit the long Raccoon Hill Road at ninety-five miles an hour. For we climbed the first two-thirds like the shot out of a gun. And then hit the steep grade that curved like a rainbow as we neared the top.

"Look back and see if you can see anything of Marvin Clayton's ambulance," Franklin said. "Here's a good place to see if he's coming! You can see two miles beyond the foot of the hill! Hurry! I'll soon be at the top!"

I looked back over the winding stretch of narrow surfaced road. In the far distance I saw a car that looked like an ambulance coming at a terrific rate of speed.

"I think I see 'im," I said. "Looks like an ambulance to me! And it's really moving!"

"I told you he'd be along," Franklin grunted, puffing on his cigar faster than ever. And there was that worried look on his face that is on any man's face when he is about to lose a big deal to his competitor. "He's a hard man to beat, I'm telling you."

"Wonder who tipped him off?" I said as we topped the mountain, and it seemed to me, as we went over the gap and started down the other side, our ambulance leaped forty feet through space and hit on all four wheels at ninety miles an hour.

"Tipped off nothing," Franklin grunted. "I told you he had an instinct about death! He's been at this game so long that he just feels when a person has kicked the bucket. Something tells him. Maybe it's Death himself what warns old Marvin. I've often thought he give 'im sort of a signal like causing little bells to ring in his ears. Ain't you never heard of the death bells? I think old Marvin hears 'em!"

We had reached the foot of Raccoon Mountain and we were now crossing Tibert River Valley. Here we left the hard-surfaced road and hit the graveled turnpike. The gravels flew from our wheels like hailstones fly in a storm. Only the gravels didn't come down like hailstones; they flew from behind our wheels in two big streaks, pelting anything and everything along the road that we passed coming or going. That didn't bother Franklin Foster! We were going after a body. And going after bodies is what he had done since he had been a young man! It was his life's work, and to get the body before his rival got him was the height of his ambition. It was his joy and exultation!

Before we had crossed the valley, Franklin nudged me in the ribs with his elbow. "Look back," he said. "See if you see him coming? It's the last place we can look back!"

"Yonder he comes at the foot of the mountain," I said. "Look at the clouds of dust!"

"I don't have time to look back," Franklin said, bearing down on the accelerator. "No time now to look back. Must gain some on 'im here!"

And that is what we did. Clouds of dust rose like smoke from battle and the clouds of dust were filled with flying rocks from our rear wheels like bullets flying through battle smoke. We were going up Tibert River Turnpike and the ambulance was given free reins and the whip. Old Franklin Foster's cigar was just a stub and the fire was gone, but he was still chewing it. This short man, round as a barrel, and three times as heavy as he should be for a man of his height, gripped the steering wheel firmly and looked at the road ahead. His face was lit up like a lantern in the dark. I had never seen him as full of life as he was now that he was beating his old rival, Marvin Clayton, to get the prize.

"Old Sartin Sandless," Franklin said, "the greatest outlaw Blake County has ever seen, will have Franklin Foster's twenty-seven funeral services when the end comes. And it won't be long! Sheriff Bert Saddler left an hour before we started! He took a posse of seven men! Sartin Sandless escaped the state pen and then broke our county jail. Said he'd never go back to prison. Said they'd take him dead if they got 'im. And when a Sandless says anything, he means it! You can bet on it! He's better known to the world beyond than any man in Blake County! Papers all over America carried his picture and told of his daring escapes! He's a man worth going after! And old Franklin will be there to get him when the end comes!"

"If we keep going like this we're liable to overtake Sheriff Saddler and his men," I said.

"They're already there," Franklin grunted as we slowed down to fifty miles to make the sharp turn up Slush Creek. "Won't be long now for us! We've got old Marvin bested now. I'll bet he's five miles behind. Didn't tell you but I had this old dead-wagon up to a hundred-and-ten! Some going for a gravel road!"

"We're lucky," I said.

"I say we are. Now you've begun to see the light! See why I'm after old Sartin! Look at the publicity that man got! It's an honor to bury 'im!"

Up the Slush Creek jolt-wagon road, over the chugholes, and around the curves Franklin slowed the ambulance down to fifty miles an hour! At the slow speed of fifty miles an hour, it didn't take long to reach the head of Slush Creek, where old Sartin Sandless had grown to be a man and where he killed his first three enemies, Tom, Mart, and Seldon Shelton the same day. And he shot at Eif Shelton, who was running, and put a bullet in his heel. Sartin had never robbed; he just killed his enemies, the Sheltons, instead of a lot of arguing with them.

"Yonder's where we get the body," Franklin said, pointing to a log shack upon the steep hill above the Slush Creek jolt-wagon road. "That's the old Sandless shack!"

"And look," I said, "I see men behind trees aiming guns!"

"Yeah, there's one behind a pile of posts," Franklin said. "Maybe we did get here too early!"

"The battle's just now started," I said. "Let's stop here!"

"And let Marvin Clayton get the body," Franklin said. "I won't do it."

And as we drove toward the steep foothill with the shack clinging like a big brown rock upon its side, Franklin said thoughtfully, "Who knows, we might get more than one body. Sheriff Saddler might get popped! And when the end comes for him, I want 'im. He's important. Sheriff of Blake County, Bert Saddler, Lonesome Hill Cemetery, under the direction of Franklin Foster's Funeral Home. That wouldn't look bad in the paper. And who knows," Franklin Foster spoke hurriedly, "we might get the Sheriff and his deputies and a few others. One never knows how many he'll get when he comes to a thing like this. A pitched battle ready to start any minute!"

"How could we take that many back?" I asked.

"Stack 'em in the ambulance and haul 'em back to Blakesburg," Franklin Foster said. "How do you think I'd get 'em back? Carry 'em? Or, do you think I'd give part of 'em to Marvin Clayton? Not me! He's in business to get me and I'm in business to get him!"

When Franklin pulled the ambulance up to the foot of the hill, stopped, and killed the hot engine, he jumped out in a hurry and started up the narrow footpath and I started up the hill after him.

"If you don't come out, Sartin, we're comin' in after you," Sheriff Bert yelled. "Give up before it's too late!"

"Come on, I dare you," we heard Sartin yell from inside the house.

Then Sheriff Bert gave orders for his deputies to move as he did and to keep behind cover. The men ran from tree to tree, getting closer to the house.

"Won't give any of you low-down polecats the honor of killing old Sartin Sandless," we heard Sartin scream. "I'll do that myself!"

"He's got his wife barricaded in there with 'im," one of the deputies said in an awed voice.

"Go easy, men," Sheriff Saddler said after he'd threatened to take his life. "He's not going to do what he said!"

And then we heard four shots fired inside the shack. And again we heard two shots fired. In less than a minute, while Sheriff Saddler and his deputies looked at each other and signaled from behind trees, old Jarvis Sandless, Sartin's father, opened the door and came out with his hands up.

"You can have Sartin and Rosebud, too, Sheriff," Jarvis said. "He kilt her and then he plugged hisself. It's safe now, men!"

"I'll take 'em now," Franklin said, getting his breath hard after climbing the hill and putting a new cigar in his mouth.

"But who are you?" Jarvis asked. "Is he one of your men, Sheriff?"

"Nope, he's the undertaker," Sheriff Saddler told Jarvis.

"I'm always there when the end comes," Franklin said. "I'm right at your service. Burial with twenty-seven services."

"But who told you to come?" Jarvis asked. "Who sent for you?"

"I got a hot tip about what was going to happen," Franklin stammered, for he'd never got a reception in time of death like this.

"We bury our own dead here, Mr. Foster," Jarvis Sandless said. "We've had enough killings fer one day. You'd better go back. And go in a hurry!"

Jarvis lowered his hands to each hip and laid his right on a big bulge under his clothing. His lips trembled, and the wind moved his uncombed gray hair and his long, tobacco-stained white beard.

"Go, Mr. Foster, before it is too late," Jarvis warned. "We've already got the double coffin made for Sartin and Rosebud."

When he said these words, I knew he meant business. I started running down the crooked path so fast that my knees nearly buckled under me. I looked back once. I saw Franklin Foster trying to run, but he was too big and heavy to run down a mountain. He was holding on to saplings to keep from pitching headfirst down the path.

"Take it easy, Franklin," I said.

"But I see Marvin Clayton a-comin'," he grunted. "Run to our ambulance and pull down the curtains quick as you can. Hurry, before he gets here!"

I ran like a young rabbit to the ambulance, jumped inside, and lowered the curtains. Franklin waddled up with a fresh cigar in his mouth. He was getting his breath hard, chewing one end of the cigar, and jerking small clouds of smoke at the same time. He climbed in the ambulance, stepped on the starter, and gunned his engine. When Marvin saw us coming with the curtains down, he crawled over on his side of the narrow road as far as he could. He stopped his ambulance, rolled the side glass down, and stuck his long, skinny, red face through the opening.

"Well, did you get 'em all, you old hog?" Marvin yelled above the roaring ambulance motors.

"Nope, there's been a big gun battle over there," Franklin answered with a look of triumph on his jolly fat face. "And I left two bodies for you!"

Marvin pulled his head back in at the window. There was a puzzled look on his face as he gunned his ambulance past us. We drove down to the bend in the road. We didn't stop to look back.

Governor Warburton's
Right-hand Man

THE door to Al Winton's office opened suddenly, and Chad Burton poked his head inside.

"Oliver, what's the matter?" Chad asked me. "Aren't you going to Maitland tonight?"

"I wouldn't miss the show for anything," I laughed. "But I've got these deeds to record before I can go."

Chad Burton knew I didn't belong to his Greenough party. He knew I didn't belong to the Dinwiddie party either. I was one of the few Independent voters in our Commonwealth. I just couldn't go for politics and politicians. Chad knew that, too. But the Greenoughs and the Dinwiddies did things that made me laugh. I could laugh louder at some of the things they did than I could at the comic strips in our newspapers. And I was in the right place to see everything that was going on, for I had my desk in Al Winton's office where I worked recording deeds most of my time. The rest of the time I laughed at the Greenoughs and the Dinwiddies. I knew I'd never be connected with either party or be a politician.

I would have asked Chad to come inside, but I knew Al wouldn't like it, and I didn't want to contrary Al, since I had to use his office. Chad Burton didn't hold any county office, but he was a lawyer and an important man in the Greenough party. He had never held an office, but he saw to it that his friends got nominated in the Greenough primary. Then if his party beat the Dinwiddies in the November election, Chad Burton's friends were in office.

But I'd better explain what happened. For years we'd not had a Greenough governor in our Commonwealth, for the Dinwiddies were a powerful lot, to take them state-wide. They could muster up an overwhelming vote and beat the Greenoughs. But one time they didn't beat them. The Dinwiddies had a hot primary election and split their party. And the Greenoughs elected Ezekiel Warburton governor by a comfortable majority. And then something happened we'll never forget. Right after the first reports of victory, Al Winton and Chad Burton each claimed the honor of electing Governor Zeke. Governor Zeke was the first man in the party they had both worked for. Now, each wanted to be his "right-hand man" to give the local jobs to his friends. Each claimed the honor of getting the most votes for our governor, and each wanted to be the closest to him. Each craved the power Governor Zeke could give him.

This fight between Al and Chad split the Greenough party. There was Al's Faction and there was Chad's Faction. If Governor Zeke leaned just a little toward Al's Faction and give someone an appointment, such as road boss or caretaker of the Commonwealth's road machinery, Chad's Faction got sore. And they let Governor Zeke know how they stood about such matters. For there was greater rivalry between these Greenough factions than there was between the Greenoughs and the Dinwiddies. And if you'd see the Greenoughs fight the Dinwiddies at the polls, then you could understand how bitter the fight was between the

Al and Chad Factions. They were toting guns for each other.

"My boys must make a showing tonight," Chad said. "We've got to show Governor Zeke that we appreciate him and all he's done for the Commonwealth!"

"Yes, I know you have," I laughed. "But, Chad, who do you think the Governor will select to sit on his right?"

"Come over here, Oliver," Chad spoke in low tones, motioning with his index finger for me to come to the door since he wouldn't enter Al's office. "I'll be that man," he whispered. Then he winked. "We'll show Al's crowd something," he whispered and winked again.

Just then Al came from the front office and Chad slammed the door tight and went down the courthouse corridor.

"Who was that, Oll?" Al asked. "Was that old Chad Burton?"

"That's who it was," I said.

"Was he telling you he'd be Governor Zeke's right-hand man tonight?" Al asked as he took his cigar from his mouth.

"That's what he said."

Al laughed like I'd never heard him laugh before.

"You know who'll be Governor Zeke's right-hand man?"

"No, but I'd like to know," I said.

"A man from my outfit," he said with a wink as he put his big cigar back between his lips. "And the reason is as simple as adding two and two. My crowd controls the most Greenough votes in this county! And you know who the leader of my crowd is, don't you?"

"Yes, you are," I said.

"That's why I want you to go to Maitland tonight," Al chuckled, showing his smoke-stained teeth. "I want you to see me sitting on Governor Zeke's right!"

"How can you and Chad both sit there?" I laughed loudly.

"Chad won't be there," he said. "Chad is up for a fall tonight. This will be a test of strength. It will end Chad Burton's election-fixing for all time to come. I'll be the man in Blake County after tonight! Chad's gang will all come back to the real Greenough party. They'll come begging and crawling to me."

Maybe they will, I thought.

"See, Governor Zeke will go the way the most votes go," he said, knocking the gray ash from his cigar with his index finger.

"I'll see either you or Chad on the Governor's right tonight," I said as I picked up my briefcase and left Al's office.

"You'll see me, Oliver," Al winked, as he proudly puffed a cloud of smoke from his cigar.

When I stepped out into the courthouse corridor, it was like a crowd running to a Blakesburg fire. I'd never seen anything like it and I'd been in Blake County all my life and had lived many years in Blakesburg. Men, women, and children were running from one office to another. They were talking to this one and that one. Of course, each person was talking to the members of his faction. For this fight, this hatred of one side for the other, was carried back home by the men to their wives and it was inherited by their children. It had caused trouble in the schools, where the children had quarreled and fought.

Everybody was getting ready for the Greenough Regional Rally, to be held at Maitland, eighty miles away. Each was going to see the real representative of his Greenough party, the one that would be selected to sit on Governor Zeke's right. All afternoon people ran helter-skelter through the courthouse corridors, gathering "their own," and getting automobiles ready for the two automobile cavalcades from Blakesburg to Maitland. Members of Al's Faction were trying to beat members of Chad's Faction. It was a wild race.

County Judge Rabbit Bascom, a member of Al's Faction, bumped into me in the corridor.

"Ain't you a-goin', Oliver?" he asked.

"Yes, I'm going," I said.

"We invite you to go in our cavalcade," he said. "Don't you be seen with that Chad Burton."

"I won't be ready by the time you are," I laughed. "Besides, I'll bring up the rear of both cavalcades."

Judge Bascom looked strangely at me. He didn't know what to say. But he was still smiling. It was his smile, everybody said, that got him votes. He always looked like he was laughing. When he had been elected County Judge for his first term, he had two rows of pretty white teeth. But now the judge had lost one or two of his front teeth and he'd never bothered to have them replaced. When he smiled, as he did to everybody, all one had to do was peep through the hole where the teeth were missing to see his tongue. And since he had promised to grade and gravel every road in Blake County, and he had failed at this big undertaking, he reared back in his swivel chair when men come to see him about his getting their roads graded and graveled before winter came and told them it would not be a rough winter, we would have only two snows, for them to go home and take it easy. That was why they'd started calling him Judge Rabbit Bascom. For only the rabbits could prophesy the weather, as any of the Blake County farmers could tell you. The rabbits gnawed on the tender sassafras as high as the snow would be deep and as many circles around the slender sassafras stems as there would be snows.

"Ollie, you ought to go along with us," Judge Rabbit smiled as I looked at his tongue. "You'll see Al Winton made Governor Zeke's right-hand man as sure as there are stars in the sky."

"I'll be there to see him," I said.

"Be good to everybody but Chad's gang," Judge Rabbit said as he turned and ran stiff-legged down the corridor.

In a few minutes I heard the automobile horns honking. I looked from the courthouse window and I saw Al's caval cade start. Al led his cavalcade in a long black limousine. He had his subordinates of leadership in his limousine. In the next car was Judge Rabbit Bascom with the little precinct leaders of Al's Faction. When Al's chauffeur gunned the big limousine, Al Winton and his subordinates waved their hats to the watchers-on, mostly Dinwiddies. Then Judge Rabbit's car leaped as if doing the standing broad jump. Car after car in the long cavalcade jumped after each other like rabbits in the brush in spring. Each car was loaded to capacity. Everybody was screaming and waving his hat. Women were waving handkerchiefs and children were waving their hands. Each driver bore down on his horn as the long Winton cavalcade left Blakesburg.

On the other side of the courthouse square there was a great noise. Chad Burton's cavalcade had not started yet. They were almost ready. Everybody was getting impatient since Al's cavalcade was roaring out of Blakesburg. Chad had for his chauffeur Willie Pratt, the Blake County speed king. Chad had his subordinates around him in his limousine, which was the same make, size, and model as Al's.

Before Al's long cavalcade was out of Blakesburg, Chad's cavalcade was off. Willie gunned Chad's limousine and it jumped like a gray-throated bull frog. It never stopped jumping while other cars jumped behind it and everybody shouted, waved, and screamed. The drivers bore down on their horns, and a few members of Chad's Faction hadn't forgotten to bring along cowbells. It was the more colorful cavalcade of the two, though it was running two or three minutes behind. Each cavalcade was over two miles long.

Willie Pratt shot down the inner track on the four-lane highway like a bullet. The few of us left in the courthouse hugged around a window to see the dangerous race.

"We're liable to lose a lot of good Greenoughs before next election," Tom Hendrix said.

But they were fighting the highway harder than they had ever fought the Dinwiddies on election day. It was something to see, cars running at full speed, two lines of them, each one on the other's tail, running at such tremendous speed and all horns going at full. People were screaming. The whole highway from Blakesburg to Maitland belonged to the factions in the Greenough party. Other cars going from Blakesburg to Maitland dared not get into either Al's or Chad's cavalcades.

It's time for me to be getting in my car, I thought, as the last car in each cavalcade was running neck and neck out of Blakesburg, where there was a speed limit of twelve miles per hour. This was a time when Blakesburg speed laws didn't matter, for it was Blakesburg's populace, the ones who had made these laws, on their way to see which faction would gain the power from the Giver-of-Power. It was a great holiday; it was a great celebration. It was the maddest time in the history of Blake County. The early ancestors of our Greenoughs had had their Sunday horse races, their mule races, and buggy races, but they had never had a race like this.

I jumped into my car and followed the cavalcades. But I held to the Commonwealth's fifty-mile speed limit and I

never gained sight of an automobile until I saw a Greenough car parked by the road. It was Sam Litteral.

"Anybody hurt, Sam?" I asked as I drove up beside him.

"Nothing but a blowout, but I held 'er," he said.

I left him changing a wheel and drove on. Burt Middle-
ton, one of Al's Faction, had left the road. He said Mart
Higgins, one of Chad's Faction, crowded him from the
road. No one was hurt, and I moved on until I came to
Maitland. All along I saw dark streaks of burnt rubber on
the gray concrete where drivers had skidded their wheels.
Often I whiffed the scent of burnt rubber along with the
lingering gasoline fumes.

I had to park a half mile away from Maitland City Hall.
Cars had lined the streets. Parking lots were full. Cars were
double parked. I'd never seen anything like it, and I wondered where all the Greenoughs came from. I wondered
why Governor Zeke had such drawing power. But I stopped
wondering when I walked down the street toward the City
Hall. I heard men on the streets talking about Al's Faction
and Chad's Faction. They speculated whether Governor
Zeke would select Al or Chad from this powerful Blake
County, the one that gave the biggest majority of Greenough voters in the Commonwealth. Our county was the one
everybody was watching in our Congressional district.

When I walked inside the City Hall, I saw a magnificent
spectacle of Greenough power. There were eighteen counties in our Congressional district. And each county had
its group. Each group sat directly behind its county banner. And people were streaming in all directions to fill
the empty seats behind each county banner, while upon
the stage in the largest auditorium in any building in the
Commonwealth sat Governor Zeke, looking out over the
massive auditorium at his children. That's the way he had

addressed them in his political rallies before he had been elected governor. Governor Zeke looked the part of a governor. He was a big man with a smooth, pleasant face, with a smile not half so pleasant as Judge Rabbit's, and with hair as white as clean-washed sheep wool. He was a fine-looking man with big, soft blue eyes and heavy black eyebrows which were in contrast to his white hair. His cheeks were rosy, for the autumn wind had whipped some color there.

Men formed a long line in the middle aisle and went up to greet Governor Zeke before the meeting began. These men were all "next to the Governor," leaders in each county, officeholders and champion vote getters. I didn't fall into either of these and I hadn't any intention of going up to greet the Governor, but I got caught in the line and couldn't free myself. I was caught among members of the Chad Burton Faction. Chad was leading it with a smile from ear to ear, long cigars stuck in his vest pocket, and a diamond stickpin in his necktie.

I soon learned I was not the only one caught in this mad whirl-stream of political-minded human beings. But we couldn't free ourselves. We followed the stream. Governor Zeke greeted each man, shook his hand, said a few words, and the man went on. If he tried to linger to have more words with the Governor, he was shoved on by the eager line. As the line shortened, I got closer to the Governor. I was a little shaky; I didn't want to be with either group and here I was with the Burton Faction.

When I reached the Governor, he looked me over with his soft blue eyes.

"Oliver Timmins, Governor," I introduced myself. "I'm from Blake County."

"From Chad's Faction?" he asked.

"From neither—I just came to look on," I said, and then I was shoved along by the people behind me.

After we were back in our seats and everyone was seated behind his county banner, except those who had to stand in the aisles, the Governor made a rousing talk about the power we had captured in the Commonwealth under his administration, having taken Dinwiddie county after Dinwiddie county. He spoke of the greatness of our Commonwealth in our great Republic.

He was a fine-looking man, and Old Glory and the Commonwealth flag were behind him, while to his left sat the Greenough dignitaries and candidates for the November election. When the Governor began to talk about the November elections when they would all go out to fight the Dinwiddies, a shout went up almost loud enough to raise the top from the Maitland City Hall. Finally the Governor had to ask for silence, and then he went on to blast the Dinwiddie party, and the eager listeners cheered and shouted.

While the cheers were dying down again, I began to hear whispers around me about the vacant chair on the Governor's right. There were seventeen chairs filled with Greenough leaders from each county in our Congressional district. Only the Blake County chair was vacant. I decided he was in a spot I would not want to be in. No matter whether he chose Chad or Al, there was going to be trouble, but when he had finished his speech and sat down, the crowd applauded and whistled and stomped their feet and rang cowbells. The Governor drank two glasses of water, then wiped the perspiration from his face with his handkerchief. I looked over toward the Blake County section and saw a smile come over Chad Burton's face. And Al Winton, who sat in the front row of his Faction, was chewing a cigar.

A few important announcements were made about the

places the Greenough speakers would appear in before the November election, and several people went over to whisper to Governor Zeke. Two men from his left hurried over to him, and whispered excitedly.

"Whatever plans they had," a big man next to me said, "they're changing them. He'd better be mighty careful what he does—half the people won't like him if he names Chad and the other half will be mad if he names Al. I wouldn't want to be in his shoes."

"Sure—they're just stalling for time," another man said.

Finally the Governor arose, and held up his hand for silence.

"We have a vacant chair up here," he said, "and it hasn't been easy to find the right man to fill it."

Both Al's Faction and Chad's Faction stood up silently and faced the Governor.

"Unfortunately we have two Greenough parties in Blake County. Each party has good men, but having only one chair I cannot name a man from each party to fill it."

The silence seemed to me ominous, and I wished I was outside the building. Then the Governor called out in a loud voice:

"Oliver Timmins!"

I sat, almost terrified, then I decided I must have misunderstood him.

"We have selected Oliver Timmins from Blake County to fill this vacant chair tonight," the Governor said.

"Who is he?" someone shouted angrily.

"Where is he?" someone else shouted.

"Does he belong to Al's or Chad's Faction?" another shrieked.

"Neither," Governor Zeke said.

Then the applause went up from all over the auditorium

—and both factions cheered—and the people in the aisle were now motioning toward me and making a path so that I could reach that vacant chair.

I was trembling on my way up there. I had never made a speech in my life and I knew they would expect it. When I got up there, the Governor shook hands with me, quieted the audience, and said, "Oliver Timmins." They applauded and shouted again, and I had stage fright. I couldn't speak and I didn't know what I should say. The Governor quieted them again by raising his hand, and he indicated me with a sweeping gesture.

Finally I stammered, "Well folks, I only regret that everybody is going to forget what a handsome fellow I am beside this fine-looking gentleman on my left." And with my own sweeping gesture toward the Governor, I sat down in the vacant chair, and I must say the audience cheered and whistled again louder than ever. I could tell by the smile on the Governor's face that he liked it, and I had the sinking feeling that I had already become a politician.

The Anglo-Saxons of Auxierville

As the much-welcomed sun rolled high enough to penetrate a pocket of earth walled in by mountains, its bright beams evaporated the clouds that had come to roost for the night in the great recession of earth where Auxierville was nestled like eggs in the bottom of a nest. A stranger watched the screeching wheels of a loaded coal buggy roll down the mine track to the tipple. The danger of the cable's breaking didn't matter to a small boy near by. Tiny rivers of muscles in his young, sun-tanned, and shirtless shoulders moved in perfect rhythm as he raised the foot adz high above his head and let it fall to the cinderish earth. The mad whistles of the screeching engines on the eleven railroad tracks across the narrow-gauged valley, the zooming of the coal trucks heading for a dozen or more coal-loading ramps along the railroad spur, didn't bother the boy either. Down in this deep pocket of world he had a little pocket of his own, twelve by fifteen feet, where there wasn't a miner's shotgun house, railroader's shack, coal truck, railroad track, pigpen, hen house, coal tipple, coal ramp, coal car, truck, or a pile of junked steel wearing away with rust.

"Good morning, young man," the stranger said, breaking the silence as he walked toward the boy. "Ground is pretty hard there, isn't it?"

"Yep, purty hard," the boy grunted. Then he looked straight at the two-hundred-pound, square-shouldered stranger. "Who air ye, mister?" the boy asked, looking straight at him with keen blue eyes.

"Shan Powderjay," the stranger said. "My cousin Mick Powderjay lives here. I'm visitin' 'im."

"Oh, I know Mick Powderjay," the boy said. "I've fished with 'im in the Sandy. I've helped 'im work in his garden thar on the mountain," he pointed to an indentation of trees, high upon the great wall, midway of the mountain, up near the coal tipple. Shan then observed something he hadn't noticed before. There were many of these indentations in the scrub forest that covered these rugged and infertile slopes.

"My name is Billie Auxier," the boy volunteered.

This young boy, wearing only a pair of yellow cotton pants tied about his narrow waistline with a string, leaned on his foot-adz handle and looked Shan Powderjay in the eye. He wasn't quite sure of this man who had disturbed his little world. The blue steady eyes that looked at Shan were bright pools of doubt.

"Digging up a garden here, Billie?" Shan asked. He was curious why the boy was digging among the dry cinders and pulverizing the clods with his tough-skinned dirty little hands.

"Nope," said Billie. "Couldn't raise nothin' here. Dirt won't even sprout nothin'. Too much cinders in it, I reckon. I'm lookin' fer worms. Won't grow them neither," he said, his voice rising in a tone of disgust. "I ain't found a worm yet and I want to go fishin'. Johnnie Newsome ketched a mudcat in the Sandy that weighed twenty-two pounds and six ounces. Ye could git the end of a fence post in its mouth. Biggest fish ever ketched over thar," he pointed toward the river, where two thin rows of bankside trees walled in the muddy and brackish water that split the narrow-gauged valley in the center. "Gee, I wish I could ketch a bigger fish than Johnnie Newsome did."

"You're not goin' to find any worms here," Shan said. "This ground is too dry for worms. Why not dig up there between the garden and the road?" Shan pointed to a narrow strip of land that belonged to the highway. "Looks like we ought to find worms there."

"Just as you say, mister," said the boy, picking up his foot adz and a little tin can.

They waited for the six coal trucks, that had just unloaded at six coal ramps and were almost touching each other, as they moved on toward the truck mines in clouds of road dust that rose up to meet the coal smoke and float over the miners' shotgun houses and the railroaders' shacks. There was definitely a distinction between these abodes. The shotgun house was just like the long barrel of a shotgun, with one, two, three, four rooms, one behind the other. The railroaders' shacks were squat little things, one, two, three, four, and six rooms. They were square like boxes. There were two rooms in front and two rooms in a lean-to behind. The larger shack had four rooms below and two rooms upstairs. Often two families lived in these larger shacks. Any stranger would notice the difference in houses where the coal miners lived and the railroad workers lived.

When the last coal truck zoomed through the dust, the man and boy looked up and down, perhaps forty feet each way, then dove through the dust across the road. Billie carried the foot adz across his shoulder and the tin can in his hand. Shan asked for the foot adz. He started digging between the paled-in little garden four rows wide and the dust-clouded graveled highway. He lifted a big lump of

loam-wash at the foot of the mountain wall that was pocketed with dark, ugly, gaping mouths of coal mines above.

"Oh, a big white grubworm," Billie exclaimed. He was more pleased than if Shan had given him a bar of candy.

When Shan came down with the second lick, he lifted a great clod of loam-wash and Billie went down to his knees.

"Red worms," he cried, until he could be heard by the coal miners who worked at night and were out sitting in the shades of their shotgun houses, squinting their ferrety eyes at God's light. "Red worms! Red worms!"

"Say, mister, ye know where to dig fer worms," Billie shouted.

"Just call me Shan. Don't call me mister."

"Ye know how to dig fer worms, Shan," Billie repeated somewhat reluctantly as he tried to break the clod with his hands to see if there were more worms. He couldn't pull it apart with his tough little hands, so he braced his knee and came down with all his power. It crumbled into pulverized garden silt and six slimy worms lay sprawling and squirming. "Worms! Worms! Worms!"

"Shan, how did ye know thar wuz worms in this here ground?" Billie asked. His eyes were no longer pools of doubt.

"You're talking to an old fisherman now," Shan answered, as the foot adz lifted another clod with a dozen or more worms half hidden. The worms were trying to pull their bodies back into the clod, their clod of native mountain earth, all but the mineral rights, to hide themselves from God's light. "You and I, Billie Auxier, are goin' to try to catch the biggest mudcat in Sandy this afternoon."

While Shan lifted the clods and Billie broke them apart to get the cutworms, grubworms, red worms, and lost locusts that had forgotten to rise every seven years, the coal miners, enjoying the morning shadows, sat silently on their little porches and listened. They looked at the freedom of the big man and the skinny boy, digging worms to go fishing, until their eyes hurt and they shaded them with the backs of their calloused hands. Little girls, by twos, threes, fives, sixes, walked barefooted down the dusty road, with autumn-dusty frosted-sedge-grass-colored hair loose to the wind. Their little dresses were tattered and loose. And their little sweaty legs absorbed layers of dust.

When these little girls saw Billie they stopped. Billie explained to them what he and Shan (the first cousin of Mick Powderjay, that lived in the second house below him) were going to do that afternoon. They were going to catch a bigger mudcat than Johnnie Newsome had. It would weigh, he didn't know exactly how much more, over twenty-two pounds and six ounces. The little girls looked at each other, smiled, and went their way down the dusty road.

"Billie, doesn't your dad ever go fishin' with you?" Shan asked, as he stopped to wipe his radish-red face with a big white bandanna.

"He's too busy a-workin'," Billie answered as he looked admiringly at his can three-fourths full of writhing worms. "He works every day over thar at the roundhouse, see." Billie pointed to the big coal-colored steel structure filled with silent and half-panting engines. "He works every day."

"Work on Sunday too?"

"Every day," Billie repeated. "Takes all the overtime he can git too."

"Are you the only child in your family?"

"Me, the only child?" Billie repeated. He was puzzled as

he looked at Shan. He wondered why his new-found friend would ask him this question. "I'm number twelve. Pa ust to call me Dozen. But that was when I was little. Thar were sixteen in our family. Sixteen besides Pa. Four air dead now."

"Is your mother living?" Shan asked.

"Nope, she's dead," he said. "She died three years ago when Tinnie wuz born."

"Did Tinnie live?"

"Yep, see her a-playin' down thar in the yard?"

Shan looked across the highway, now that the dust had cleared again, at the railroader's shack whose little front porch almost touched the highway and whose back porch was within four feet of a railroad track. It was a little squat, square, unpainted, four-room shack. In this tiny yard, bordered on the south by the highway, on the north by the railroad tracks, on the east by a coal tipple and a coal-loading ramp, and on the west by another railroader's shack, children were like stairsteps at play. The smallest of these was little Tinnie, wearing a dress that had once been white and riding a broom handle for a horse. The natural color of her hair must have been blond.

"Where is your mother buried?" Shan asked, becoming more interested in Billie Auxier's family.

"I can almost show ye," Billie said, pointing to the top of an Appalachian foothill where the white marble and brown sandstone markers emerged from the low brambles. "I remember when Ma died. I remember a-goin' up thar and lookin' down in the grave. They cut it down through sandrock. They made her coffin and it wuz shaped like a guitar box. Little at the head and feet and broad at the shoulders. I saw 'em let it down with ropes and shovel the sandrock down on her. Preached her funeral right out thar at the

Baptist Church, see," Billie said, pointing to the little unpainted house built on the steep mountain bluff with long legs below and short legs above. "Took three preachers four hours to preach Ma's funeral. That wuz one place where all my brothers and sisters were together at one time. Biggest funeral we ever had in these parts."

"Say three more in your family have died since your mother's death?" Shan asked.

"Yep, three brothers air dead," Billie said, watching the writhing worms in the can. "Tom, my oldest brother, wuz 'lectrocuted up thar in that coal mine. Teched a live wire with his head and that wuz the end fer 'im. Preached his funeral at the Baptist Church yonder but buried 'im in a store-bought coffin. The company paid his funeral expenses. Then, brother John, the third in our family fer sister Wilma is betwixt Tom and John, was kilt one night when he was a-switchin' cars over thar and a big engine backed into 'im and cut off his legs. He didn't live till they got 'im to the hospital, he bled so. But they buried 'im, cut-off legs and all but his blood that splattered on the crossties and T-rails. It never did entirely disappear. Ye can see it fer yerself if ye want to go over thar and look. Company buried 'im purty in a store-bought coffin with a lot of ruffles and laces to it. But brother Jim, he was the fourth down from the top in our fambly, he didn't die a-workin'. He died a-fightin'. He was stabbed with a knife at a place where they sold whisky and he wuzn't buried in a coffin as purty as Tom's and John's. He wuzn't buried in a nice suit of clothes either. Pa couldn't git the best fer 'im because he had thirteen besides himself to feed and not another one of us big enough to take a job and help. Buried Tom, John, and Jim over thar on that pint beside Ma and I looked into thar graves too before they let them down in the sandrock."

"Any of your sisters married?" Shan asked.

"None big enough to marry but sister Wilma, and she can't git married because she has to fill Ma's shoes!"

Shan stood thinking as he looked at Billie, standing there contented with a can three-fourths filled with fishing worms. Billie never took his eyes off the worms. They were more precious to him than black gold, yellow gold, or bars of candy.

"Do you own your home down there, Billie?" Shan asked.

"Own the shack but we don't own the land."

"Looks like it would be better to own the land where your house is built."

"See all the shacks on the other side of the Sandy?" Billie pointed to more than a hundred shacks. "See all of this row of shacks from the coal tipple to the Sandy? The Railroad Company owns all the land they're built on. But th' land's been condemned and we won't have to move our shacks any more. Ye ought to 've seen the shack we had before we had to move. We had a nice place. Yer cousin Mick Powderjay had a nice place, too."

"He told me he had a nice shack and a little garden," Shan said.

"Everybody had to move his shack when the Company built nine more tracks. More coal from these mountains. More railroad tracks to haul the coal."

"But I wonder why your father and cousin Mick didn't buy lots to build on."

"See that old shack thar?" Billie said. He pointed to the shack above the narrow garden. It was propped up with planks to keep it from falling. There was a mountain behind it. The coal tipple was in front of it. "Guess what that man was offered fer that little lot and that old shack."

"Hundred dollars," Shan guessed.

"He was offered seven thousand five hundred dollars," Billie said. "He laughed at the man who offered 'im so little. He'll git fifteen thousand. Shotgun houses on little lots that the companies don't own sell fer thirty thousand and up. Poor people can't buy land here. They can't buy a house. A lot down in Auxierville sells fer a hundred thousand dollars. This is the heart of the soft-coal field. Thar's eighty thousand people in Auxier County and thar ain't a thousand acres of bottom land. A bottom at the head of one of these valleys, twenty miles from Auxierville, sells from one to twenty thousand dollars an acre."

"Did your father always live here?" Shan asked.

"Nope, he wuz born on a farm," Billie said. "But all of us wuz born here. Pa often talks about how they ust to farm fer a livin'. But everybody sold the mineral rights on his land from twenty-five cents to a dollar an acre. Pa sold all the land the Govermint give his great-grandpa fer fightin' in the Revolution. He sold the mineral rights fer a quarter an acre. Then he sold the land. Thar are mines all over the land he ust to own and the train backs up Dry Fork twice a day to haul the coal. Not anybody here owns the mineral rights on his land."

"Who does own them?"

"I don't know. The Clean Coal Company owns Dry Fork, the land Pa's great-grandpa got from the Govermint. Great-grandpa owned Dry Fork from head to mouth. Owned all the land in that watershed. The railroad wuz built up thar to git the coal. Now they build more tracks to git more coal and everybody digs coal 'er works fer the railroad. They don't farm any more here. A lot of people work around the oil fields and the gas wells, too. We've got a lot of them here and a lot of people and money and not many places to build shacks, so ye see why we moved the scraps of our old shack onto this level spot of cindered ground the Railroad Company condemned so we could keep a place to live and work fer 'em and not have to move again."

"Let's finish fillin' the can with worms, Billie," Shan said. "Then let's go to the Sandy and get the big fish."

After they had finished, Shan and Billie crossed the dusty highway. They opened the little gate to a little fence that enclosed the tiny cindered yard, where lawn grass wouldn't grow around the Auxier shack.

"Reason yer cousin Mick gits grass to grow on his lawn, he hauled truck loads of mountain dirt and spread over the cinders," Billie said. "Paid twenty dollars a truck load. He ain't got but two young'ns and he's got money to spend fer dirt. He makes the same money Pa makes."

In the Auxier yard, the stairstep children, from Wilma down to Timmie, regarded Shan with suspicion. Wilma didn't come outside the four-room shack. Two young women, about seventeen and eighteen years of age, sat in one porch swing. Two other young women, about fifteen and sixteen, sat in another, while three small boys, all younger than Billie, played in the yard with five small girls. They were all Anglo-Saxons all right. One could tell by the blue eyes and the frosted-sedge-grass-colored hair. These were the marks. That color of hair, blue eyes, ferret-colored eyes, elongated gray eyes, brown and black eyes, and any other color of eyes.

These young Anglo-Saxon girls will marry Anglo-Saxon boys and like their mothers they will reproduce, Shan thought. The young boys, now in dresses and rompers, will throttle the big engines, oil their pistons, build new tracks, and run the electric motors in the mines. They will go back under the mountains and grovel the coal with picks, coal cutters, and load it with shovels and loaders. They will bring the coal from the bowels of the mountains. They will load it in buggies and shoot the black diamonds down to the empty cars from the tipples. They will die natural and unnatural deaths. They will be buried deep in Anglo-Saxon sandrock, under Auxier County skies. . . . Their spirits will leave their temples of clay for one of the eight Baptist Heavens. The last remnants of merry old England under the wide and spacious skies of great America! These old pioneer Anglo-Saxons walled in by the high unpenetrable walls that God made when He created this haven for the last remnants of a fighting, working, dreaming mongrel race.

Shan waited in the yard until Billie came out with a wad of fishing lines and hooks.

"Wilma, don't worry about me," Billie called back to her, "I'll be all right. I'm jist a-goin' over to the river with a great fisherman. He knows how to find worms. He'll know how to ketch the biggest mudcat left in Sandy."

Shan followed Billie around the shack to the back yard fence. There were not more than three feet between the back porch and the first railroad track. Billie led the way with a can of bait and rolls of hooks and lines. Shan followed across the eleven sets of railroad tracks toward the little river of muddy and brackish water, flowing in the center of the narrow-gauged valley, walled in by two thin rows of dwarfish trees.

Evidence Is High Proof

Eif Cluggish rode Thunderbolt, his white horse with flaxen mane and tail, in front of the long wagon train. He sat up straight as an iron poker, on one of the best saddles that money could buy, with polished black bridle reins held loosely in his gloved hands. Thunderbolt, considered the fastest horse in Blake County, lifted his feet proudly as Eif turned in his saddle to look back over his mule teams, plodding along wearily through the November moonlight, along the Little River Road from Blakesburg to the Tibert River Valley.

When Eif looked back at his twenty-three good mule teams, with twenty-three good wagons loaded with supplies, it gave him a feeling of happiness that made him puff his dollar cigar with pride. He sent up small clouds of smoke that faded on the chilly November wind. For Eif Cluggish owned everything he saw in this wagon train but the drivers, sitting on the front seats like soldiers on horse-drawn artillery pieces. And he nearly owned them. They owed as much allegiance to him, to fight for him and "the business," as soldiers owed to their country in a time of war. Eif Cluggish's business was almost war. The Law was after him. And Eif and his men knew it. But that didn't bother them.

Herbie Cluggish, Eif's oldest son, rode behind his father on a blazed-face pony that he called Rock. Eif would never let Herbie ride in front of him. That wasn't Herbie's place. Herbie's place was between Eif and the wagon train of mule teams. When a driver needed help the word was grapevined from driver to driver until the news reached Herbie. Then Herbie rode back to the supply wagon to get an extra part for a broken wagon and was back in a jiffy, so he kept the wagon team rolling along.

"I like to hear the wheels roll over the frozen dirt," Eif said to Herbie as he blew a cloud of fragrant cigar smoke. "And never once has my train been stopped by the Law! It's allus been a breakdown that stopped us. And it didn't stop us long."

Eif Cluggish carried extra parts for his wagons and harness in the last wagon on the train. He carried supplies for the men and mules in this wagon too. And behind this wagon was an extra mule that just followed along for use if one of the work mules got sick or died in the harness. Everything was worked out in "the business" to perfection except one thing. Eif Cluggish hadn't thought of any way to handle Keaton Battlestrife, a deadeye shot, fearless as a lion, and the smartest revenue officer in the mountains.

"We've got the Blake County officers sewed up, Son," Eif told Herbie as they rode along together. "They've got to be re-elected and we've got votes enough to do that. They like their offices and we like them as long as they leave us alone. And revenooers from out-of-way places," he talked on as he puffed clouds of smoke from his cigar, "can't hook up with our local law and get us. So they stay away. But the one officer who won't hook up with anybody is that 'Old Keat' Battlestrife. He'll bring his own men and they're as dangerous as a pack of copperheads. They'll strike before they give warnin'!"

When Eif spoke of Old Keat Battlestrife, his beardy lips quivered and his keen black eyes danced in their deep sockets like wind-blown embers returning to life. Herbie knew that his father was afraid of Keaton Battlestrife, and he wondered what they would do if this revenue officer and his men ever attacked their wagon train.

"Pa, would you know Keaton Battlestrife, if he 's to ride up here?" Herbie asked.

"Shore I would," Eif said as he removed his glove and took another long cigar from his inside coat pocket. "I've seen his picture in the paper so many times I think I'd know his face any place. Remember that time a shiner nearly got 'im and he lay in the hospital at Auckland with a bullet hole through his middle and how the papers carried his picture every day and told about his condition? I made it my business to study his face so I'd know it!"

"What would we do if he did attack us?" Herbie asked Eif.

"That's just what I've been a-thinkin' about," Eif said. "It's hard fer me to think until we get into a pinch. Then the thoughts come fast. You know all the pistol signals?"

"Yes," Herbie said, as he slowed his pony back to second place and let Eif lead the train. Herbie could hear a few of the drivers behind him speak gently to their teams. Many he could hear cussing their mules and slapping their rumps with the leather checklines. And always he could hear the turning of wagon wheels. He heard them night and day. For when he slept he heard them. And when he was awake he heard them. It didn't matter when he slept, day or night, he heard the turning wheels. But on this night the lonesome

November wind whipped through the sycamore trees along Little River bank and often drowned the sound of wheels but never the voices of the drivers. For their rough words would pierce any wind. And that is why he never saw the man on a horse ride past him. But that wasn't anything to think about. It happened often when they were on the road. And often the man would ride up beside his father as this man had, ask him a question, and then move on. But when this man rode along beside Eif, Herbie saw his pistol in his right holster. Then Herbie rode his pony up beside the stranger.

"You don't act like a stranger," Eif said. "I want to know just what your business is."

"I know what *your* business is," said the tall man, sitting in a screaky saddle on a long-legged raring-to-go bay. "I've seen too many of these wagon trains but I'll admit this is the best one and the biggest one I've ever seen!"

"You're Keaton Battlestrife!" Eif's voice was a whisper. "I'd know that face in daylight or moonlight."

"And you're Eif Cluggish," Keaton said. "You have the biggest dairy in the Kentucky mountains and you peddle a very expensive and powerful brand of milk."

"How do you know so much about my business?"

"Your 'business' is to 'make,' " Keaton Battlestrife said, "and my business is to get you. That's why I'm here. I'm taking you back with me, Eif!"

"That's what you think." Eif spoke with more confidence. "But I don't think you are. My customers have to have their milk! Remember, I sell good milk!"

"But the price is a little steep," Keaton Battlestrife said. "Forty dollars a gallon!"

"More than that," Eif boasted.

"And you don't pay any State and Federal taxes," Keaton

Battlestrife said. "That's why you've bought half the land in Tibert River Valley and why you've been able to run the legal liquor stores out of Blakesburg! Now you're goin' with me."

"You can't take me," Eif said. "Look at the men I've got!"

Then he quickly whipped his pistol from his pocket and shot twice into the air. This was the signal for his wagon train to stop. In the sudden silence Eif heard the hoofbeats of a cavalry of horses. They galloped up along the left side of the wagon train.

When Eif saw Keaton Battlestrife's men riding up from the rear, he held his pistol in the air and shot three times. This was the signal to his men that he was leaving the wagon train.

He reined Thunderbolt to his right and Herbie followed on Rock. Thunderbolt knew that there was trouble. He'd heard this signal before. He streaked like a white ghost on the wind down the other side of the teams so Battlestrife's men couldn't get him. Rock streaked out after big Thunderbolt who was laying his hoofs to the ground like the low sounds of thunder. Eif lay down almost flat on his back and gave him full reins, his long coattail flying behind him like a black flag. Herbie leaned forward in his cowboy saddle and gave Rock the reins and whip. He had to have both to keep up with Thunderbolt.

"Pow," Eif shot one time for the wagon train to start moving when they could. But the two riders never heard the wheels start rolling for the sound of hoofs hitting the frozen ground. They cleared the end of the wagon train before Keaton Battlestrife's cavalry could turn to pursue them.

When Thunderbolt turned the curve in the turnpike

Rock was at his heels. Eif and Herbie heard the pistols barking then. But these sounds didn't bother them. Eif reined Thunderbolt down the first road to the left. They were riding for Little River. Eif pulled the pistol from his left holster, as Keaton's cavalry came charging down the road, and fired four times. That signal meant for Herbie to follow him.

When they reached the river, they heard bullets hissing through the treetops above them. Thunderbolt let out a big snort, but he took to the river like an impatient diver. Herbie dreaded the plunge when he saw Thunderbolt and Eif go all the way under, but when they arose Eif was still in his saddle. Water spouted from Thunderbolt's nostrils.

"Swim down the river and not across," Eif yelled to Herbie.

Herbie caught his words just as Rock hit Little River going all the way under, and he went down in the icy water to his neck. But when Rock came to the surface he followed Thunderbolt down the river. And when they were two hundred yards or more down the river and the wind had quieted for a minute they heard Battlestrife's men back where they had hit the river. They heard them open fire into the bushes on the other side. While they were shooting, Eif and Herbie reached Put-Off Ford, and Thunderbolt was walking from the river, up the jolt-wagon road. Water was rolling from his body like it does from a duck's back in the rain. Water was dripping from Eif's soggy clothes. He had his nice clothes wet and his dollar cigars were ruined. Eif pulled his pistol from his holster and shot twice.

"Why do you shoot now?" Herbie asked.

"I want 'em to follow us," Eif said. "We'll lose the whole pack on one of these roads!"

"What will happen to the wagon train?" Herbie asked Eif.

"Don't worry about that, Son," Eif said. "Only time to worry about the wagon train is when we go to Blakesburg with a load of precious milk. Old Battlestrife would have the goods on us then. He doesn't have anything on us now 'cause all we've got on the wagons is cracked corn and sorghum molasses. Come on, Son," Eif said as he gave Thunderbolt the rein, "can you take it?"

"Sure can," Herbie said, his lips trembling with cold.

It was fourteen miles across the hills and hollows to Tibert River Valley. And Eif and Herbie raced against time. Thunderbolt galloped up hill and down with a water-soaked rider wearing black gloves, but without the familiar cigar in his mouth. And Herbie followed on Rock, one of the toughest ponies in the mountains.

Once they stopped on a high ridge to let the horse and pony wind. And while they rested Eif wiped the water from his pistols with dry leaves, fondled them as if they were his children, and then he filled their magazines with cartridges. Then Eif leaped back into his saddle and was off like the wind. Herbie laid his hands on Rock's rump, leaped over his back into the saddle, and was off. They followed the ridge, a divide between the two watershed rivers, and after a mile or so, turned left again. And now their going was easier, for they were riding down, down, down, gently down but with full speed!

In a few minutes Herbie recognized Rockford's barn. He knew they were on Turkey Creek where his father had first established "the business." Since it was walled in by high cliffs, the only way one could get into Turkey Creek was to go down from the Divide or come up from the mouth.

"See, this'll save a lot of time," Eif said. "We can send the boys our signals and move on!"

"D'you reckon Battlestrife and his gang are on our trail?" Herbie asked.

"Not when we come this way," Eif said. "They'd have to track us, and that wouldn't be easy to do! He went back up Little River Road and will go over Barton Hill and come down Tibert River. He'll be here to visit us. Don't you doubt it!"

"But he doesn't know where we live," Herbie said. "And he doesn't know the different creeks and deep hollows where we've got 'the business.' "

"Don't fool yourself," Eif said. "He'll know where we live. He'll know where I've got my stills. And he'll go to each one before daylight! That's why we must hurry on to signal the men!"

"How has he found out, Pa?" Herbie asked.

"Stool pigeons, Son, stool pigeons," Eif said. "Battlestrife thinks he's smart, but let's beat him at his own game!"

When they reached the Right Fork of Turkey Creek, Eif pulled the pistol from his right holster and shot six times. His shots were about two seconds apart so the men could get the signal.

"Nine men working at three stills on Right Fork," Eif said. "Bill Sneed, my tenth man, sits on a cliff and listens for signals. He grapevines them to the men! All will be well here!"

On the Left Fork of Turkey Creek, Eif emptied the pistol from his left holster. He only had two stills, six shiners, and a listener on Left Fork. Then they rode down the sandy road, crossed Tibert Bridge, where they turned right toward Shelf's Fork. They rode up Shelf's Fork a half mile or more before Eif reloaded his pistol. He fired six times very slowly, each shot breaking the silence of this quiet hollow where even the wind couldn't penetrate for the overhanging cliffs. Here was the place Eif got most of his precious milk, for thirty selected shiners and two listeners worked here where he had ten stills.

They rode back to the turnpike, turned right, and rode two miles up Tibert Valley. Then they came to the narrow gorge where Culp Creek followed into the Tibert and they turned right. They didn't ride more than a half mile until Eif emptied his pistol into the still night. This valley, too, was walled in by cliffs against the wind.

"That's got 'em," Eif said. "Last three stills warned! The listener got that message and he's a-grapevinin' it to the men. I think we've won our fight. We'll go home and go to bed!"

As they rode down Culp Creek, Herbie thought of the money his father had made. He owned nearly all of Turkey Creek, all of Shelf's Fork and Culp Creek. He thought about the time, after they'd been in "the business" a little while, that his father sent him to get his hunting coat he'd left hanging on a tree by the Tibert. The coat was so bulky he thought it was filled with birds. When he lifted the coat it felt light and he looked inside where the dead birds should have been and the coat was filled with tens, twenties, fifties, and hundred-dollar bills. He was still thinking about how his father had worked to build "the business" and to make money when they reached the Tibert Turnpike and started for home.

"Look, Pa," Herbie warned his father as their tired animals walked slowly up the road.

"Keaton Battlestrife and his cavalry have arrived," Eif said as he looked at the many horses and riders in the road in front of his house.

"So you thought you'd fox me, Eif," Keaton Battlestrife said as soon as they rode up to the house. "But we got here! And you can wait with us a few hours!"

"Say, what is this?" Eif asked innocently.

"We'll show you by daylight," Keaton said. "Men, you know where you're going. You've got your maps and directions! Now get going and good luck!"

Seven men rode off in the first group. "Turkey Creek," Eif heard one whisper. Ten men rode away in the second group to Shelf's Fork. And four men rode away in the last group. They were going to Culp's Creek. Two men stayed with Keaton, Eif, and Herbie.

"We'll have the evidence on you, Eif, by four o'clock," Keaton Battlestrife said. "You thought we didn't know where you lived and you'd shake us off the trail. But we've found you. And we know where the evidence is!"

"What did you do to the wagon train, Keat?" Eif asked.

"We know better than to fool with that," Keaton said. "We just inspected it. Found quite a few barrels of sorghum and plenty of cracked corn. You fellows really like your sweets for breakfast out here! And you must have a lot of chickens and cows to feed! No," Keaton Battlestrife talked on, "we didn't bother your wagon train. It's on the way here."

"I'm glad to hear that," Eif said.

"You fellows certainly did some fancy riding," Keaton laughed.

"I'll say you did," said one of Keaton's men.

"Fastest horse and pony I ever saw," said Keaton's second man.

"In my business I need fast horses," Eif said.

Keaton and Eif talked on about "the business" calmly and quietly as two old friends, while the moon went slowly down and darkness replaced the floods of moonlight. Finally the seven riders sent to Turkey Creek returned. One man dismounted his horse and gave his report to Keaton. "We found where three stills had been on the Right Fork of Turkey Creek. But we couldn't find any men, still-worm, or any barrels of mash."

"What about the Left Fork?" Keaton asked in a disappointed tone.

"We found where two stills had been," the tall beardy-faced man reported, "but it was the same as on Right Fork. Not one bit of evidence could we find."

"That's funny," Keaton Battlestrife said.

Just as day was breaking, ten tired horses bearing their riders came up the road.

"What report do you have?" Keaton asked.

"The ten stills had been there all right," a short heavy man said as he rocked disgustedly in his saddle. "We found little furnaces where they had been. But we didn't find a still-worm nor a still, nor a barrel of mash. Not one bit of evidence."

"And the air in that still hollow is so thick from moonshine perfumes that it will make you drunk to breathe it," another rider said.

"We didn't even find a furnace on Right Fork of Turkey Creek," the man said who had first made his report.

"And we didn't find one on Left Fork either," said one of the first seven men to ride away.

"That's funny," Keaton said thoughtfully. "I can't understand it!"

"You won't find anything, fellows," Eif spoke with a note of triumph. "You won't find anything on Culp Creek either. You'd as well ride your tired horses back to Blakesburg and give them some hay."

While they waited in their saddles for Keaton Battle-strife's four men to return from Culp Creek, the tired and impatient horses pulled at the reins and pawed the earth. And morning was coming over the high hills into the valley, tinting the leafless trees and the small stubble fields a pale red.

"What can be the matter with my men?" Keaton Battle-strife said. "I'm uneasy about them! Do you suppose that they've gotten lost?"

"They can't get lost," Herbie said. "Can't get into Culp Creek but one way!"

"Shut up, Herbie!" Eif warned as he fingered nervously at the bridle rein.

"You seem to know that valley pretty well," Keaton Battlestrife said.

"Look, Pa! Look!" Herbie shouted, for he was the first to see them coming around the bend.

Nine men were walking in front with their hands up. One was walking a few feet behind with a Winchester in his hands. Two men rode horseback with guns pointed ready for action while one man rode a horse with still-worms and moonshine jugs tied to the saddle and led a horse with a moonshine still roped to the empty saddle.

"Stand still, Eif," Keaton Battlestrife said. "Don't you move. They're not only bringing your men but they are bringing the evidence as well!"

"But you gave the right signal, Pa!" Herbie said. "I know it was the right signal!"

"I don't understand what happened," Eif spoke in defeat as Thunderbolt pawed the earth and champed at the bit.

"Don't forget, Eif," Keaton Battlestrife said, "six shots means to stop making. But seven shots means to keep on making. Just one of your men got away from Culp Creek.

Five of those men are my men! I had an extra man in Culp
Creek!"

"Why in Culp Creek and not Turkey Fork?" Eif asked.

"Because you can't hear a shot fired from that creek after
you reach Tibert Turnpike," Keaton said. "We let you do
your shooting and reach the turnpike, then my man did
his shooting! So, Eif," Keaton spoke victoriously, "we must
be on our way to Blakesburg with you, your men, and the
good evidence."

Battle with the Bees

THAT makes us a hundred stands of bees," Pa said as we stood the sourwood bee gum on a flat rock in the corner of our yard.

"You're not a-countin' the bees we got upstairs," I said. "How many hives do you think we got in that press?"

"I don't know," Pa said, lookin' at the beehives lined around our yard palin's. "All I know is, we don't have a beehive too many."

I'd never seen a man as wild about honeybees as Pa. No wonder all our neighbors called Pa "Drone," Mom "Queen Bee," and my oldest sister "Honey"; they called my second sister "Bee's Wax" and my baby sister "Little Honey." I was called "Little Drone" and my brother was called "Bee Bread." Not one of us had the name of "Working Bee." Maybe it was because that we didn't bother to farm; all we did was hunt wild honey.

"Before I die," Pa said, "I hope to have a thousand beehives around this house."

"It's dangerous now, Pa," I said. "What will it be with a thousand beehives?"

"Afraid of a bee," Pa said. "I'd be ashamed. Bees love me. They won't even sting me."

"But they sting me," I said. "Mom can't pick a flower

that grows in this yard without gettin' a bee sting. We can't play in this yard without our gettin' five or six stings apiece. The bees have the yard and we have to go to the woods to play. They not only have the yard but they have part of the upstairs."

Pa lit his cigar and watched the bees we'd just brought from the woods start workin' from the sourwood beehive. It was just a cut from the sourwood tree we'd sawed down and Pa nailed planks over the end. He'd found the tree on Toab Gilbert's farm and we'd slipped in with our ax, crosscut saw, and log chain. We wrapped the chain around the trunk so when we sawed the tree Toab wouldn't hear us for the log chain silenced the sound of the crosscut saw rippin' through the wood. These were th' tools we used when we slipped on other people's farms to cut the bee trees we'd found. Pa didn't want anybody to have bees but himself.

No wonder Pa was called "Drone," for he was like a drone bee, he wouldn't work at anything but huntin' bees, hivin' bees, robbin' bees. But I couldn't understand why I was called "Little Drone" at school and every place I went when I had to cut wood, feed the hogs and chickens, and cut the wood and keep the fences mended.

"All I have to do is touch a beehive with my hand," Pa bragged and puffed on his cigar, "and I have luck with the bees. Seems like my bees know me. All bees in these parts know me and love me and work for me. That's why I don't have to work. That's why I can make a livin' sellin' honey, beeswax, and beebread."

Pa put his big thumbs under his suspenders and pushed them out and let them fly back while he stood watchin' the bees work and while I carried the log chain, crosscut saw, and ax to the shed. Pa was proud of the row of beehives all the way around the palin's that fenced our house on all sides. He was proud of the bees bendin' the tops of Mom's flowers all over the yard and the lines of workin' bees flyin' to and from the beehives all over the yard. Honest, the sun could hardly shine on our house, for the air was always darkened with a cloud of bees.

"You'd better do something with that press upstairs, Mick," I heard Mom say just as I stepped inside the kitchen door. "I sent Lavinia upstairs to get some clothes and she got two bee stings. She found bees in her clothes. I think there's a leak where the bees are comin' through."

"I don't think so, Queen Bee," Pa said, ticklin' Mom under the chin with his long index finger. "I saw my bees workin' in and out at the auger hole bored into the press from the outside. I'll have Shan go upstairs and look the press over."

"It's hard to live here," Mom said. "Children can't get out'n the house. I live in misery from day to day. I fear somethin's goin' to happen."

"What will happen?" Pa asked. "What can happen with a few hives of friendly bees around the house?"

"Plenty can happen," Mom said. "Plenty has already happened. I can't gather a bouquet from my flowers and put it on the table unless I gather it at night after the bees have quit work. Young'ins can't put on their clothes unless they turn the wrong side out and the right side in lookin' for bees. Then they get stung."

Pa puffed on his cigar stub and started to say something, and Mom had just put a pan of cornmeal dough in the oven to bake when it happened. I was the first one to see Gilbert's hogs come into our yard.

"All of Toab Gilbert's hogs are out," I said to Pa.

"They've come through the yard gate."

"Get 'em out, Shan, you and Finn," Pa said. "Get 'em out in a hurry."

"Come on, Bee Bread," I said to brother Finn.

We ran out into the yard and tried to shoo the hogs back through the gate but three brood sows and their litter of pigs took right along the yard palin's where we had the beehives. And I don't know what made the sows so nosy unless they were hungry, but they run right along rootin' over the beehives, and clouds of bees rolled from the hives and covered the sows and their pigs and the few shoats that were with them. I never heard such squalin' in all my life. Sows, pigs, and shoats were takin' off down among the rest of the beehives, upendin' 'em as they went. Toab's big male hog just stood and chomped his long mouth while the slobbers flew. He was a-tryin' to fight the bees, but there were too many of 'em.

A mad cloud of bees had me covered and I yelled tor Pa. I looked tor Finn and he was gone. A pig tried to break out of the yard and he couldn't find the gate, so he was stuck between the palin's and the bees were lettin' him have it. I tried to get to 'im but I couldn't. I met swarms of bees on my way. They hit me like hailstones in a storm. Then I turned back toward the house and I saw Pa comin' ringin' cowbells that he used to settle the bees. But the bees didn't pay any attention to the bells. They didn't pay any attention to Pa, their master, but they covered him like drops of rain in an April shower and popped their stingers into him as they were doin' me. Mom knocked the bees off'n me as I reached the kitchen door before she let me in the house.

"Bees are riled upstairs," Mom said. "They're comin' through the press somewhere. I've had to shut the door up-

stairs to keep 'em from comin' down. The house is full of
mad bees. Lavinia and Lucretia are swattin' 'em with the
fly-swats."

Just as I entered the house, Pa rushed to the kitchen door
with a cowbell in each hand. He was covered with bees, and
Mom beat 'em off with a broom the best she could. All th'
time she was beatin' 'im with the broom, Pa was yellin' to
Mom to let 'im in the kitchen.

"Not until I get these bees off'n you," Mom told 'im as
she beat 'im harder with the broom. "The house is already
filled with bees. You've got a whole hive on you, Drone."

"It's tough out there," Pa said. "My pets 're riled. Toab
Gilbert's hogs 've caused it all!"

I ran to the front room to look out at the window while
Mom let Pa inside the kitchen. She slammed the door
against a swarm of mad bees chasin' Pa and buzzin' like
hissin' vipers. When I looked out the winder I saw seven
pigs stuck between the palin's, covered with bees. Toab
Gilbert's big male hog was still standin' in the yard covered
with bees, chompin' with white foam flyin' from his mouth.
He wouldn't give an inch, and the bees were pourin' their
stingers to 'im. Sometimes I heard his grunts above the roar
of the bees. The brood sows were still runnin' wild among
the bees but not as fast as they'd run before. They couldn't
see as big a thing as a gate they were so excited, but I saw
two shoats make it through the gate with their tails curled
over their backs. They took off up the road toward Gilbert's, leavin' little clouds of dust behind 'em.

"Gilbert's hogs 'll remember the next time they get into
our yard," Pa said.

"And we'll remember Gilbert's hogs a long time," Mom
said.

"Toab's hogs 've ruined me," Pa said.

"I believe your bees 've ruined his hogs," I said just as I saw Toab Gilbert's big male hog fall over dead like he'd been shot between the eyes with a rifle. I didn't see the pigs that were stuck between the palin's movin' either.

"I don't care if my bees kill all his hogs," Pa said. "Toab ought to keep his plunderin' hogs at home. I've told 'im before that we had a stock law in Kentucky."

"You don't keep your bees at home," Mom said. "Toab told you he'd keep his hogs up when you kept your bees at home."

Mom was mad, for she'd been fightin' bees with a fly-swat until her arm was so tired she could hardly raise the swat to slap another bee; yet they buzzed all over the house. Mom put Little Honey in bed and put heavy quilts over 'er, since that was the only place she could hide 'er from the bees.

"Where 're you goin', Pa?" I asked, as I saw him put on his overcoat, hat, gloves and tie a scarf around his face.

"I'm a-goin' out to try to settle my bees," Pa said.

"You'll get stung to death," Mom said.

"What's a bee sting?" Pa said bravely as he darted out, slammin' the door behind 'im.

I watched Pa from the window. He threw sand up amongst the bees. He screamed at them. But the bees wouldn't settle. And I saw one of Toab's brood sows fall over at Pa's feet and kick a few times. Then Pa started back to the house, covered with bees. Mom met 'im at the kitchen door and broomed 'im again before she'd let 'im in the house.

"Give me my double-barrel shotgun," Pa said. "It's my last chance."

I gave Pa his double-barrel and two boxes of shells and he went out again to settle the bees. I never heard such shootin' in my life. First he fired one barrel up among 'em, and then he fired two barrels until he shot away all the shells. But his shootin' only made the bees madder than ever. They blackened our windows tryin' to get inside the house. Pa finally got inside the house and Mom had to swat the bees that had crawled up under his overcoat.

"What will we do, Drone?" Mom asked.

"Never in my life have I ever seen bees get this mad," Pa said. "Must 'a been the smell of Toab's hogs that riled 'em this way."

"Won't they settle sometime?" I asked.

"Not until night," Pa said.

"But they'll get us before then," Mom said. "They 're a-gettin' inside this house faster 'n I can swat 'em."

Pa took the swat and I took a pillow from the bed and we fought bees.

"Can't something happen to settle these bees?" I asked Pa. "We can't go on fightin' 'em all day."

I'd never in my life seen Pa as scared as he was. His lips quivered. Pa couldn't talk.

"Mom, I've swatted bees until my arm's so tired I can't lift the fly-swat," Lavinia said. "The bees are about to sting me to death!"

"I can't swat any longer either, Mom," Lucretia screamed. "What'll I do?"

"Make for the bed," Mom said. "Get under the quilts!"

"Mom," I heard Little Honey call from under the cover.

"You lay still there, Subrinia," Mom said. "Don't move the quilts. If you do, the bees will get you!"

Lavinia and Lucretia ran to the bed and dove under the quilts, covering themselves from head to foot.

"Where's Finn?" I asked Pa.

"I don't know," Pa said.

"Here I am," Finn answered from the clothes press. "But don't anybody come in here! I'm goin' to haf to get out! The bees are findin' me. Crawled up my pant legs and stung me five times!"

"Oh, mercy me," Mom shouted.

"Look out the winder, Pa," I said. "Toab Gilbert's comin' after his hogs!"

"He'll haf to haul most of 'em back," Pa shouted as he hurried toward the window with a pillow in his hand, sweat streamin' from his beardy face.

We watched Toab Gilbert walkin' in a hurry toward our house. Suddenly he stopped and swatted at somethin' around his face and then his leg. Then we watched 'im take off up the road with his hat in his hand and we heard his screams above the roar of the cloud of bees.

"Serves 'im right," Pa said, laughin' as I'd never heard him laugh before. But his laughin' stopped suddenly when he slapped at a bee under his pant leg.

"Did one sting you?" I asked Pa.

"What's one bee sting," Pa said. "I'll bet I've got over a hundred!"

"Oh, mercy me," Mom said, standin' with her tired arms limp at her sides with a fly-swat in each hand. "I can't do any more!"

"Mommie," I heard Little Honey callin' from under the cover.

"You be quiet there, Subrinia," Mom said. "Don't you move that cover!"

"Look, Pa, at old Rags and Scout," I said as I watched them come into the yard.

"Poor dogs," Pa whispered as he watched the bees cover 'em.

We saw our hounds take off up the road yellin' every

jump, their mouths open, their tails tucked between their legs, and their hind feet touchin' their forefeet as they leaped through the wind.

"Oh, Lord," Pa said, slappin' at a bee that was tangled in his whiskers.

And then Pa slapped at another one tangled in the whiskers on his other cheek.

"When will this thing ever end?" Mom asked, knockin' a knot of bees loose from her leg where they were tryin' to settle.

"Not until nighttime," Pa said. "If it would rain and wet their wings and cool them off it would be God's blessin'."

"Not a rain cloud in the sky," I said.

"I feel like gettin' down on my knees and prayin'," Pa said.

"Don't be a hypocrite," Mom said. "You've never prayed before and now don't ask th' Lord to save you since you've got us into this mess."

"Oh, Mommie," Subrinia called again from under the cover.

"You be real quiet, Subrinia," Mom said. "Don't you make a move."

"I've thought of everything I know to do," Pa said as I saw Finn make a break from the clothes press and run and dive headlong into the bed where Lavinia and Lucretia were and jerk the quilts over his head.

"I can't stand it any longer, Drone," Mom said as she made for the bed where Subrinia was under the cover.

"Mommie, tell Daddy to get the Flit gun," Subrinia said. "I've been tryin' to tell 'im for a long time but you wouldn't let me talk!"

"The Flit gun, Drone," Mom said.

"Oh, what a relief," Pa said as he ran to the kitchen to get it.

Little Honey, only four years old, thought of something we'd never thought about.

Inside our house it was like a beehive. Bees were flyin' over the rooms buzzin' louder than redbirds sing in April. They flew around until they got tired. Then they'd lit any where, on the beds, walls, furniture, and on us. And as soon as one lit on one of us and smelled our sweat, he popped a long stinger into us.

Pa came into the room as I was tryin' to lift my pillow up to bring it down on a knot of bees that were tryin' to get under the bed quilts at Mom's feet. Pa had the Flit gun in front of 'im, pumpin' it with all the strength he had left. It was sprayin' a sweet-smellin' cloud of fog into the room. And as this fog hit the bees, they made funny little noises and hit the floor.

"Glory, glory," Pa said, sprayin' until the room was filled with fog. "It works!"

"But I don't like the smell," Finn said.

"But it's better 'n bee stings, Bee Bread," I said.

"The room's gettin' cleared of bees," Pa said. "Somebody will haf to sweep 'em from the floor before they come to life again!"

"I'll sweep 'em up, Pa," I said, grabbin' a broom and sweepin' a roll of senseless bees across the floor.

"When had we better get up?" Mom asked.

"When I use this gun on all the rooms," Pa said. "Then we can't get outside until dark."

"Young'ins, lay under your quilts until dark," Mom moaned.

"We'll be after dark gettin' our work done up," I said,

sweepin' the roll of bees into a bushel basket so I could carry them outside.

While Pa used the Flit gun, I swept until we'd gone over every room in the house. Then Pa stood at the window, pressin' his face close to a pane, lookin' at the darkness that was gatherin' over the land.

"Glory, glory," Pa whispered, "night has come!"

Hot-collared Mule

KEEP that mule a-goin'," Pa hollered as I passed by where
he was sitting on a log under the shade fanning himself with
sourwood leaves. "Run 'im until he's hot as blue blazes!"

I couldn't answer Pa. My tongue was out of my mouth
and I was getting my breath hard. If you have never owned
a cold-collared mule then you wouldn't understand what a
job it is to run one long enough to get him hot so he'll work
in the harness. What you do when you run him is put a
collar on him and run along behind and slap him across the
back with the lines when he begins to slow down.

The bad thing for Pa and me was, we had a mule we
couldn't ride or work until we got his collar hot. Pa had
tried to ride him. Pa went over his head when he bucked
and came down belly-flat on the hard road in front of the
mule, knocking all the wind out of him. When I had him
galloping, he stopped suddenly with me. I bounced up in
the air like a rubber ball. It was done so quickly I couldn't
come down to the ground on my feet. I came down a-sittin'
in the middle of the road. And I sat there seeing stars.
Of all the trading Pa had done, he'd never got a mule like
Rock.

"He's a-gettin' warmed up," I grunted to Pa as I passed
him on the second lap.

243

"Fetch 'im around agin and I'll take 'im," Pa said. "Just be keerful and don't do any hollerin'."

If I had wanted to holler at Rock I couldn't, for I was so short of breath. I was running Rock up a logging-road to the turn of the hill; there we turned right up a cowpath that wound up the hill and connected with another logging-road which ran parallel to the one below and then turned perpendicular down the hill and connected with the first road. The circle of narrow road looked cool, for it was bordered by culled trees whose clouds of green leaves sagged in wilted pods. These leaves were so thick they not only obscured the sun but they kept out the little August breeze that idly swayed the wilted pods of leaves. It was a close smothery warmth down under the trees that heated up a man faster than it did a cold-collared mule.

"All right, Pa," I grunted as I came in on my last lap. "It's your time now."

"Hit'll be the last time one of us has to run this mule," Pa said as he took the lines.

I dropped down on the log where Pa was sitting and picked up the sourwood fan. Sweat ran from my face like little streams pour from the face of a hill after an April shower. I'd run Rock three laps around the circle. Now Pa would run him two. Pa couldn't run as well as I could, for he was older and his legs were stiffer and his breath came harder. While I sat fanning, I watched him go out of sight, running stiff-legged like a cold buck rabbit in the winter-time. The twist of burley leaf was jumping up and down in his hip pocket as he made the turn to climb the hill.

"Hit's a hard way to git a mule to work," Pa grunted as he passed me going into his second lap.

I was fanning fast as I could fan. I had cooled down some,

but my clothes were as wet as if I had jumped into the river.

When Pa came around on his second lap, I didn't think he'd make it. But he did. His face was red as a sliced beet, and his clothes were as wet as mine were. But a sweaty foam had gathered under Rock's flanks and his shoulders were wet around his collar.

"He's in shape to work now," Pa said as he dropped to the ground. "I'll wind a minute before we hitch 'im to the drag."

But Pa didn't wind very long. He sat there long enough to catch his second wind. We couldn't wait until Rock's shoulders cooled. We threw the gears over his back, hitched a trace chain to the singletree, and let him draw the log chain to the dead oak that Pa had chopped down for us to haul to the woodyard.

"When Cyrus sees my mule pull a log like this," Pa said as he wrapped the log chain around the log, "he'll swap that good mule o' his 'n and give me ten 'r fifteen dollars to boot! See, this log 's heavier than Rock. He'll be a-pullin' more than his weight on the ground," he went on as he fastened the log chain around the drag. "I'm a-goin' to ast 'im twenty-five dollars to boot. Then, maybe, I'll drop to fifteen dollars. Remember, I'm through runnin' a cold-collared mule. My ticker ain't good enough for it and my legs won't stand."

"It's some job for a young man," I said.

"All right, Rock," Pa said, slapping him with a line. "Git down and pull!"

Rock squatted, braced his feet, and pulled, shaking the big log from where it had indented the hard earth. Then, without Pa's telling him, Rock pulled again, and the big log started sliding along while sparks flew from his steel shoes.

"If he wuzn't cold-collared I wouldn't trade 'im fer any animal I ever laid eyes on," Pa said, holding the lines up from the briers.

I walked behind Pa as he drove Rock toward our wood-yard.

Maybe our timing was just right. We pulled into our woodyard under the sour-apple tree just as Cyrus Broad-foot rode his harnessed mule up and stopped.

"That's some log, Mick," he said.

"Well, it's purty good-sized," Pa said. "But Rock's pulled a lot bigger logs than this 'n. I'll pull 'im agin any mule of his pounds. Do you want to pull your mule agin 'im?"

"Not necessarily, Mick," Cyrus said, dismounting his mule.

"I thought if you wanted to hitch yer mule to my mule's singletree, we'd let 'em pull agin each other," Pa said as he unhitched the log chain from the drag. "If yer mule pulls mine backwards," Pa went on, "I'll give you my mule. If my mule pulls your mule backwards, then ye give me yer mule! That's fair enough!"

That was the way Pa always started a trade. He would always put the other fellow on the fence. He'd set a price, give or take. And he'd trade at sight unseen. That's how we'd got old Rock. He'd traded with Herb Coloney. Herb told Pa he had a mule that could pull his weight on the ground. That was enough. Pa traded him a two-year-old Jersey bull and got ten dollars to boot right there. Now he was going after Cyrus.

"I don't keer much about tradin' that way, Mick," Cyrus said, pulling a big knife from his pocket with one hand as he picked up a stick with the other.

"Yer mule's bigger 'n mine," Pa said.

"I know that," Cyrus said, whittling a big shaving. "But he ain't as old."

"How old is yer mule?" Pa asked.

"Rye's a-comin' five in the spring," Cyrus said, his words muffled as the sound of his voice was strained through his big mustache.

"Rock ain't but four," Pa bragged. "He ain't shed his colt's teeth yet."

Then Pa picked up a stick, pulled his knife from his pocket, and began to whittle. While Pa whittled big shavings from a poplar stick, Cyrus opened Rock's mouth and looked at his teeth.

"He's still got his colt's teeth all right," Cyrus said. "Don't ye want to look in my Rye's mouth, Mick?"

"I'll take your word fer his age, Cyrus," Pa said, whittling away. "Ye've allus been a good neighbor and a truthful man!"

Pa's words didn't please Cyrus. Maybe Cyrus was thinking about the last time he had traded with Pa. Pa had said these same words and patted Cyrus on the back when he sold three steers for a hundred and forty-three dollars. Cyrus kept them all that winter, put them on grass next spring and summer, and sold them late in the fall for a hundred forty-four dollars. He knew Pa was a good trader, the best among the hills.

"Jist how much boot are you a-goin' to ast me, Mick?" Cyrus asked.

"Tell you what I'll do, Cyrus," Pa said, laying his stick and knife down so he could pull his galluses out and let them fly back like he always did when he was trading. "Since it's you, I'll take twenty-five dollars to boot and trade."

"That's a lot of boot, Mick," he said.

"Won't take a cent less," Pa said.

"I won't give you a penny," Cyrus said, whittling a long shaving.

"I'll tell you what us do," Pa said. "Let's split the difference!"

"Okay," Cyrus said.

Cyrus pulled a ten-dollar bill, two ones, and a fifty-cent piece from a Bull Durham tobacco sack he was carrying in the little watch pocket on the bib of his overalls.

"Jist a minute," Pa said, before he took the money. "That means we're trading harness too!"

"Right," Cyrus said.

Then Pa took the money. I knew Pa had got a barg'in on the harness. Rock's harness was wrapped and tied in many places with groundhog-hide strings.

"You've got a pullin' mule," Pa said as Cyrus picked up the rope lines to drive Rock away. "He's the only mule in these parts that can pull his weight on the ground."

Then Pa looked at me and winked. I knew what Pa meant, for Cyrus didn't know how we had to run old Rock to get up steam. In a cold collar he wouldn't pull the hat off a man's head.

"I'm satisfied, Mick," were Cyrus's last words as he drove Rock up the hollow.

I wasn't sorry to see Rock go.

"Now we've got a mule," Pa said. "We'll hitch 'im to the express wagon and take that load of melons to town."

With all the confidence of a strutting turkey gobbler, Pa drove Rye to our express wagon. He was proud of his trade, and I was too. I never wanted to see another mule that I had to run to get steamed up like I had to run Rock. I never wanted to see another cold-collared mule.

Our express wagon was loaded with watermelons and

parked under the shade of a white oak in our backyard. When Mom saw Pa backing the new mule between the shafts she came out at the door.

"I told ye, Sall, I'd have a new mule to take these melons to Greenup," Pa bragged. "I really set Cyrus on fire in that trade! I really give 'im a good burnin'. One he'll never forget!"

"I guess it's all right to do that, Mick," Mom said. "Men do such things. But one of these days you're goin' to get a good swindlin'."

"Not me," Pa said, laying the lines down and pulling at his galluses. "I've made you a good livin', ain't I?"

"Yes," Mom agreed by nodding her head.

"And I've done hit mostly by tradin', ain't I?" Pa went on bragging as I hitched the trace chains to the singletree.

"Yes, by cheating people," Mom said. "I feel bad about Cyrus Broadfoot's six little children. Never have a pair of shoes on their feet all winter!"

Then Mom turned around and went back into the house.

"Funny how softhearted wimmen are," Pa said as he fastened a chain through the loop while I fastened the other. "If wimmen had to make a livin' and men stay in the house, wouldn't that be funny? Could ye imagine yer Mom out a-mule-swappin'?"

Pa laughed at his own joke as he climbed upon the express seat and I climbed up beside him. With a light tap from the line, Rye moved the loaded express wagon across the yard and down the road toward Greenup. Pa sat straight as a young poplar with his whip across his shoulder and a chew of burley leaf under his sun-tanned beardy jaw.

As we drove down the sandy jolt-wagon road, I never heard such bragging as Pa did. He talked about the trades he had made in his lifetime, how he had cheated people from the time he began mule trading. That was when he was sixteen. He would tell about cheating people, then he would laugh. And when he spoke of how he had traded a cold-collared mule to Cyrus, he would bend over, slap his knees with his hands, and laugh until people walking along the road would stop and look at us.

"When old Cyrus starts runnin' Rock . . ." Pa would never be able to finish what he started out to say for laughing. He laughed until I had to take the lines and drive so he would have both hands free to slap his knees.

"Old Cyrus will get hot under the collar," Pa went on. "I can just see old Cyrus a-takin' off behind old Rock. . . ."

The tears rolled from Pa's eyes down his sunburnt face.

"Wonder if he'll know what's the matter with . . ." and Pa got down on the load of melons and rolled around like he was crazy.

At first it was a little funny, but after I thought about what Mom had told him I couldn't laugh any more. And I was ashamed of him the way he rolled over the watermelons, laughing. The people we passed would stop and look at him like he was out of his head. I'd never seen a man in my life enjoy a barg'in like Pa was enjoying his trade with Cyrus.

And Pa had made a barg'in, for Rye pulled the load easily and smoothly along the jolt-wagon road until we reached the turnpike. Now we were on the road to Greenup, where we would soon sell our melons. When we reached the turnpike where there were more people traveling, Pa got back on the seat beside of me, put a cigar between his beardy lips, and took the lines. He would never chew burley when we got near town. He would always light up a cigar, though Pa enjoyed a chew more than he did a smoke. He thought he looked more important with a cigar in his mouth.

Rye had pulled steadily along for three miles or more, and now I noticed there was foaming sweat dripping from his flanks and oozing from beneath his collar and dark shades of sweat on his sleek, currycombed and brushed brown hair over his ribs. Pa didn't notice the sweat on Rye. He just sat upon the high springboard seat with a whip over his shoulder that he carried for an ornament, a cigar in his mouth to make him look important, and looked down at everybody we passed.

"Pa, you'd better let Rye take it a little easy," I said. "He's gettin' pretty warm!"

"A mule can stand an awful lot of heat," Pa said, driving on.

But when we reached the Lottie Bates Hill, Rye braced his feet and wouldn't move a step.

"Wonder what's wrong with Rye?" Pa asked me.

"I don't know," I said.

"He needs a little ticklin' with the whip," Pa laughed, pulling it from over his shoulder and tapping Rye on the back.

Then Rye started going backwards, shoving the express wagon zigzagging from one side of the road to the other.

"Slap on the brakes," Pa shouted to me.

I put on the brakes as quickly as I could and stopped the wagon. People passing us along the road started laughing. And Pa was really embarrassed. His sun-tanned face began to change color into a pawpaw-leaf crimson.

"He's a mule that goes backwards," a man said, laughing.

"Somethin's wrong with the harness," Pa said. "Here, take these lines. I'm gettin' down to see what's wrong."

I held the lines while he started to examine the backband and the trace chains. When Pa put his hand on the backband, Rye kicked up with both hind feet and squealed.

"What's the matter with that mule?" Pa said, jumpin' back in a hurry while the strangers walking home with loads on their backs stood at a safe distance and laughed. "He acts like he's crazy. I'm sure it's his harness hurtin' 'im or a blue-tailed fly on his belly."

"See if the bridle bit is cutting his tongue," I said.

When Pa started to open his mouth to look, Rye lunged forward with both front feet in the air and tried to hit Pa, but he side-stepped just in time.

"That mule's dangerous," Pa wailed. "Git this near town when we can see the smoke from the chimneys, then he acts up like this!"

The words weren't out of Pa's mouth when Rye lunged forward and I pulled back on the lines. Then he started going backwards and the express wagon started rolling down a little hill. The endboard came out and the melons rolled like apples from the wagon bed, down the hill into Town Branch.

"There goes our melons," Pa moaned.

Twenty people, who had stopped to enjoy our trouble, all made a run for the melons that were broken and ruined. While all of them but one old beardy-faced man ran for the melons, Rye jumped forward again, veered to one side, and broke the shafts from the express.

"Hold 'im," Pa shouted.

"I'm doing my best," I said, rearing back on the lines until I brought the mule under control.

And now it worried me not so much that the people were eating our melons, but that I was providing entertainment for them while they ate. They could hardly eat our melons for laughing at us. But Pa puffed harder on his cigar and there was a worried look on his face.

"Say, stranger," the old man with the beardy face said as he slowly approached Pa, "I don't want to butt into yer affairs. But I'm an old mule skinner. I ust to drive a mule team when they had the furnaces back in this county. I drove mules fer forty-three years and hauled cordwood," he went on talking, "and I can tell ye what's the matter with that mule. I've seen four 'r five like 'im in my life-time!"

"Hit must be his harness that's a hurtin' 'im, Dad," Pa apologized for Rye.

"Nope, that ain't it, stranger," the man said. "He's a hot-collared mule!"

"Never heard of a hot-collared mule," Pa said, throwing up both hands. "I've heard of a cold-collared mule!"

"Well, that's what he is, stranger," the old man said. "Somebody's give ye a good burnin'. He's sold ye a hot-collared mule. And this one is a dangerous animal!"

I looked at Pa and he looked at me.

"And I can prove to ye he's hot-collared," the old man said.

"How can ye do it?" Pa said, turning around to face the old man.

"Take this bucket and go down to the crick and get a bucket of cool water and throw hit over his shoulders," the old man said, as he emptied his groceries so Pa could use it. "Ye'll see that he'll pull when he gits cool shoulders!"

"I'll try anything," Pa said. "I'd like to git my express wagon back home."

Thirty-five or forty people who had now gathered to eat our watermelons looked strangely at Pa when they saw him dip a bucket of water from the creek. They watched Pa carry the water up to the road and throw it on Rye's shoulder, while the mule stood perfectly still as if he enjoyed it.

"It'll take more water," the old man said.

While the people laughed at Pa carrying water to put on a mule's shoulders like he was trying to put out a fire, I thought of what Pa had said about Cyrus's having to run old Rock to get up steam. And the people with watermelon smeared on their faces laughed at Pa more than he had laughed at Cyrus. But after Pa had carried the tenth bucket of water the old man said, "That's enough now, stranger. Ye've put the fire out!"

And when the old man smiled I could see his discolored teeth through his thin dingy-white mustache.

"Now try to drive 'im, young man," the old man said to me.

"Get up, Rye," I said, touching his back lightly with the lines.

The mule moved gently away, pulling the express wagon with the broken shafts which made it zigzag from one side of the road to the other. And when I stopped the mule, Pa came up and said, "It's a new wrinkle on my horn. I never heard of a hot-collared mule but we've got one, Adger. We'll haf to wire up these shafts someway until we can git home. I'll haf to do some more swappin'. Yer mom was right."

Old Gore

Good mornin', Shan," Old Gore said as he came through the toolhouse door.

"Good mornin', Gore," I said.

"See you're a-puttin' our tools away," he said, watching me put away tools we wouldn't use during the winter.

Old Gore watched me work while the winter wind whipped the barren treetops unmercifully. I knew on this kind of day he hadn't come to work.

"Shan, I've come to see you about rentin' your house next year," Old Gore said thoughtfully. "This year is about over and I'd like to know what I am a-goin' to do."

"I have to keep Uncle Jeff," I said. "He's been with me eleven years. Old Alec's been with me ten years. You've been with me only a year."

"Four years," Old Gore corrected me.

"But I was in the Navy when Pa brought you here," I said. "You've only been here one year with me."

"I'd like to go on with you," Old Gore said. "I know Jeff and Old Alec have been here longer than I have. I thought you'd keep them. And that is right."

"And since I won't have work for you," I said, as I watched Old Gore scuff his brogan shoe over a knothole on the toolhouse floor, "I'll want possession of the house. I want to rent it for cash rent."

Old Gore didn't speak when I asked for possession of the house. His lips trembled like a white-oak leaf in the winter wind. His mind was trying to think of words to say, and his trembling lips were trying to shape them. I knew Gore wouldn't want to rent the house for cash rent.

"I hate to lose you, Gore," I said, to break the silence. "You're a good worker and a good neighbor. It's my fault I haven't managed the farm better!"

"That means I'll have to vacate your premises by March first?"

"That's right."

"If you need me, let me know."

"All right," I said as he closed the door behind him.

Through the window I watched Old Gore plod up the wagon road where mule tracks and wagon ruts were frozen into the earth. I heard his big brogan shoes whetting against the frozen ground as I stood watching him swinging his big gorilla arms by his sides as regular as clock pendulums. His big hands, broader than small fire shovels, were pulling against the icy wind.

Two weeks after I had told Old Gore I would want my house, I was in Greenwood to get grass seed. While I was in Dawson's Hardware, Willie Felty slapped me on the shoulder.

"Shan, I want to ask you about a man by the name of Chris Gore," Willie said. "He's been up on Cane Creek tryin' to find a house to rent. Wants to work for some farmer by the day. He tried every farmer on Cane Creek. Started at the mouth and went to the head of the creek. He told everybody he lived on your place and he had to get out by March."

"Did he find a house?" I asked.

"No," Willie said.

"Not any empty houses on Cane Creek?"

"Two or three," Willie said.

"Didn't they need any help?" I asked.

"They need help all right," Willie said,

"Then why didn't they rent to Old Gore?"

"See, about everybody on Cane Creek knows you," Willie explained. "They think when you tell a man to go, he's not much good."

"I never thought of that," I said.

"And they didn't like Chris Gore's looks," Willie said.

"He's the kindest man that ever lived on my farm," I said. "He's the best man to a team I've ever known. He never whips a team. You never know he's plowin' in a field unless you see him. You never hear him. The reason he's leavin' my farm is, I have too much help. The men I'm keepin' were with me long before Old Gore came."

"I'll admit, I was afraid of 'im when he came to see me," Willie said. "And I knew if I ever saw you again, I'd ask you about this man. Big shoulders, big arms, legs, and feet, and when he walks he swings his arms like a gorilla. I never saw him smile."

I thought about Old Gore as my car bumped over the frozen dirt road toward home. I knew he would find a house to rent and work to do, if he'd go up some of the hollows in Greenwood County.

It was the middle of January before I saw Old Gore again.

"Thought I'd come down to tell you about a piece of fence that needs fixin', Shan," he said. "It's the dividin' fence betwixt your big pasture and the field where you raise your tobacco!"

"What's wrong with that fence?" I said. "We built it only six years ago!"

"But remember, you used chestnut posts after the chest-nuts had been killed by the blight," he said. "They've all rotted off even with the ground. Quarter of a mile of fence that's a-layin' flat on the ground!"

"I thought that fence was perfect," I said. "How'd you come to find it?"

"I was back on the ridge cuttin' stovewood," he said. "Just got to thinkin' that on one side you pastured thirty to fifty head of cattle. On the other side you raised tobacco. I wondered what would happen to a field of green tobacco if fifty head of cattle got into it. They'd destroy it in three hours."

"Now's a good time to fix it," I said. "Get Uncle Jeff and Old Alec and repair it."

Before Uncle Jeff, Old Gore, and Old Alec had finished repairing this fence, I was in Greenwood one day when Hill Porter stopped me.

"Shan, what kind of men do you have workin' for you?" he said.

"Good men," I said. "The very best."

"That fellow Chris Gore went all the way up Maple Branch here a few days ago," he said. "Said he lived on your place and had to move by March. He was tryin' to find a house. Wanted to work for some farmer by the day. Everybody wondered why you's a-lettin' 'im go, since they know people live on your farm until they get ready to leave."

"Lettin' him go because I have too much help," I said. "I'm losin' money on my farm. And the other fellows have been with me longer than Old Gore. That's why I'm lettin' him go!"

"Quit your kiddin', Shan," Hill laughed. "Who'll believe that story?"

Hill laughed as he turned and walked away.

Old Gore, Uncle Jeff, and Old Alec found more of the division fence flat on the ground. The chestnut posts had not lasted as long as we had expected. Frozen ground and a couple of snows delayed their getting the fence repaired until February.

After I paid the men, I didn't see Old Gore again until the middle of February. That was on a bright sunny day when a high wind was blowing and the vegetation on the ground was dry as powder. Old Gore sent a fox hunter, who was looking for a stray hound, to summon all the fire fighters in the neighborhood to Seaton Ridge. When Uncle Jeff, Old Alec, Pa, and I got there, Old Gore, singlehanded, was holding back a line of fire a mile long. He had raked a ring along the ridge and had fired against one of the most dangerous forest fires we had ever had. In one place it had crossed the ridge into my young timber, and Gore had stopped it just in time. If he hadn't, it would have ruined five hundred acres of timber and it would have burned two barns and a house.

"Gore, how in the world did you find this fire?" I asked. "How did you know it was comin' up this side of the mountain?"

"When I saw the smoke rise up," he said, "I whiffed the wind and I smelled burnin' leaves! I knew it wasn't smoke from a chimney. I grabbed my rake and come out here just in time to keep it from a-comin' over the ridge."

Gore's face was flushed with heat. His eyebrows were singed. His hands were burned. Gray wind-blown ashes had stuck to his sweaty face and pieces of burnt leaves were hanging to his winter beard. He had fought fire and had held the ridge and had done without water to drink. All that afternoon and until midnight we fought fire. We finally stopped it by raking a ring down the mountain to the river and firing against it. Old Gore had saved us.

What a good man Old Gore will make some farmer, I thought, as I walked back home after twelve hours of fighting fire. Then I thought about Old Gore's fighting fire for eighteen hours. He had not only fought fire to save my barns, house, and timber, but he had fought fire to save fifteen other homes on our side of the ridge.

On March first I walked up the hollow to see if Old Gore had moved from my house. On the road between where we lived, where the creek flowed toward the road, I noticed somebody had dug a channel across a spur of ground that jutted from the opposite hill and had turned the creek to keep it from cutting any more of the roadway. This was a job I had planned to do but had never done. I was glad someone had done it and I wondered if it had been Uncle Jeff, Old Alec, or Old Gore. I didn't have to wonder after I examined the tracks in the soft dirt. The tracks were unmistakably Old Gore's, for he wore the largest shoes of anybody that lived on the farm. When I went far enough to see the smoke coming from Old Gore's chimney, I turned back toward home.

When I passed the barn, Old Gore was unhitching my team from the plow.

"Thought I'd better get the barnyard manure turned under on that bottom," he said as he stopped the team. "Lot of cutworms in that ground and I'd better get it turned, for we might get another little ground freeze and kill the cutworms. I would have plowed it long ago but. . . ."

Old Gore stopped talking. It was my turn to talk. For I knew Old Gore must have known I'd found out how hard he'd tried to rent a house and find work. And he must know why he couldn't rent a house and find work, I thought, as

I looked at the steam rising from the sweaty mules and Old Gore's sweaty clothes.

"Yes, Gore," I said, "plow that bottom. Then, plow the next bottom and the next and the next! Freeze the cutworms in all of my bottoms."

Old Gore smiled. First time I'd seen him smile in months. He tapped the mules gently with the lines and spoke to them softly. I watched him drive them through the shadows of dusk toward the big barn.